MONA

at

SEA

Elizabeth Gonzalez James

Library of Congress Cataloging-in-Publication Data

Names: Gonzalez James, Elizabeth, 1982- author.
Title: Mona at sea / Elizabeth Gonzalez James.
Description: Santa Fe, NM : SFWP, [2021] | Summary: "In this sharp, witty
    debut, Elizabeth Gonzalez James introduces us to Mona Mireles—
    observant to a fault, unflinching in her opinions, and uncompromisingly
    confident in her professional abilities. Mona is a Millennial
    perfectionist who fails upwards in the midst of the 2008 economic
    crisis. Despite her potential, and her top-of-her-class college degree,
    Mona finds herself unemployed, living with her parents, and adrift in
    life and love. Mona's the sort who says exactly the right thing at
    absolutely the wrong moments, seeing the world through a cynic's eyes.
    In the financial and social malaise of the early 2000s, Mona walks a
    knife's edge as she faces down unemployment, underemployment, the
    complexities of adult relationships, and the downward spiral of her
    parents' shattering marriage. The more Mona craves perfection and order,
    the more she is forced to see that it is never attainable. Mona's
    journey asks the question: When we find what gives our life meaning,
    will we be ready for it?"—Provided by publisher.
Identifiers: LCCN 2020027382 (print) | LCCN 2020027383 (ebook) |
    ISBN 9781951631017 (paperback) | ISBN 9781951631024 (ebook)
Classification: LCC PS3607.O56267 M66 2021 (print) |
    LCC PS3607.O56267 (ebook) | DDC 813/.6—dc23
LC record available at https://lccn.loc.gov/2020027382
LC ebook record available at https://lccn.loc.gov/2020027383

Published by SFWP
369 Montezuma Ave. #350
Santa Fe, NM 87501
(505) 428-9045
www.sfwp.com

Contents

January 2009

Sad Millennial

The room in the church annex is small and smells of burnt coffee. Someone's thoughtfully hung the wood-paneled walls with inspirational posters promoting Courage, Teamwork, Perseverance, and in one corner, a disturbing painting of Jesus kneeling over someone shooting heroin. There's a toddler story time happening next door and every minute or so I hear an explosion of maracas and the phrase, "Shake that silly boo boo!" I'm sweating through my clothes; the backs of my thighs are wet inside my leggings. It's ten in the morning and because of a freak winter heatwave, the temperature's almost a hundred. Goddamn Tucson.

The flier promised refreshments. I suppose a half-eaten box of animal crackers hastily dumped onto a paper plate technically qualifies as food, but I don't know that I'd call it refreshing. There are about a dozen other job seekers hovering near the cookies, wistful, unpretentious people who look much more alive than I am this morning. I hear snippets of conversations about television, barbeques, and college basketball. Pleasantries. It's so easy for everyone else. They seem like nice people, but we have nothing in common. I want to run.

My mother forced me to come, badgered me until I gave in,

promising I'd get a lead on a job or at least find comfort in the company of others. "Better than holing up in your room," she said.

"I like my room."

"It's not healthy."

"Neither is that Diet Coke."

"Are you smoking marijuana again?"

"With what money?"

"Go to the meeting or I'm taking your car."

Transportational coercion, the threat of last resort. After graduating from Arizona and trekking the eight miles back to my parents' suburban hacienda, reattaching myself to the familial teat through which flowed food and air-conditioned shelter, I had little choice but to suffer these extortions. So, I went.

Folding chairs are arranged in a semi-circle and I grab the one closest to the door. As I'm chewing on a cuticle and trying to divine shapes in the brown grain of the carpet, a guy about my age sits next to me and, in between guttural attempts to clear his throat, I hear a wet clicking sound that I identify as a tongue ring being rapped against teeth. Cringing at each thwack, I slouch lower in my seat, hoping he'll take the hint. He doesn't. "Hey," he says. I ignore him so he tries again. "Hey," and he jabs an elbow into my arm. "Do I know you?" he asks. I look at him without blinking but, undaunted, he tries again. "Did you go to Marana? Class of '02?"

"No," I say, "I didn't go to Marana."

"Do you know Pokey? Worm's little brother? Did you used to party over at their place? Or the Pita Pit. Did you used to work at Pita Pit?"

I sit up straight and face him, too under-caffeinated and over-stressed to continue this line of questioning. "I don't know you," I say. "I don't know Pokey or Worm or the place where they used to party."

But he only shakes his head and sits back in his chair, pulling out his phone. "Nah dude," he says. "I know you. Imma figure it out. Don't worry."

Mercifully the door opens and an older woman with orange, fluffy hair and red paisley pants strides in and asks us to sit down. My seat companion pockets his phone and I resume chewing my cuticle, praying we won't have to give introductions.

"Welcome, job seekers," says the woman with a smile. "My name is Paulette. Before we get started this morning, I want to give you one piece of advice." She reaches for a binder under her chair and removes a piece of paper, the word, 'BREATHE' written across it in black marker. She holds it forth like the eleventh commandment and nods while we take in the power of her message.

"I want to tell you that I know where you're coming from. I was a legal secretary for seventeen years, and got laid off after a merger. I searched high and low for another job, but at my age," and here she points to her head so we can all see her gray roots and know she's deliberately chosen carrot-colored hair, "at my age, it's hard to convince employers to take a chance on you. So, I started coming to church…" and here I tune out for a while. I told my mom the meeting was a thin ruse to pack the pews on Sunday, but she wouldn't listen. "…and Jesus led me here, and I've been running these workshops for the last three years." Paulette finishes her spiel with a quick glance heaven-ward and says, "Now let's get to know one another, shall we?"

A thin man, fiftyish, with long, scraggy hair stands and fingers his tie, looking like he'd feel more comfortable in a t-shirt with a monster truck on it. "My name is Randy. I'm originally from Kingman. I sold wheelchairs for twenty-five years, but I'll start anywhere." He looks to Paulette for approval. She nods and motions for him to continue. "My brother-in-law's got a power washing business, so I've been helping him out with that, but it's not very steady. I don't do computers too much. Oh, and I can play the flute," he says and sits down.

Next a woman in a tracksuit speaks. "My name is Dara. I was late because my ex forgot to pick up my daughter for school." Her body is powerful under thin cotton clothes. She shakes her wrists and rolls her neck from side to side like she's getting ready to enter the ring. "Two months ago, I was laid off from the airport. I was a baggage handler for five years, but I'm trying to get into cosmetology." She holds out her hands so we can admire her manicure and it is something to behold: every nail boasts a different character from *Sesame Street*, Oscar and Grundgetta receiving the coveted thumb spots. "I can't afford the tuition for beauty school so I'm trying to teach myself, but no one's hiring anyway. I hostess sometimes at the Smokehouse on Campbell. But damn, it gets to you. You start thinking you'll never find a job."

The others stand, one by one, give their name and sad situation: laid off, downsized, restructured, redundant. The day I started my senior year at the University of Arizona, France's largest bank halted withdrawals from three of its biggest funds citing fears about a looming subprime mortgage crisis, effectively setting the stage for the Great Recession. How's that for a bad omen? As my turn to speak approaches, I consider running, but I only have two dimes in my purse. Where would I go?

Tongue ring is next. He's wearing white Pumas and the kind of denim pants that inhabit the strange, unnamed sartorial category between shorts and capris. His goatee tapers into a thin line that connects with his sideburns and, though he's dressed in 'athletic apparel,' he looks no stranger to the Taco Bell drive-through. "What's up?" he says. "I'm Chasen. I work at Safeway. I used to do sheet metal fabrication, but I got fired." Here he pantomimes smoking a joint. "I like working on cars and, uh, I guess I'm a people person." He looks at me and winks and I'm so appalled I can't even roll my eyes.

I shouldn't be here. This feels too much like accepting defeat. I can't shake the image that somewhere in lower Manhattan there's a building full of desks, and on one of those desks is a little brass and false-wood nameplate that says Mona Mireles. Maybe they even spelled my name wrong, Morales instead of Mireles, or Mirles or Mireless, but I'll know it's me, my desk, my chair, my Bloomberg terminal. And eventually the space under my desk would blossom with pairs of sale-rack luxury shoes, and beside the nameplate would sit a little gilt-edged business card holder, and a dopey mug with cactuses on it that says, Looking sharp! If someone would have only shown me to my desk, if they'd only opened up the building—

It's my turn. I rise and face the room. Besides Chasen, I'm the youngest by at least twenty years. And looking down at my flip flops and the Princess Jasmine t-shirt I slept in, I think the age difference is apparent to everyone else in the room, too. "My name is Mona Mireles. Eight months ago, I graduated from U of A with a major in finance. I got recruited out of college to work at an investment bank in New York, but that kinda fell through. So here I am."

My heart is clanging so hard I can see it rising and falling under the swoop of Princess Jasmine's bubble braid. Since September, I've spoken only to my parents, my brother, and my best friend, Ashley. Even the guy at the liquor store and I have worked out a system of grunts and head jerks. Thirty unblinking eyes are making me bury my fingernails sharp into my palms as sweat trails down my sides. I can see the panic attack like it was a freight train and me, my feet wedged between the rails. I suck in a breath and hold, hold, hold before letting it out slowly, trying not to look like I'm practicing Lamaze.

"Which bank?" Paulette asks.

My face reddens. "Bannerman," I say, addressing the floor.

There's a murmur. Dara whistles and lets out a low, "Shiiiiiiit."

Paulette tsks and I can practically hear her face fall in pity. Truly my story is the saddest of them all. "So. You're looking for something in finance?"

"That's the plan."

"I may have a lead for you." Paulette rummages through her binder and I look up, my heart mustering one faint leap. "How would you feel," she asks, holding out a brochure, "about selling car insurance?"

I take the brochure and stare at her, unsure how to explain in under a thousand words the vast differences between investment banking and property insurance. I sit down and, to keep my pulse even for the next fifteen minutes, spend the rest of the meeting naming beers in alphabetical order.

When we're finished, I grab my purse and try to exit before anyone can speak to me, but I'm blocked by the other job seekers lingering to chat. In my haste to leave, I drop my keys, and when I come back up, Paulette is there holding her binder to her chest like a life preserver and giving me a warm, expectant look.

"So, what did you think? Are you going to join us next week?"

No.

"Yes, for sure. It was great. I definitely learned a lot."

Paulette lets out a big breath like she'd been worried. "I'm so glad. This is such a lonely process. It's good to be around other people who are going through it with you."

I'm nodding, one eye on the sunlight streaming through a glass door. I'm about to thank her and make my escape when the light disappears behind Chasen, his arms folded and a smirk brightening his face, goatee to eyebrows.

"Sad Millennial," he says firing two finger-guns at me. "You're 'Sad Millennial,' aren't you?" He punctuates his question by sucking saliva through the tongue ring and, getting too much at the back of his throat, coughs into the crook of his elbow.

My face is so hot I think it might be glowing. "I don't know you," I say, trying to avoid eye contact.

"What's 'Sad Millennial'?" Paulette asks.

Chasen's face brightens more. "Dude, me and my boy watched that video a hundred times. And the autotune version? That was my ringtone!" He pitches his voice up and sings, poorly, "It's not faaiiir, I ate my veggies!"

"This is something on the internet?"

"You gotta look that shi—" Chasen catches himself before a disapproving glance from Paulette. "You gotta look it up."

Bannerman had been cagey about a start date, a move I'd assumed was some abstruse hazing ritual inflicted on the new class of junior analysts. I'd been out of town with my parents, one last jaunt to Puerto Peñasco to see the dolphins, and when we got back to Tucson there was an email from HR demanding I be in New York the following morning. I don't remember packing. I don't remember how much my parents had to pay for a last-minute ticket or what Ashton Kutcher rom-com played on the in-flight headrest screens. I don't remember the cab ride to Bannerman's Wall Street headquarters other than the red wall of brake lights and car horns screaming infinitely before us. All I know is that the front doors were locked, the side doors were locked, the back doors were locked, and by the time I woke up and took a look around me, I realized I was surrounded by well-dressed people hugging cardboard boxes and potted plants while they cried and cussed and smoked like it was some great, unplanned funeral.

Then there was the woman in a pink jacket and a small, mean face. Like a terrier. She practically kissed my lips with a microphone, a strong astringent funk like mouthwash coming off its foam head. A black-framed camera floated over her shoulder.

"Today was supposed to be your first day at Bannerman. You've got your suitcases—you must have just come from the airport. I hope you won't mind me saying, but you look young. This may have been your first job out of college. Coming here and finding out you no longer have a job: How does it feel? What's going through your head right now?"

"It sucks," I said, blinking far too many times. I remember I couldn't look straight into the lens.

The reporter slit her eyes, unimpressed with my brevity. "Can you elaborate?"

I opened and closed my mouth a few times, trying to condense a brewing ten-minute polemic into a few sentences. I must have packed the breathing exercises I used to hold back my anxiety inside my bag with my pin-striped pants, because as I began to speak I was aware that I was not taking in air, that the words were getting squeezed out in one long, terminal gasp. "It's not fair. I worked really hard to get this job. I was valedictorian. I was president of the Investment Club. I did everything right, you know? Everything. I said no to drugs, I stayed in school, I got straight A's and ate my veggies and now I just want my job. I had seven interviews to get this job, I beat out I don't know how many people—you know I'm the first person Bannerman hired from Arizona in ten years? I'm probably the only Latina in the new analyst class, because you *know* all those investment banks are old boys' clubs. I came all the way out from Tucson. Tucson! My plane landed this morning. I don't have anywhere to stay; I don't know anyone in New York. I've got everything I own in these two suitcases and I just, and I just—" Halfway through my speech I'd felt my throat tightening and even though I'd fought off the tears until then, they finally sputtered out of me as the horrible woman pushed the microphone closer, making sure no pathos went un-filmed. "I don't know what to do," I sobbed. "I don't know what I'm supposed to do."

The annex room has almost cleared. Dust motes pirouette in the morning sunshine. My face must look severe, because now Chasen clears his throat and looks down at the carpet. "For real that sucks, though. Did you get any money from the video?"

Yeah, I copyrighted it. "What do you think?"

"That's messed up. But hey," and Chasen cuffs me lightly on the shoulder like we're friends, "someone'll do something else stupid and pretty soon no one'll remember you. There's always someone more screwed up than you."

"Thanks, I guess?"

Chasen moves off and Paulette gives me a small, encouraging smile that feels confidential, only for me. "Do you know I saw Monica Lewinski on TV?" she asks quietly. "Remember her? I didn't know this but she was only twenty-four when all that happened. Can you imagine?"

"Yeah, that's a lot."

"She was the only thing people talked about—it seemed like years, didn't it? And in all that time, the story was the same over and over—that homewrecker, that blue dress. How could she? Nobody ever bothered to look at it a different way, that here's this young woman and the most powerful man in the country. That maybe there was something else we weren't seeing. How did the reporter say it? Something like, 'What is it like to be the biggest punchline in the world?'"

My eyes hurt and I realize I've stopped blinking. I'd underestimated her with the 'BREATHE' sign but Christ, this lady is good.

"Do you have a journal? It might help to write down what you're going through. You might not ever share it with anyone, and that's fine, but there's something about getting things down on paper that really helps you see the whole story. Even if you're the only one reading it."

"I haven't but thanks, that's a good—I'll think about it, definitely."

Paulette looks past me through the door. "It's a beautiful day," she says, still smiling. "There's that."

* * *

My dad snuck me forty bucks to fill up my car, so I spend thirty on gas and use the rest to buy a fifth of bottom shelf tequila. Colima is the name on the bottle with a little, sleeping Mexican man stenciled on the label. Soon, my friend, we'll both be passed out.

In my bed, with my tumbler of tequila and orange juice, I scan the headlines on my laptop. Already calling it the Great Recession is a little presumptuous if you ask me. It could certainly get greater. The year's only just begun and inflation is up, jobs are few, there's a drought in the Midwest. Horse starvation rates are through the roof. I read an article entitled, 'Millennials More Narcissistic Than Previous

Generations.' "Lazy, illiterate, slack-jawed phone jockeys," the author calls us, "addicted to the morphine-drip of social media validation." Spend one day in my flip flops, buddy. The morphine part is right, though—Quod me nutrit, me destruit. I scroll through photos of old classmates, smiling, successful people in Oxford shirts grabbing drinks with co-workers or spending newly-acquired paychecks on gadgets and cars. It should have been me.

I apply for my three hundred seventy-seventh job, something called an FP&A Specialist, and I have no idea if I remembered to change the objective on my résumé from my last application. Not that it matters.

Before I fall asleep, I turn on the news only to turn it off a second later. When Bannerman Financial Services filed for bankruptcy, they were carrying a debt-to-equity ratio of 60 to 1. The anchors were in the middle of a skit where Bannerman's demise had turned into a scary story that investment bankers told their kids around a campfire—"They wish the call *had* been coming from inside the house, Jim!" I fantasize about firing a gun straight into the TV, imagine the crackle and hiss of exposed wires and the silent malevolence of mercury gas filling my bedroom, but satisfy myself instead with hurling the remote control into a pile of dirty laundry.

I'm unemployed, I've never had a boyfriend, I live with my parents in the most boring town on the planet, and I hate myself. I sing myself to sleep with these facts every night. I started the list with good intentions. I thought if I could name my problems, catalog my failings in one concise mantra, I could tackle them one by one. But eight months after graduation I'm still here, still stuck, and each repetition only chisels the words deeper into stone. I'm unemployed, I've never had a boyfriend, I live with my parents in the most boring town on the planet, and I hate myself. The shame turns physical, a cold, liquid pain flowing through my bones, down my spine, and into my joints. My whole body aches. I press my hands into my eyes until I see spots, hoping by some magic of brain chemistry the spell will pass.

It doesn't.

I throw off the covers and go to my desk. The scent of chocolate hits me when I open the drawer—soaps shaped and scented like truffles spill out of their box and mix with pens and paper clips—and I reach my hand all the way back, past the graphing calculator, past the blank CDs, and feel the cold vinyl of the pencil case. The red chalk face of Leonardo da Vinci looks out from the case, over my head and off into the distance, sullen that his image has been reproduced and printed on thousands, millions of identical pencil cases to be shipped anywhere and everywhere.

He is the pin to my grenade, the Hoover Dam to my Colorado River. I open the case and lay out the materials: rubbing alcohol, gauze, new razor blades. I take a deep breath and begin my routine. My pulse slows, my hand steadies, my mind clears, and the warm assurance that soon I'll feel better wraps me like a blanket.

I am Mona the Mutilator. Mona of the Lancet. Mona, High Priestess of the Clan Tiny Cut. I'm hunched over my leg working, telling myself I'll make one more cut before I'm done. The only sounds are my low, steady breaths and a motorcycle idling somewhere down the street. I can't feel the carpet under me, can't hear the steady breath of the air conditioner. I feel nothing except the bitter steel of the razor and the sensation of tumbling Alice-like, down to another place.

In ten minutes, I'm back in bed. And if not fully restored, the boil reduced to a simmer.

* * *

The first thing I see every morning is my trophy wall. Opposite my bed, from about two feet off the floor and stretching up to the ceiling, is every major award I have received since the first grade. Some notable highlights include Outstanding Delegate in Model UN, first place in the Junior MBA Club's Emerging Entrepreneurs Expo, Blue Ribbon in the Arizona State Science Fair four years in a row, Best Oil Painting in the Southwest Young Artists Showcase, and my personal favorite, fourth place in the National Spelling Bee, just three spots shy of the big prize. In one sweep across the twelve-by-ten-foot space I can relive my entire childhood.

I blink, my brain dull from bad dreams. It's been the same one for months, the nightmare that frightens me for reasons I can't articulate. It's an encroaching presence, a texture more than anything else, like tightly woven, porous, dark grey mesh. The entire dream is that I sit in some formless, abstract place and watch as the texture moves closer. And whatever is contained in the dark grey, whatever it is or represents, I know I don't want to find out what happens when it reaches me.

Getting out of bed after a tequila night is always a frightening proposition: You never really know if you have a hangover until you stand up. Sometimes I lie there for fifteen minutes, stock still, trying to suss out what hurts. Today I hold my breath and decide to do it quickly, rip off the covers and put my feet on the ground and outrun the headache, the sour stomach, get some coffee into me before I survey the damage.

I'm dizzy—that's bad. My head doesn't hurt, though. I drape my comforter over me like a shroud and pad to the kitchen in my socks, hoping I've missed my parents. I peer around the corner at the coffee maker. No one.

I'm working on an itch inside my armpit and I have a cold tortilla hanging out of my mouth when my mother appears in the doorway like Jacob Marley come to bring ill tidings.

"Good morning," she says, though she's already moved past the greeting and is looking around at the counters, making sure I haven't left crumbs or upset the stacks of paper and journals she's left at neat intervals. She takes off her glasses and rubs the bridge of her nose. Her close-cropped brown hair gleams even in the grey morning light. It's new since Christmas and the only option left after she spent 2008 as a blonde, a redhead, and, for a few months, possessing some bang-heavy layered thing that made her look like Pete Wentz.

"Hmhmm." I point to the food in my mouth.

"What's on your schedule today?" she asks and I shrug. *Price is Right* at ten, *Dr. Phil* at eleven, long shower, *Oprah*, staring wistfully out the window, the evening news, some self-loathing before dinner, obligatory family interaction, cocktails, and then cat videos until I fall asleep with my face mashed against the keyboard.

"Same thing I do every day. Applying for jobs."

"Is there anything I can do?" she asks. "Is there a class you could take? I can get you books or find out if there's a networking seminar through the school."

I don't notice that my father has slouched into the kitchen until I hear him pouring himself the last cup of coffee. I put down my empty cup a little too loudly, but he doesn't notice anyway. My mother clears her throat with a small, pointed sound. My father looks up from his coffee and her expression seems too weary for this early in the morning.

"Didn't the steering committee meet half an hour ago?" she asks. "Aren't you late?"

My father is a weathered, turtle of a man. He brings his watch close to his glasses with feigned indifference.

"I didn't want to go," he says.

My mother blinks several times before answering. "It's not optional. Some things aren't optional."

My parents are medical researchers specializing in Alzheimer's Disease and have been on the university faculty since the eighties. Last spring my mom achieved her dream and was named director of the entire Gerontology Lab, making her my dad's boss. Some men might have balked at working for their wife but I think my dad is prouder of her accomplishment than she is. He certainly cried harder than she did at the celebratory banquet. When I compare him to a turtle, it's because he's been pulling back inside himself for years, skipping dinners, forgetting promises, spending nights in his study reading baseball card blogs. He travels to conferences whenever he can, no matter how small or arcane, and sometimes I'll assume he's out of town and then I'll startle to see him coming out of the shower or bringing in the mail. It's like I can see the edges of him blurring, fading into smoke. When I was a kid, he wasn't exactly a roll-around-on-the-ground-with-you sort of father, but he was always there, a solid form in the background, someone I'd run to with a skinned knee or hurt feelings. I half worry one day we'll open the door to his study and he'll be gone, vanished like the memories of the patients he works to save.

"Good morning," he says to me. "Necesitas algo?" he asks, meaning money. At this my mother looks disappointed like he'd just offered me weed.

"You know I can speak Spanish," she says. "You can't talk over me. And please don't give her any more money. Her room reeks like tequila and Doritos as it is."

"You should take a walk," my father says to me. "The whole day to kill—you might as well enjoy it."

I give him an aggrieved look. "Time kills you, not the other way around. All you can do is bide."

"So profound, mijita," and he musses my hair. "Try not to be so in your head. Bueno," he says to my mother, "I'll be in the car," and he goes out to the garage.

My mother rubs her nose under her glasses again. "Why don't you send me your résumé again?" she asks.

"The unemployment rate is twelve percent. It's a terrible time to look for a job, especially in finance."

"Your brother could go with you to a networking event. It would be good for him to start making contacts now before graduation."

"That's not going to happen."

"What about volunteering? You might feel better if you did some community service."

"I'll think about it."

She sighs and says, as if we haven't had the same conversation a thousand times, "This is a problem to solve. You approach it the same way we always have: you have a hypothesis, you test it, and if it doesn't work you alter your hypothesis and begin again."

Being a woman of science, she's a big believer in formulas, recipes, directions that produce predictable, repeatable results. I have to believe she saw my youth spent in accelerated classes and extra-curricular activities as a portent of success, Step One in a list of instructions culminating with me joining the tenured faculty at Princeton. How frustrating it must be for her to see me here every morning, shuffling the house in dirty socks, my future curdling and everyone, especially her, especially her hypotheses, powerless to stop it.

"If you leave the house, please take my library books back."

"I'm not."

"I love you."

"I know." I wait to see if she'll force the issue, but she doesn't. Blackberry in hand she leaves for the world of people with jobs and deadlines, self-respect, fulfillment, interesting conversations, and the leisure to say, "Ooh, what about crepes for lunch?"

The only sound in the empty house is the grind of the icemaker and the cubes falling into the catch. For a change of scenery, I bring my laptop out to the kitchen island, but once it's open, I can't bring myself to start trawling the job boards. Instead, I stare at a painting I did in the fifth grade hanging next to the refrigerator, my face in black and white like a yin and yang, and I remember what Paulette recommended yesterday: Tell my story. I open a new document. I type the words, Chapter One, and count sixty cursor blinks before I can think what to write. Finally, I decide to open like *David Copperfield*, at the beginning.

Chapter 1: I am born.

My mother's parents didn't come to her wedding, couldn't endure the shame of seeing their Irish rose joined to a Mexican-American with skin the color of a pecan shell. Within a year my parents had me and a year after they had Danny. I think my mother hastily made two new family members to replace the ones she'd lost. I grew up hearing the story, how love had bested hate. But eventually I learned the unsaid kernel deep inside the tale. The one that caused me for years to look at mirrors quickly and always at a slant, was that I now carried something inside of me that might cause others, even my own family, to turn away.

I remember the year I learned the sun was going to explode. My mother had an astronomy book that lived on the coffee table, and the back inside cover had full-color illustrations of the final stages of the sun: from yellow ball to angry giant to dead, silent dwarf. I imagined all-consuming heat scorching everything on Earth, and the forever night that would follow. I had nightmares about fireballs, melting trees, a gloom swallowing every sound. My mother hid the astronomy book in the attic and enrolled me in a few afterschool classes at the Y.

By second grade, we had a day planner in which I could see my future meted out in fifteen-minute increments. All those little blocks, equally sized and neatly labeled, made me feel secure, confident I would always know what lay ahead.

When you're told, over and over, what a smart kid you are, and when you win every science fair, every essay contest, it doesn't just go to your head—it defines you. I defined me. I became what people said I was: a winner, a genius, a singular talent. Losing becomes an abstract concept like infinity or world peace. I could think about it, but to see it or live it—that wouldn't compute.

My middle name is Lisa after my mother's mother and Mona was tacked on, I assume, in a half-cocked bid to align me with greatness. I don't know what my parents were playing at, naming me after the most famous painting in the world. But if timeless beauty and silent grace are the summits I'm meant to reach, God knows they picked wrong. I'm a one-hit-wonder, then nothing, nothing. Like the lady with the mystic smile.

You'll know
when you know

"Clucka-clucka who? Clucka-clucka moo!" The toddler story time is at it again. The walls in the church annex must be made of cardboard. Chasen and the other job seekers hover around the table in the back of the room. Today we've got Ritz crackers. Oh joy.

I told myself I wouldn't come, woke up in the morning determined not to leave the house and yet here I am, a congregant in the church of mutual misfortune looking, like any penitent, for the how, the why. Paulette's in a green dress with a wide Peter Pan collar and earrings shaped like angels. She shows us her 'BREATHE' sign again and I muster a shallow inhale.

"How's it going, guys?" Paulette looks eager to hear good news, and I don't suppose there's any chance Chasen's made store manager.

Randy stands and gives a half wave. His hair is twisted into a bun that hangs over the collar of his windbreaker. "My brother-in-law and I are offering a discount on power washing, if anyone's interested. It'll make your home look brand new." He pushes his sleeves up before he sits down and I glimpse a tattoo on his forearm—a silhouette of a longhaired man playing the flute.

Dara is wearing a different tracksuit and dozens of gold bangle bracelets that jingle like Christmas. "It's hard, you know," and Paulette and the others nod. "Things are getting so expensive. Milk, eggs, gas— it's all going up. I only get unemployment for another three weeks, so time's running out. My friend, she's going to beauty school, and she's been showing me some stuff at night, how to do acrylics and all that, but it's hard. No one's hiring." She throws up her hands and sits down.

"Unemployment is hard," Paulette says, addressing the group. "And what I want you to understand is you're not in this fight alone. You can't give up. You will get a job. It may not be the job you want," and for some reason she looks at me when she says this, "but you will not fail. Repeat after me: *I will get a job.*"

This feels less like a networking seminar and more like a group therapy session.

"Mona," Paulette says, "let's hear from you."

"I'm applying," I say, rubbing my hands down my face, "but sending résumés out feels like throwing pennies down a wishing well." Paulette nods and motions for me to continue. I don't want to be here. I'm not supposed to be here. But going all Ignatius-Reilly-bemoaning-Fortuna is not really a good look either. "I don't know what else to say."

"Are you customizing your cover letters?"

"Yes."

"And are you networking?"

"I appear to be doing that right now."

"Have you thought about volunteering?"

"My calendar's pretty full."

Paulette ignores this obvious lie. "And internships?"

"Already had one."

"Are you able to relocate? You might try looking in a bigger city."

"I should be so lucky."

"Are you only applying to jobs in finance? Have you tried branching out?"

"I want to work in finance."

"You can always come back to it. Get your foot in the door another way."

"My degree is in finance," I say, hoping she'll give up.

"What do you like to do? What's your favorite pastime?"

"I watch a lot of TV."

"What I mean is, what would you do if you didn't have to work? How would you spend your life?"

This is going nowhere and I've had enough. Thirty unblinking eyes stare like dead fish behind glass and I can feel my rapid pulse throbbing down in my fingertips. "I can't do this anymore," and I reach for my purse. Paulette means well but this is a waste of time.

"You *can* do this," Paulette says, and her expression is firm but kind. I hold the purse a second, deciding, and then drop it back on the floor with a thud. She starts again, her voice measured and soft like a hypnotist. "If I'm a genie who can grant wishes, what's the thing you'd like to do most of all?"

"I want to work in finance," I say, and I wish those eyes would stop beaming their judgement like floodlights. "It's a good job, it's something I'm good at. It pays well. It's prestigious. It's everything I want."

"Why?" Paulette asks. She is sympathetic, nodding her head, but I don't think she grasps the depth of my predicament.

"I'm trying, don't get me wrong. This morning I hit four hundred applications. Four hundred. I've had ten in-person interviews, six phone interviews, one Skype chat, and I've gotten nothing." I cross my arms over my chest and stare down the orange halo over Paulette's head. "So, what am I supposed to do? Breathe more? It's not helping."

I take my seat and watch an ant hurry across Paulette's binder. No one speaks. The only sound comes from Chasen's tongue ring rapping his incisors. An automatic air freshener hisses and suddenly the room smells like sugar cookies.

"I know you're under a lot of stress," Paulette says, smoothing down her hair. "Why do you think I start my sessions with relaxing breaths? I lost my condo last month. I had to move in with my daughter. I'm sleeping on a futon in my grandson's room. Everyone's going through it. But lashing out isn't the answer. Because you can spend all your time assigning blame for this and that, and at the end of the day, you're still unemployed."

The others are silent, waiting to see what she'll do next. I don't move my eyes from the carpet, too ashamed at my outburst to make eye contact. "I'm sorry," I say, and long for the isolation of my car.

"UPS is hiring," Randy says, looking at me. "I've got an interview next week. Go to the website. Ten bucks an hour is better than a kick in the pants."

"Can you do makeup?" Dara asks. "They're hiring a part-time Clinique girl at the mall. I can see if the Smokehouse needs another hostess."

"Thanks," I say meekly, touched and mortified in equal measure.

Later, as we file out, Chasen taps my arm. "You shouldn't be so hard on yourself. But four hundred applications? Shit, I woulda gave up after fifty."

"Yeah, well, if at first you don't succeed..."

"Safeway's hiring for deli prep. I can get you an interview if you want."

"Thanks," I say. "I'll let you know."

The sulfur sun is high when I step out into the parking lot and the air is drummed by the buzz of a cicada somewhere over my head. I look at my phone and see I have texts from Ashley, my best friend and college roommate. She needs me to come over and help her put together a portfolio of her work so she can apply to graphic design jobs. I groan. I love Ashley, but I'm not in a helping mood. I sit in my car, angling the air conditioning vents up the sleeves of my t-shirt and stare out the window at a woodpecker hammering away at a saguaro. I will never understand why the American Southwest was colonized.

I sit a for few minutes, making up excuses, but realize Ashley will just keep asking. It's easier to go. With a sigh I put the car in drive and head to Ashley's tony apartment complex on River Road. On the way I pass entire housing tracts aborted and forsaken, model homes proud and erect near the main road and sadder, lesser homes trailing back into the foothills, diminishing block by block so that some lack roofs, some walls, some no more than concrete slabs marooned inside pools of compacted brown dirt. CASH FOR GOLD!! I pass a dozen yellow signs fronting a dozen different pawn shops, spun by lackluster people with sunburnt hands, and I wonder if they, too, lost amazing jobs, now forced into the role of human billboard. At a stoplight I watch a man crawl into the narrow space between a highway overpass and a retaining wall and settle in for a nap.

When I get to Ashley's I key a pin number into a call box set in a faux rock, and stop in the lobby for a complimentary cappuccino and to steal the latest issue of *The Economist*. I have a key so I give a perfunctory knock and let myself in, dropping my shoes in the designated basket, then open and close the kitchen cabinets in a fruitless search for cookies.

"I need help," she calls from another room.

"Don't we all," I say to a pantry stocked only with Crystal Light and miso broth.

Ashley emerges from the bedroom in a pink sundress, two cloth waxing strips stuck to her upper lip. "I'm too scared," she says, offering up her face so I can be the one to rip the hair from her mustache. We've done this dance before and I still hate to cause her pain, however superficial.

"On three," I say. "One, two…" And I tear the first side.

"Cocksucker!" she shouts, and brings a cotton ball soaked in baby oil up to her mouth.

"Are you done crying?" I ask. "You're not supposed to let them dry that long."

She nods and puts her head back again.

"Okay," I say, "one, two…"

"Fuck on a fucking fuck!" A second cotton ball is produced. "This is why they don't let me do this at the salon. They don't let you back if you're a screamer." She tucks a lock of limp hair behind her ear and sips a Diet Coke. Her long arms and legs jut out of her body like insect appendages, all joints and angles, and her bony proportions are only magnified by her oversized shearling slippers. There are throw pillows flung about the hallway and I can see that Ashley's been stuffing her clothes again.

When I met Ashley, she was larger. Two hundred pounds larger. She had gastric bypass surgery midway through our freshman year of college, and at first the weight loss had the effect of ice melting from around her, releasing something that seemed to have been bottled. Gone was the quiet art major content to spend Saturday nights locked in the studio making wheat paste collages. By the end of our sophomore year, armed with new breasts bought by her proud parents, she was dragging me out of my homework and into off-campus parties with muscled but flavorless men, with dates who followed us back to our apartment and would barge into my room at four in the morning looking for the bathroom, then not bother to tell Ashley goodbye when they left.

But after about a year with her new body, Ashley was down on herself again. She'd sit at the mirror fretting that her knees were too bulbous or that her hair wouldn't hold a curl. I came home from class one day and found her, in the middle of a warm spring day, wearing a sweatshirt and sweatpants she'd filled with pillows and rolled-up towels, mimicking the Rubenesque splendor of her former self. She knew she had to stay thin, that neither she nor her parents could forgive the loss of control implied in regaining the weight, but she said she missed the luxury of her old body, its velvet folds and luscious, convex topography. I'm the only one who knows her secret, that when she's home she puts on her old skin and delights in the feeling of being so, so grand. I look away from the pillows and pretend I saw nothing. I've always been grateful for her friendship, for the random housing assignment that allowed it to happen, and I realized over time she's just as grateful for mine. Pre-Ashley, I had made it to eighteen without a best friend.

"I need to figure out what to put in the portfolio," she says, motioning for me to follow her into the bedroom. "I need a real job. If I have to keep driving up to my parents in Scottsdale to beg for money, I'm going to kill myself."

If my parents rewarded me with thousands of dollars and shopping bags of new clothes every time I drove home, I wouldn't be contemplating suicide over it, but I hold my tongue.

We sit on her bed where her laptop is open to a painting I remember her making shortly after losing the weight. She stands naked in a field of flowers, her arms spread as though she's poised to take flight. The painting is well-executed, though more than a little derivative of Frida Kahlo.

"I think showing your potential boss a naked picture of yourself is an interesting move," I say, scrolling to the next image, "but I doubt your graphic design clients are ever going to need a nude in flowers. Do you have anything more commercial?"

"This one," she says, pointing to a picture of a daisy made of flip-flops.

"Yeah, that's good. How many do you need?"

"My advisor said twelve."

I come to one picture I remember from freshman year—an acrylic of a woman buried under an avalanche of cosmetics. She's barely visible under boulder-like powder compacts and tubes of mascara. Her eyes, which are large and dark like gemstones, are positioned in the center of the painting, angled in such a way that they seem to follow the viewer left to right. The piece is nicely done, though the message is so obvious it beats one healthily over the head. I zoom in and can see the pencil marks where Ashley didn't apply enough paint. I zoom closer still and the woman dissolves, lost in a tortoiseshell mélange of beige-brown-black. I notice I've been biting my cheek and I let go; a second later I have to bring my shoulders down as well. The closer I zoom into the painting the more keenly I feel a growing agitation, the source of which I cannot locate. In and in I go, and I wish I was alone so I could slam shut the laptop and hurl it down into the soft bosom of the duvet.

"…and I can't with her," Ashley is saying. "I'm tired of her making it *my* job to make *her* feel like a good mother."

From a dark and pulpy place inside me I hate this picture. I zoom out and click on another and hate it just the same. Ten paintings and my hatred grows tenfold.

"Can I block her number?"

I don't like this feeling but it's as though I'm no more in control than a child pounding the floor with hard, sticky fists.

"…over it and once I get a job, she can stick her little text messages right in her eye."

This is just unemployment rage. This is the displaced anger I've been wearing for months. It's jealousy and anxiety and fear and resentment and justified and unjustified rage at a system that once worked in my favor and now won't let me even peek over the rim of success. And to sit here in Ashley's luxury apartment with dirty laundry spilling out of an open closet and the only decorations consisting of magazine pictures of Jason Statham scotch-taped to the wall while I'm still sleeping on the same pillow I used to stick my baby teeth under, I can't help but feel that however much she dislikes her parents, I'd gladly trade places with her. And when I think of how in college one of us popped No Doze to ace quantitative analytics while the other got third place in a sexy footwear contest, and how many panic attacks I had before exams and how many times Ashley turned in late work because she was hungover or tired or just because…

I shove the laptop back into Ashley's hands and stand up to leave before I say something stupid and start a fight.

"The makeup one is good. They're all good. Just don't use the naked ones."

"You're the best," she says, and I wish I could believe it.

* * *

That night I go into the kitchen and find my brother Danny leaning against the counter looking at his phone. He's wearing his El Presidente sweatshirt, one of the many gifts and honors conferred unto him after assuming the presidency of the Chi Chi Theta fraternity.

"Don't talk," he says, holding up one hand. I peer over his shoulder. A teenage boy sits in a shopping cart perched at the top of some concrete steps. The boy finishes a beer, tosses the can, someone off camera starts a countdown, and the shopping cart begins its inevitable flight. I look away. Seeing someone break their neck is not going to improve my day. "These pledges are nuts!" Danny screams a second later. Then he puts the phone on the counter and appraises me. "Who sucked the cream out of your Twinkie?"

"Why are you here?"

"I want to remind Mom and Dad they still have one kid who doesn't suck."

He's jealous. Dyslexic and popular, Danny's grades have always tended toward the left side of the bell curve. "How are your classes?"

"International relations blows. Hey—did you know France and Germany are next to each other? No wonder they were always fighting."

I can't believe we have the same parents. "Yeah, Germany used to be over by Turkey but they moved it during the Schnitzel Campaign of 1812."

"Oh," he says, uncritically. "How's the job search going?"

"I don't want to talk about that."

"It must be hard. I mean, if you can't get a job, I'm pretty much screwed, huh?"

"Probably," I say, appreciating the compliment while still coming down off nearly blowing up at Ashley.

"Mom said she wants us to go to a networking thing together." I shake my head, physically shuddering at the idea.

"Do what you want, but I never woulda made President if I didn't leave my room."

"Thanks, but I don't think I need advice from someone whose résumé includes judging a wet t-shirt contest."

Being only sixteen months apart, Danny and I have been side by side for over two decades, and yet the gulf between who we are and how we live in the world seems to widen year by year. As Danny likes to point out when I decline picante sauce or come back from the beach with sunburned shoulders, our parents had one Mexican kid—him—and one white kid—me. Looking at a family photo it would seem my father and mother independently budded us like hydra, Danny growing from a lump on our father's neck and me from our mother's. His gentle teasing is well-intentioned but underscores the truth that my skin tells a different story than my last name, a contradiction I wear into every job interview and family reunion. Danny has always seemed to me by contrast more united, his body and spirit not bifurcated but complete. He carries this harmony inside his relaxed posture and easy smile and I've secretly always envied it, would love to know what it's like to be taken, better or worse, for who I am.

The garage door groans awake, signaling my parents' return from work. My dad enters first, car keys between his teeth, clutching file folders and the travel mug I gave him in the ninth grade printed with the periodic table. My mom follows a minute later, face down and navigating by periphery as her thumbs pound the keypad to finish one more email before dinner.

I plan to decline this opportunity to dine with my entire family, but my mother holds white plastic bags of Mexican takeout and I can smell the cheese enchiladas snug in their Styrofoam beds. The temptation is too great—melted cheese always wins.

I watch my brother use a toothpick to spear out all the green peas from his rice while my father flips through the mail and my mother resets the table, eschewing the plastic cutlery from the taqueria and laying down silverware with a resentful thwonk, her small protest at the unfairness of the second shift. I never noticed it until I moved back in after college but my mother has always worked two jobs, finishing her day at the university to then come home and cook and clean and pay bills and undertake the general air-traffic-controlling of suburban life. It's surprising in a woman who lists Betty Friedan as a personal hero, and yet this is how it's always been, almost as if arrangements were worked out long ago, compromises calcified into law. I bring a mug from my room half-full of rum and Dr. Pepper and take several nourishing gulps. There is a vile mood rising in the room like bad cologne.

I open my box, ready to flood my body with delicious casomorphins, but there on top of my enchiladas, splayed haughtily across my food like a Grande Odalisque, is the thickest, longest, blackest hair I have ever seen, its contours glistening in congealed grease and its aberrance set in high definition against the soft orange of the cheese.

"Oh my God," I say, shutting the box and standing up from my chair, "I'm gonna be sick."

"What's wrong?" my mother asks as I stalk to the trash.

"There's a *hair* in my *food*," and I shove the box down amongst coffee grounds and used tissues.

My mother tsks. "Just one little hair."

"It. Was. Massive."

"You could have pulled it out," my dad says. "You didn't have to waste a whole meal."

"I don't have to eat hair-covered garbage food."

I don't have to turn around to know my parents are exchanging a look, but I pretend to myself that I'm being perfectly rational and reasonable as I drop a bagel in the toaster and open the fridge to look for cream cheese.

"So," my mom asks with soft sarcasm, "how was your day?"

"Thrilling," I say. "Transcendent. Splendid beyond compare. Where's the cream cheese?"

"Dad, did you see the Diamondbacks traded Loyce?" Danny asks. "He was their best shortstop."

"You think we can hit up spring training next month?" Danny dips his head slightly and looks up at our dad with hope. "We can go to that steakhouse with the curry fries."

"Maybe," my dad says into his food and I see Danny's shoulders drop. The irony is Danny told me once he doesn't even like baseball. "We'll see. I might be traveling."

"Do we have any cream cheese?" I ask again, a little louder. The refrigerator is actually empty. Someone has to be responsible.

"Mona, do you remember my friend Belinda?" my mother asks. "She throws the Fourth of July party every year."

"Are we out of cream cheese?" I reply.

"She drives the Corvette," she says.

I'm not responding until my question is answered. Cream cheese is a small ask.

"We had dinner with her at that Greek place."

"Cream cheese," I say. "Do we have any?"

"I think her oldest daughter is Jana or Jenna, Jeanine—"

"Catherine," my dad says.

"She was a year younger than you at school."

Still waiting for an answer.

"Her husband owns the pottery shop by La Encantada...Pottery Fantasy, Pottery Factory..."

I can't stand it any longer. It's like they can't hear me unless I'm screaming. "Oh my God, Mom, yes I remember her. What's your point?"

"Okay. Well, she's got a little telemarketing business over by the airport, and she told me they have a call center position open. It's nothing exciting—just making phone calls, helping out around the office—but it would help, you know, get your feet wet."

"I don't want a telemarketing job," I say, rubbing my hands down my face. "I didn't get straight A's for seventeen years to work for minimum wage." I don't add that surely, in the time she spent shuttling me from one résumé builder to another, she never imagined it was all to prepare me for a life of shaking down strangers over the telephone. "Do you want me to work all day and get home too tired to look for a better job? Where's the cream cheese?"

"It's been eight months," she says. "Maybe it's time you revise your expectations."

"Where's the cream cheese?" I ask. My bagel is losing critical heat, the doughy insides hardening, turning my dinner into a hockey puck.

"I don't want you to settle, but taking a job, any job, would get your confidence up. You've got to start somewhere." She pauses and then adds, "And I think getting your own place would make you feel better, too."

The truth comes out—she wants to get rid of me. "Do we have any cream cheese?" Can't they see there's a time limit on eating a bagel? You get, like, five minutes max out of the toaster before it's inedible. This is agony.

"I don't think she should take that job," my dad says, and I look over to see my mother pinch up her face like a coin purse. "God forbid she find herself. Why not get her a job spinning a sign out front of a pawn shop?"

"I don't want to find myself. I want money. But I do want to find the cream cheese."

"You're too young to know what you want," and my father dismisses my words with a wave. "You have an opportunity here most people would kill for. A chance to really find out who you are. You can choose to see this from another angle."

"You could sell your plasma," smirks Danny, showering his food with Tapatío.

"I'm not saying she should degrade herself," my mom says. "I'm only suggesting she cast a wider net."

"Are we out of cream cheese?"

"You're telling her the opposite of casting a wider net," my dad says. "You're telling her to crawl into a casket and close the lid."

"You're so hyperbolic," my mother says. "I'm just saying it's time she learned how to swim."

"I'm standing right here."

My mother turns and speaks slowly like I'm stupid. "It's time you learned how to swim. We can't keep you afloat forever. It's not good for you and it's not good for us. I've offered you help a million different ways but you don't want it. And you need to realize your father and I have lives of our own. You're not going to hold us hostage with your bad attitude while you work this out. I refuse to get sucked down into your void."

"My void? My bad attitude?" I have a small moment of clarity, my first journal entry flashing in my brain like a Vegas billboard. "If I'd been allowed to fail at something when I was a kid maybe I would have learned how to do it better. I don't need to learn how to swim. I need to learn how to drown."

"That's enough," my dad says. "I just want to enjoy the rest of my dinner."

"I was kidding about the plasma thing," and Danny looks like he blames himself for the spiraling conversation.

"I don't know where you get this ego," my mother says, shaking her head.

"Uh, maybe from being told a gazillion times how good I was at everything?"

"And the sarcasm, the constant wisecracks. Always having to have the last word."

"Yeah I have *no idea* where I got that from."

My father looks down into his food and doesn't say anything. My mother leaves her plate on the table and gets up, pushing her chair hard against the Saltillo tiles.

"I finished the cream cheese," Danny says into his dinner.

I've had enough family fun for one night so I take my hard, dry bagel back to my bedroom.

"Bon appétit," I mutter at my laptop screen.

Before he returns to his frat house, my brother stops by my room to get my take on dinner. But I'm into my second or third cocktail and my mind has already slid eel-like out of those muddy waters.

"Have you noticed Mom and Dad sniping at each other more than usual?" he asks.

"Stop babysitting them. They're not your responsibility."

But Danny isn't convinced. "The lab's losing funding because of the Recession. Mom said there's gonna be layoffs for sure and she said something about maybe having to pull people off Dad's team."

"Well I guess it's good he's already sleeping with his boss."

"Can you just try to be a little nicer? It wouldn't kill you."

"It might, actually."

He gives me a hard look and I tighten my lips until I finally break. "I will agree to a ten percent increase in familial-directed niceness."

"Twenty."

"Twelve percent, and you have to bring weed the next time you come over."

When Danny's gone and my parents have settled into their postprandial routines—my mother howling at late-night men on the couch, my father cloistered in his study—I venture out for either more food or more alcohol, whichever of the two I see first.

I'm almost to the kitchen in the dark hallway when I practically knock over my father backing out of his study. In his green socks on the thick Berber he can move quiet as a ghost.

"Thanks for sticking up for me with Mom," I say, uncomfortable and unsure where to put my eyes. My father holds his shoulders up and his face tight and he gives the impression of wishing dearly he was elsewhere.

"It's your life. Only you can decide what to do."

"She wants me out of the house."

"You take your own time. No one's kicking you out. Though," he adds, "your mother's usually right."

I speak slowly, partly because I'm drunk, and partly because I feel childish. "How did you know what you wanted to do? Like, how did you decide you wanted to work on Alzheimer's?"

"It was a long time ago."

"But how do you know what you're meant for? How did you choose from literally every career in the world?"

"It's hard to say," and he looks as though he wants to say more, but he closes his mouth and looks over my shoulder back to his study, the room of his own. "No one can tell you what the right answer is, but this is far from the worst time in your life. I think I would say that you'll know when you know."

Feeling apparently that the matter is settled, he moves around me down the hall toward the bathroom, leaving me with no answers and an empty mug.

Chapter 2: Ad fundum.

When I was a senior in high school, I told my mother I was planning to major in finance and her face brightened like Christmas morning. "A smart choice," she said. "Another crack in the glass ceiling." But when I told my father there were no high fives or blessings of good luck. He was quiet a moment and then he said, "You're not supposed to say this to your child, but if you do, I will hate who you'll become."

Conquering Fears, Capturing Wealth

If you grew up in the fifties or sixties you probably got to experience Frank Sinatra music as it was intended: on the radio or a large walnut hi-fi or maybe even performed live by some fifteen-piece swing band. And maybe his music was good, at least relative to acts like Pat Boone. Maybe his music takes you back to strawberry malts at the pharmacy counter or Sunday drives along a serene lake. No one sells one hundred fifty million albums without anchoring themselves deep inside people's lives.

But if you grew up in the nineties, like me, and lived in a suburb characterized by sprawling, dough-colored strip malls of varying age and quality, as I did, your sole experience of Frank Sinatra would have been contained to trips to mass-market, upscale-casual corporate chain Italian restaurants like Carrabba's, The Spaghetti Warehouse, Buca Di Beppo, Brio Tuscan Grille, Johnny Carino's, Olive Garden, Maggiano's Little Italy, and Macaroni Grill. And as if on cue, as I push through the heavy wooden doors, nod at the orange-faced hostess sweeping farfalle into a bus tray, and get smothered by the thick, sweaty smell of fried garlic and burned rosemary, "Fly Me To The Moon" hits its big swinging crescendo, assaulting my ears and making me loathe the marketing team that coldly calculated same-store sales would rise three tenths of one percent if they always played up-tempo standards.

Far in a back corner of the restaurant, partially hidden behind a wall of tinned olives, is a sign that reads, 'Job Hob-Nob' and I wonder how I'm supposed to get help finding a job from people who can't even spell the word hobnob. It's a networking mixer, a cattle call of the dispossessed lured by free appetizers and a reason to put on pants, and a necessary evil born in the bowels of economic desperation. My brother follows me inside and, spotting a different tangerine-skinned hostess he knows from school, leans up against the bar stand and flirts, leaving me to scan the room and anxiously tug at the hem of my skirt. I didn't want Danny to come but my mother insisted, perhaps believing his charisma would rub off on me, that I could be cool by association.

"Come on," I say to Danny and march across the restaurant, imagining the pitying looks I must be getting from the other gainfully employed diners. I'm given a nametag and a reassurance that, "Things'll pick up after the Wildcats finish." The crowd is thin. In five minutes, I've introduced myself to everyone, eaten several handfuls of calamari, and listened to three different pitches from insurance carriers looking for new franchisees.

"You find a job yet?" Danny asks, eyes on the basketball game on a TV above the bar.

"Well," I say, "I've got several people eager to give me my own insurance brokerage for the low, low rate of sixty thousand up front."

"The calamari's good, though," he says.

"Did you find a job yet?" I ask, a little afraid the answer might be yes.

Danny looks at me over his Jack and Coke, eyebrows raised. Of course, he didn't even try to network, and why should he? Danny convinced our high school to build a hot tub in the natatorium.

"Did you call that chick?" Danny asks. "About the telemarketing job?"

"No," I say, indignant. "And I'm not going to."

"A job's a job," he says, still watching the game.

"Yeah and the first rule of the tautology club is the first rule of the tautology club." I sit down at a table and pull my pinched toes out of my Cole Haan's. A man in a leather cowboy hat walks by and starts chatting up a short, defeated looking ex-software engineer. They finish and Cowboy Hat ignores me because we've met before, twice, at other networking events. He sells used office furniture and comes to these things looking for leads on companies that are laying off. A thin, grey-haired Frenchwoman in a fraying sweater nods at me and moves on as well. I've met her before, too. She has cases of diet pills in the trunk of her car and is looking for some sucker to buy into her exciting new direct selling opportunity. These are the remoras, siphoning off the leftovers of our crumbling economy. The room fills eventually—men and women with hunched shoulders who go through the routine of handshakes and business card exchange—but it's all futile. Everyone is unemployed. How do you get a job by speaking to a bunch of other unemployed people?

I'm mingling again, listening to a woman tell me her idea for a new frozen yogurt parlor/belly dance studio, when I hear my name and turn around to see Paulette and Randy waving and smiling. Paulette appears to have forgotten my outburst from the other morning because, as usual, she seems genuinely thrilled to see me.

"What a great turnout," she says.

I nod and try to think of a way to apologize when Paulette is tapped on the shoulder and excuses herself.

Randy's in good spirits. His tie has a picture of a grinning fish on it, 'Kiss My Bass' scrawled underneath. He's rocking back and forth on his feet and telling me a rousing tale about being bitten by a rattlesnake when I spy Paulette being chatted up by the Frenchwoman.

And I can't explain whether it's out of guilt over how I've treated her, or because I'm discovering that her desire for what's best for me is actually mutual, but when I see Paulette, her hair a Dorito-colored halo atop her sainted head, I know I have to save her from suffering financial ruin at the hands of this scheming continental. I wonder if this makes me a hero.

"Oh, hell no," I say, excusing myself and pushing through the crowd. The woman is crouched over Paulette like a vulture getting ready to tear open a carcass. As I approach, Paulette is asking if the woman accepts personal checks.

"She's not interested," I say as Paulette sputters and looks confused.

The Frenchwoman turns and glares. The whites of her eyes are yellowed, the muscles in her face are visible under taut, gray skin, and I can imagine that, like a vulture, she's spent her life surviving on scraps. "You're very rude," the Frenchwoman says and attempts to maneuver around me and continue her drug sale.

"It's a scam," I tell Paulette, physically blocking her from the Frenchwoman. "It's a pyramid scheme. She's trying to take your money."

"No," Paulette says, but I can see my words sink in as she knits her brows. "These are European. They're the fastest growing herbal supplements in France and it's all women selling to women. I can take them to my church group."

"You are police?" the Frenchwoman asks, poking a bony, bejeweled finger into my sternum. "FDA? No? Then fuck off."

"Okay," Paulette says, smiling nervously and holding out her hands to separate us, "we don't need to get heated…"

"You're a leech," I say to the woman, pushing her finger aside, aware I'm raising my voice and attracting an audience. "You prey on these people because they're desperate and they have no other options. And to sell diet pills? It's an unregulated industry—there could be crack cocaine and horse shit in there." Her face is venom; her arms fold up against her black sweater and she shrivels before me. "You're a bad person," I say. I spot the man in the leather cowboy hat watching me and point to him. "And so are you."

Danny is already heading for the door, no doubt trying to distance himself from his crazy sister. I take one last look at my captive audience and, deciding I've already burned the bridge, point to the sign above my head, add, "You misspelled hobnob," and leave.

"That's Amore" pipes into the parking lot and I wish I'd had a chance to eat more before leaving. Danny is waiting under a streetlight, his arms crossed. "Are you happy?" he asks. "You looked like a psycho."

"Oh well," I say. "Now everyone knows."

The restaurant door opens and Randy and Paulette come out. "Mona!" Paulette shouts, though I'm only ten feet away from her. She runs up and hugs me and, though her frizzy hair is smothering my face and making it hard for me to breathe, I allow the embrace to continue until she relinquishes her hold. "That was such a sweet thing to do," she says, her hands still on my arms. "Thank you so much for looking out for me. You were right. It was possibly a scam—"

"Definitely a scam," I correct her.

"It was probably a scam," she concedes, "but I wanted to let you know I appreciate the gesture." She pauses a moment before she says, "You remind me of my daughter. Very…oppositional."

I'm not sure how I'm supposed to respond, so I just mumble goodnight.

I'm walking to the car when I hear Paulette call out, "You're a good person!"

I wave goodbye and close the car door before the moment can get any more saccharine, before anyone can notice the blush I feel creeping up my cheeks. Fortunately, Danny rescues me by smirking and saying, "You're my hero, Mona."

And I look at my reflection in the car window and smile, just a little bit, just for me.

* * *

"And that's why I'm not allowed at the waterpark anymore." Chasen, looking satisfied, sits back in his chair. The chair gives an audible creak under his weight and everyone in the room is silent, digesting the story and waiting for Paulette to speak.

Paulette stares at Chasen a moment longer and then clears her throat. "Well, I think that's a good place to stop," she says. "I was glad to see some of you at Job Hob-Nob last week," and she smiles at me. "By the door I posted a list of upcoming networking seminars. I hope to see you at some of them. Thank you for coming and have a blessed day!"

As I'm gathering my things, Paulette catches my elbow. She says quietly, like she's about to share a secret, "I don't know if you'd be interested but I have an extra ticket to a motivational speaker tonight. She's talking about women in business and I thought, with your finance background, maybe you'd be interested."

I'm not. But I can't exactly say I have other plans: drinking rum and playing Bejeweled is not an excuse I think I can tender. "Oh, thanks. Who is it?"

"Laura Horn. Have you heard of her?"

I do a double take. A literal actual, sitcom-styled double take. "Laura Horn? *The* Laura Horn? She's going to be here, in Tucson? And you're offering me a ticket?"

Paulette smiles. "Yes, are you a fan?"

I own seven of her books, four audiobooks, and a Barbie doll Ashley personalized for me a few birthdays ago wearing a power suit and Laura's trademark blonde coif. I'm no stalker but I'd say I'm a little more than a fan. "Yes," I say, returning Paulette's smile and feeling my eyes grow wider as I plot out what I'm going to wear, "I'm familiar with her work."

"Great," Paulette says. "Meet me at seven."

This feels big and portentous, like things are happening. For the first time in a long time, I feel the wheel starting to turn.

* * *

Laura's speaking at one of the hoity resorts out in the desert. At a quarter to seven I'm ascending the wide, saguaro-lined driveway. At the top I give my keys to a valet, having nicked my mom's credit card before leaving. A pianist in the lobby is playing some familiar classical tune, a song both violent and sweet that tells me I've wandered into a gathering of my socio-economic betters. This looks like a place that might spring for prosciutto.

The ballroom is bright and filled with middle-aged, mostly white women in black, red, and blue suits. My wish for dinner is fulfilled: the air is thick with mushrooms and a cart of sizzling chicken satays wheels past me while I look for Paulette.

Aside from seeing Laura in person and asking her to tell me explicitly what I can do to achieve fulfillment and financial independence within the next six months—low expectations, all—I don't have any objectives for the evening. How often do we get to meet our heroes?

I don't see Paulette so I choose a table near the food and eye the caterers in their black aprons, guarding the pans and shooing away hungry guests like they were patrolling goddamn Checkpoint Charlie. Finally, when it seems I'll have to dine on my own hair and fingernail trimmings, a plate of lettuce and grapefruit is placed before me as Paulette plops down in the next seat.

"Oh my goodness, isn't this nice," she says and her eyes go big as she takes in the room. She's fixed her gaze above my head so I look up, too.

"Oh yeah," I say, my mouth full of salad, "frescoes. Cool."

"Isn't she great?" Paulette says, indicating a massive headshot of Laura, all shoulder pads and smiles. "I planned my retirement out of her books. Of course," she says, fidgeting with her water goblet, "that was before I got laid off but, when I get on my feet, I'm going right back to her plan."

"She's amazing," I say, nodding. "Thank you, again, for the ticket. It was really nice of you."

Paulette pats my hand and I try to take a mental picture of her face so I can recall it later: pure, unguarded warmth.

A blonde woman crosses the stage and taps a microphone. In the run-up to Laura's keynote my attention slips in and out; I spend a long time watching the woman in front of me play Scrabble on her phone. I can't believe I'm going to see her in person. This is what it must have felt like to see Elvis.

I started listening to her in high school when I inherited my mother's aged Acura and found a well-worn Laura Horn audio book in her glove box. Laura and my mother shared a passion for statement blazers. As the cover promised to teach me the secret to growing rich, and as growing rich is an objectively pure and decent aim, I put in the disc.

"Fear is the only thing stopping you from getting rich," the voice on the CD began. "Fears are the invading forces pummeling your defenses, and preventing you from erecting a sturdy castle built on sound decisions, hard work, love, and spiritual fulfillment."

A reasonable proposition. I didn't turn it off.

"And to conquer these fears, it's as simple as believing you can defeat them. If not, you deny yourself the possibility of a tomorrow blessed with more."

Well I certainly didn't want that.

"We start by first conquering our fears, and then capturing wealth, both financial and spiritual."

Embracing money necessitated embracing fear. Okay, then embracing fear meant enduring, for a short time, things I didn't want to do, and ignoring what was irrational yet deeply felt in the body, in favor of things that were ultimately to my benefit. Quod erat demonstrandum, getting rich meant doing things I was not inclined to do.

"I will show you how to confront the voices of denial, fortify yourself against new attacks, and chart a future that leaves you not only well provided for in your retirement, but that gives you the tools to capture wealth in any form, whether it's financial, spiritual, or emotional. It's only when we've achieved fulfillment in all three that we learn we are loved without reservation for who we are, and not how much we have."

But having a lot wouldn't feel too bad, either.

The blonde is back onstage. "And now, ladies, please help me give a warm welcome to our keynote speaker, Laura Horn!" The room erupts. I stand and clap until the palms of my hands go numb. There's something wet under my eye—am I crying? I sit down before I risk fainting. There she is: an angel in a St. John pantsuit, her blonde crop cut gleaming like Joan of Arc's helmet in the siege of Orléans. She dominates the stage; the other women at the podium shrink at her presence. She takes the microphone and the shock at hearing a living, breathing person intone the same voice I've had in my ear for seven years is disarming, like watching the actors from *The Simpsons* do a live reading.

"Who here is ready to conquer their fears and capture wealth?" And everyone in the ballroom is again on their feet. If beliefs were pennies everyone in the room would have a Rolex.

She begins with a story about her ascent from shoe salesman to financial adviser, getting a laugh when she says that at one time the only thing she knew about brokers was that they made you broker. Then she moves into her financial advice. We must manage our debt, she says. We must save for retirement, she says. Her facility with financial argot almost equals my own and I feel a kinship with her, the impermeable bond between two masters of the same discipline. The speech transitions from memoir to sermon as she commands—

commands!—the audience to embrace failures for their ability to bring one closer to success. The audience punctuates each message with applause and I join them. Of course, she's correct. One door closes and another one opens. I just want her to tell me when my door will open.

When she's finished, a line forms around the ballroom for autographs. Paulette and I inch through. I'm rehearsing my questions over and over, terrified I'll botch the opportunity. I've never met a celebrity, unless you count shaking Al Gore's hand, and I don't. My palms are wet and my mouth is dry. I can see her face. She really does look good for her age.

I'm next. Don't screw this up! A tall woman with a tropical scarf around her head is posing for a picture. I catch the word, cancer, as they chat and shake hands. Now the tall woman steps away, now I'm beckoned forth. Laura takes the book from my hand and flashes her champion smile: brilliant, white teeth between frosted pink lips. She's talking to me, nodding her head while she waits for my reply, but all I can hear is blood rushing through my head. Give me time! It'll come to me. Surely, I'm not the first fan to falter in your presence!

"Who should I make this out to?" she says again.

"Mona," I say. "I, uh, I'm a fan." I hand my phone to Paulette and stand beside Laura for a photo. She smells like achievement and hairspray.

"And what do you do, Mona?" she asks, sitting down.

"Well, I was *supposed to* have a job at Bannerman," I begin, waiting for the sympathetic frown I always get with that sentence. It doesn't come but I continue anyway. "I was going to be an analyst. But I got laid off when…you know. And I'm looking. I've applied to four hundred jobs, but no one's hiring. Everything sucks and I don't know what to do. What should I do?"

She narrows her eyes a little. "Did you hear what you just said? You were *supposed to* have a job at Bannerman? Stop being a victim, Mona. Holding on to the past is stopping you from moving forward."

She hands the book back to me and smiles, waiting for me to step away, but I'm not finished.

"But why can't I get a job? I had excellent grades, a sensible major, extra-curriculars. I did everything right. There's got to be an explanation."

"It's your attitude," she says, and my face freezes. "The world doesn't owe you anything. You've got to get out there and prove yourself. Stop waiting to be rescued and take control of your life. A great person gets a great job."

I close my eyes and inhale through my nostrils. I decide to try honey, not vinegar. "I'm sorry if I'm coming across as difficult. I'm drowning here."

She frowns. "Did you see the woman in front of you in line? She has Stage III breast cancer. Do you think she's sitting at home feeling sorry for herself?" She sighs and puts her hands on the table. "Why do you want to work in finance? It's the money, right? Get a job helping the elderly. Sell shoes like I did. Money's not going to make you happy. People make you happy."

She holds out her hand to take a book from Paulette behind me. I stand a moment, ten different arguments fighting to come out of my mouth, but the other women in line are giving me ugly looks so I move forward. "Thank you for coming, Mona," Laura says, looking up from the book she's signing long enough to wink at me. "And good luck." I nod and force a smile and move to the entrance to wait for Paulette, swiping two cold satays off a tray for my walk to the valet stand.

"What a wonderful woman," Paulette gushes as we walk through the lobby.

I tear a piece of meat off the stick and ignore an old woman in an Hermès scarf frowning at me. "She comes off smarter in her books," I mumble. Is that what I want to say? I try again. "I like her books more, but she's…she has this…She always has answers." Even when people don't like them.

"I sold shoes, too," Paulette says. "You meet a lot of interesting people in shoe stores."

"Really," I ask, stopping in my tracks and facing her in mock seriousness, "you think I have the right personality for direct sales?"

Paulette laughs and I do, too. "You're right," she says, "maybe you'd better stay out of customer service."

We had layoffs. Big time.

I knew another cutter once, a girl named Hayley who lived down the hall from Ashley and me our freshman year. She had chin-length purple hair and horn-rimmed glasses, and her outfits usually included some kind of stuffed animal she had reappropriated into apparel: a teddy bear backpack, a belt made of Beanie Babies, Cookie Monster gloves crowned with googly eyes. But Hayley's real flamboyance she reserved for her arms, both heavily tattooed and scattered with self-inflicted wounds that capered across her skin like shrapnel. Old Hollywood pinup girls and Hokusai's *Great Wave Off Kanagawa* were interspersed with livid, fearsome cuts that gashed over her body art like she'd tried to gouge out her tattoos with a steak knife. It was terrifying but definitely...deliberate.

I used to watch her out of the corner of my eye if we were ever at the sinks together brushing our teeth, unable to say hello because I found her revolting, intimidating, and inspirational in equal parts, and because I couldn't think of anything less trite to say than, "You have a lot of tattoos." And the fact that we never spoke only made her more mythic, for clearly there was a backstory, or if not a backstory then a manifesto, something she wrote longhand on sheets of paper taped together like Kerouac. Surely somewhere lay an explanation. If her body was a commentary she forced everyone to read, what was she trying to say? Something about violence against women? Was she redefining beauty or redefining art? Was she subverting the old, 'My body is a temple' maxim of self-preservation? Was she harming herself before the world had a chance to destroy her? Or was she altering her body to fit her own, contorted ideal? Whatever her reasons, she wasn't hiding her injuries. She wore her scars like badges, like armor, like middle fingers stationed around her body telling people to back away. But why? But why?

I tracked down photos of Hayley online and studied her poses, her facial expressions. When I couldn't learn anything more about her from MySpace I lurked through websites about cutting and burning; some people even take small doses of poison every day. I read their poetry and their stories of abuse and addiction and worse, and while studying this world felt like submerging chin-deep into a sucking swamp, I couldn't arrest my fascination with the scars, the instruments, the compulsion to indulge in something so intimately deviant, day after day after...

Sophomore year Ashley and I had an argument over a cashmere sweater accidentally shrunk in the dryer. She was a mean fighter, a dirty fighter, and she stockpiled intimacies over the years to use as emotional ammunition. She pointed her finger in my face and fired accusations like darts, targeting my insecurity over my looks, 10 points; my lack of a boyfriend, 20 points; and the fact that my obsessive accrual of accomplishments masked a sad young woman who didn't know who she was, bullseye. She had cut off my legs; I had no riposte. Not allowing her to see me cry was the best revenge I could muster.

I threw myself onto my chair, laid my head on my desk, and sobbed. When I quieted, I stayed there, listening to my heartbeat and watching dust flutter across my desk with each exhale. With one eye I could see my pencil jar jammed with pens and markers and an old X-Acto knife from a high school science class. I pulled out the knife and felt the blade. One little cut wouldn't mean much. I wasn't trying to kill myself. I was just angry with Ashley for being such a dirty fighter, and angrier with myself for not being one. I bent close to my thigh and brought the blade down. There was hesitation, some part of me pulling my sleeve and saying, no, please don't, but a more hostile element pushed the razor to the skin and held it there. "I don't care," I said aloud as I made the incision and watched blood come to the surface.

I felt so guilty after the first cut that I didn't do it again for six weeks. I could always see the little slice, about as long as a pinkie nail, peeking out from below my shorts as I sat at my desk, or during yoga, attempting downward dog. Over the weeks I watched the scar evolve from bright red to pink and white, not unlike the evolution of the sun—stormy, forlorn, and then dead. It looked strange alone, as though it required acknowledgement. Or rather, I thought, it required purpose.

Hayley's cuts were jagged lines, hardly artistic whatever their motive. But I could make something different, something with intent. Mutilation was wrong; mutilation was sick. But under another name, something less destructive, what I was about to do became body art, body modification, ritual scarification, epidermal rehabbing—the distinction between self-injury and self-expression is sometimes very thin. I'd tread the line carefully.

The first line grew into the bridge of a nose after my Mergers and Acquisitions professor said to me, in front of a class filled with myself and thirty-seven boys, that it was nice to have a pretty face to look at during lectures. The nose was joined by round cheeks when one day I could no longer zip up my favorite jeans. I carved out eyes when I saw the boy I liked from my Latin class making out with some halfwit in the dining hall, and I closed the face when I got a B on a research paper for Business Ethics. The drawing sprouted arms and hands, donned robes of heavy velvet, grew long wavy hair.

I didn't intend to make 'Mona Lisa'. In hindsight it seems pretty egotistical to carve my namesake into my leg, like all those men named John Wayne who get the Duke's face inscribed on their chests. In almost four years I've added trees and water and a winding path over her right shoulder, my scar tissue aiding in the smoky, sfumato effect. The picture has had to warp a little owing to the contours of my thigh, and I've had to sacrifice a bit of detail in favor of spatial perspective but, you know, it's my leg and I can do what I want.

I haven't yet reached her smile. When she smiles, I'll know she's done.

After I finish a section, I rub Vaseline on the fresh cuts and seal my leg in a roll of cling wrap I keep hidden in my closet. I haven't worn a bikini bottom since I was nineteen. No short-shorts in Arizona kind of sucks. I've hinted to my gynecologist that I'm a member of some obscure religion that doesn't permit exposed thighs. If my parents' cleaning lady has ever come upon my bottle of isopropyl or my economy bag of cotton balls, she's never said anything to me.

And what I've learned in four years, aside from how to achieve different color gradations of scar tissue, is that Hayley probably didn't have a backstory or a manifesto, that she probably wasn't slowly enacting some Carolee Schneemann-type performance art across her body, that she was just a fucked up person doing something fucked up for reasons too cloudy and byzantine to untangle.

I had a rotten wisdom tooth in high school that gave me so much pain for weeks I wished I could take a knife and cut the tooth out myself, just to give me some relief. I've never experienced pleasure even close to that in intensity, have never felt an enduring lightness or all-consuming mirth. Even if I did momentarily float on a cloud or see cartoon songbirds alight on my fingertips, the feeling was there and gone, replaced with tedium, sadness, and doubt. That was it. The boredom between disasters, the shuffle between school and work and the grocery store and the tire repair shop and remembering to floss and sending a follow-up email and forgetting the name of the book I read just last month. In my long unemployment, the one privilege I've had is the ability to stand still, and as I watch the world continue without me, it all seems like distractions piled one on top of the other, bricks endlessly falling from the sky like Tetris. I think if people really thought about it, really looked closely at the entire scope of their lives, no one would choose to live their life over again. It's all too much of the same. For everyone, right?

* * *

A waitress, her nametag reads Tiny, uses her order pad to swat away a fly. She waits for me to calculate if I have enough money to leave a tip if I spring for an omelet. I do not.

"Coffee and a bagel, please," and when I hand the menu back, I can feel resentment rising from her pores. While I wait for my coffee, I watch a different fly edge along the perimeter of my table before stopping at a drop of ketchup. A man in the booth behind me sneezes for the one hundredth time, the greasy lights give everyone a sickly avocado tint, and the entire place smells of bleach—hardly the glamour of Hopper's *Automat*. And it is under these auspicious circumstances that I open my laptop to the career aptitude test I've been avoiding for weeks. Paulette asked me to take it—the browser tab stares at me each time I check my email—but I haven't had the courage.

It is in your nature to assume responsibility, Yes or No. Born leader, that's me. *You prefer to read a book than go to a party.* Are there douchebags at the party? That's an important distinction. *You have good control over your desires and temptations.* Second to none.

The familiar joy of having a homework assignment creeps over me, the small bliss of a finite task, and I linger over each question, delaying the moment I have to reenter my empty house and fill the hours before my parents come home to feed me.

You think that almost everything can be analyzed. There are people who don't think everything can be analyzed? *You take pleasure in putting things in order.* I have been known to alphabetize a spice rack or two.

Personality tests are stupid. I took the Myers-Briggs in college and learned I have the same personality type as Napoleon Bonaparte, so I'm obviously destined for big things. *Please choose a response to the following scenario: Mrs. Crumb enters a baking competition. An accomplished pastry chef, Mrs. Crumb uses the best ingredients, executes her recipe without flaw, and places a picture-perfect pineapple upside-down cake before the judges. Mrs. Crumb takes second place. When she asks the judges why she did not win, they reply that the previous year's winner had been a pineapple upside-down cake, and they did not want to appear partial to fruit-based desserts. Should Mrs. Crumb: A) Accept her second place ribbon, B) Accept her second place ribbon but complain to others of her ill treatment, or C) File a grievance with the contest board and demand the desserts be reevaluated.* Poor Mrs. Crumb! C, C, a million times C!

I click for my results and sigh when I see a clip art figure of a man, with irrational exuberance, hugging a bar graph. "You are an Organizer. Conservative and introverted, you enjoy data systems, details, accounting, numbers, and accuracy. Favorite tasks include compiling spreadsheets, balancing accounts, creating charts and graphs, cataloguing inventories, and budgeting. Organizers make great financial analysts, accountants, statisticians, actuaries, bank cashiers, and IRS agents."

I scroll further however, and see descriptions for Doer, Thinker, Creator, Helper, and Persuader, with pie charts showing equal percentages for each, and I realize I've somehow scored exactly in the middle of the stupid test, that I'm intellectually, emotionally, and in all other ways suited for literally any career on earth from airplane mechanic to bikini waxer—both Helper trades, I learn.

"What a crock of shit," I say aloud, and Tiny sniffs her disapproval.

* * *

"Jalapeño croquette? Jalapeño croquette, sir? Ma'am, would you like one? Have a great day!" Since graduation, Ashley has been working as a sample girl at an upscale grocery store. For minimum wage she dispenses nibbles from a little glass booth, convincing hungry customers to buy overpriced and fatuous trifles like Manchego tarts with quince coulis, salmon mousse on brioche, charcuterie with pickled fennel—all this in a recession!

"Don't you hate your job?" I ask, swallowing a fourth croquette. Facing another afternoon at my house watching the sun wash across the stucco was too much to bear, so I came to bother Ashley at work after leaving the diner. And who can turn down free samples?

"I try not to think about it," she says, smiling as she hands a croquette to a woman bouncing a baby strapped to her chest. "It could be worse. And they let me take home all the expired coconut water."

"Wowza," I say, "try not to drink it all in one place." I yawn, stretching my arms out and cracking my neck. Then I slump over and rest my head on Ashley's counter, violating all rules about safe food handling. "I'm so bored. Aren't you bored?"

"What's wrong with you?" Ashley shoves me away and wipes down the counter. "Did I tell you my sister got engaged?" she asks in between vigorous strokes over the polished quartz. "She asked me to be maid of honor but then sent this bitchy email to me and my cousins saying we can't be in the wedding unless we're ready to spend serious money on dresses and parties and all that. She knows I'm trying to stop asking my parents for help." She yawns and kneads her knuckles into her lower back before sipping an iced coffee.

"So, don't do it," I say. "She'll probably get divorced anyway."

"No," Ashley sighs as she pulls a new tray of croquettes out of a toaster oven. "Of course, I'm going to do it. I just don't know why she has to be so unpleasant. And my parents are throwing her this big engagement party at their club, so my mom sent me this text yesterday. Tell me she's not crazy."

Ashley holds up her phone. Next to the name 'Crystal' and a photo of a triangle-faced woman in an overlarge sunhat, the message reads,

> "U need a new dress for ur sister's party. NOTHING LAST SEASON!!! Pls don't embarrass me like New Year's."

"Yikes," I say, handing the phone back to her. "I'll give you a hundred dollars if you show up in your grocer's apron."

Ashley laughs so hard she dribbles coffee down her chin.

I'm about to leave when my phone vibrates, signaling I have a new email. And though I don't dare hope it's anything approximating good news, I open it anyway.

> Dear Ms. Mireles,
>
> We request an interview with you for the position of Equity Trader. Business attire preferred. Please bring a copy of your résumé and salary requirements to our office at 10 a.m. on Thursday and PLEASE BE ON TIME.
>
> Sincerely,
>
> Jenny Nosek
> Human Resources Representative
> Phoenix X Trading Systems, Inc.

I have to read the email five times before the words sink in: interview, trader, salary. Then my shriek causes several shoppers to turn and look. The baby bouncing in the carrier looks at me and bawls, but I don't care. An interview! For a real job! A high paying, fast-paced, impressive-sounding job!

"I got a job interview," I say, delivering an awkward shuffle dance near a ziggurat of imported salami. "I never thought I'd hear from them. I sent my résumé ages ago. Who's down with j-o-b? Yeah you know me!"

"Congratulations," Ashley says, though she sounds underwhelming. "Your mom'll be happy."

"Forget her. If I get this job, I'm gonna buy so much stuff. I'm gonna get a tiny dog and cover its water bowl in crystals, and I'm gonna get eyelash extensions and a chocolate fountain and…"

"Aren't you getting ahead of yourself?"

"It's been eighty-three days since I've had an interview. Four hundred thirty-nine applications. I absolutely want to get ahead of myself, so far ahead that I wish it was ten years from now and all this was a distant nightmare."

"Well, good luck," and I can tell Ashley has more she wants to say, but she instead starts chatting up the virtues of the frozen croquettes to an elderly couple. I won't say it out loud but of course we're competing to see who will get *it* first. The good job, achievement of which implies mastery over the sucking morass of adulthood. If Ashley's jealous I got an interview, that's fine. In an arms race any escalation demands a response.

I trip out of the store checking the message one more time, making sure it isn't a mistake. Making sure they want me. They really want me!

* * *

One week later, the morning of the interview, I wake up with my bedtime mantra still running ticker-tape through me: I'm unemployed, I've never had a boyfriend, I live with my parents in the most boring town on the planet, and I hate myself. I feel a nervous dread that causes me to chew up the insides of my cheeks, but at least I'm alone in the house. My mother wanted to stay up late last night rehearsing interview questions and I had to feign menstrual cramps so she'd let me go to sleep. I tell myself the dread is nothing more than pre-interview jitters, that I want the job so badly I'm afraid I'll botch the opportunity. I shove the chocolate-scented soaps out of the way and grab my pencil case. I worry I'm forming a Pavlovian response where I equate smelling chocolate with cutting, but even after ten minutes of working on my leg the dread is still there and for a half second I wonder, am I afraid I won't get the job, or afraid I will? I try to wash out this thought as I shampoo my hair, and by the time I step into my heels, I've coaxed myself into a reasonable approximation of eagerness and confidence. Great person, great job.

I walk through the double doors of Phoenix X and almost walk right out when I see rows of empty desks, black computer screens, unplugged cords trailing from cubicles like dead jellyfish tentacles. I'd expect to hear noise—phones ringing, the tin-can voice of someone on the other end of a conference call—but all I get is an eerie, electronic hum and the click of a few fingers on keyboards. I don't see a receptionist so I lean into one of the few occupied cubicles and ask a man in a black suit and a baseball cap where I can find Jenny Nosek. He doesn't talk, doesn't look up from the screen that colors his face pale blue, just points down a hallway, so I thank him and move on. At the end of the hall, behind a dismal spider plant, is Jenny Nosek, the only worker in a space built for ten. She waves when she sees me, offers coffee, and escorts me to a conference room with windows overlooking a parched soccer field.

We make small talk—it turns out we went to the same high school and university—before she shuffles some papers and takes a long look at the back of the conference room door.

"You probably noticed there aren't many of us around."

"It does seem a little roomy."

"We had layoffs. Big time. We went from a staff of two hundred to about forty in a few months. The trading desk is still swamped though, and Mr. Ford, he's our director, he wants someone to pick up the slack." She looks over my résumé again. "You're qualified," she says, and my heart leaps, "but the decision's not up to me. I'm just a screener." She verifies my email and phone, promises she'll pass on my information to Ford, and sees me out the door.

Before she shakes my hand, she hesitates. "You are applying to other jobs, right?" she asks in a lowered voice.

"Yes," I say slowly.

"Good. I'm only telling you this because we're both Wildcats, but I'm not sure how long we're going to be around. I'd hate for you to take this job and be let go in six months."

"How likely is that, do you think?"

She looks at me sideways. "Aren't you watching the news?" She shakes my hand and wishes me well.

Outside the office I stand blinking in the midmorning sun, the heat soaking into my panty hose and wool blazer until I'm smothered. I'm not sure what just happened. Well, I know what happened, but I can't admit it yet. Red flags were thrust down my throat but I'm left still wanting the job. I'm dizzy, so on the way home I stop at a drive-thru for a milkshake. I pull off the road at an abandoned K-Mart and watch a tumbleweed roll across the parking lot. Poetic. My hands go numb from the milkshake. The tumbleweed is caught in an overturned grocery cart and a side wind tries to jerk it free. I feel something catch in my chest and I startle. I hadn't realized it, but I'd been holding my breath.

* * *

Later that night we're celebrating my father's birthday and Danny's apparently in a sadistic mood: He's booked a reservation for all of us at the local hibachi restaurant. Walking in, the place has all the cultural authenticity of an airport gift shop: bamboo plants flank the entrance and paper calligraphy scrolls the walls, exclaiming, for all I know, Overpriced meat for suckers!

My family is already here and I give silent thanks to whichever deity controls such things that they have declined the towering red paper hats some patrons wear in homage to the hibachi chef. The seating is communal and I sit down between my father and a bespectacled boy about my age in a Che Guevara t-shirt. I wish my father a happy birthday, give him the card I purchased ten minutes before, and promise to buy him a gift when I have a job.

"You don't have to get me anything," and he gives my shoulder a squeeze. "Are you ready for a show?" he asks with some sarcasm. "They're going to light an onion on fire."

"I'll try to contain my excitement. Is there a wine list?"

"How was your interview?" My mom, balancing a half-drunk martini between her fingers, leans all the way back in her chair to speak to me as the chef has begun drumming and juggling his spatulas and Danny has his elbows on the table to watch like a kid at the circus. My father, meanwhile, folds his arms across himself and watches with tepid interest.

"It was...you know. They'll let me know."

"Did you send a thank you note?"

"I put it in the mail before I left the house."

The chef drops a small mountain of zucchini on the grill and slices them longways with fluid strokes, his prongs and spatula hammering out a ticking rhythm that, combined with the sizzle from the hot grill, makes a sound like an old record spinning on a turntable, clickety-clickety-hiss.

"And you spoke about the Investment Club? How well it performed when you were in charge?"

"We didn't get to that. She was just a screener."

The chef produces a Santoku knife and filets a fish faster than Danny can pull his phone to get a picture. The fish head flops to the side and his eyes loll up toward the ceiling as though he, too, is over it.

"You could have said something. It's always worth it to chat yourself up, even if it's someone far down the chain."

Her eyes are small and gin-reddened and I nod and there passes between us a fleeting understanding of our mutual need to ease our passage through the dark night, to equilibrate and lubricate. I take my far-too-small glass of white wine from the waitress and swallow half. The one good thing about hibachi is that we're not facing one another. I pretend to be engrossed by the dragon the chef is now painting free-hand with a squeeze bottle of scrambled egg. I'm aware of a pulsing light off to my left and look up and see a teenage girl is taking my picture. The camera flashes; I cannot see.

"Sad Millennial!" she shouts in triumph. "Sing the song. Say something funny. Did you ever get a job?"

I drop my head and let my hair curtain me. I've learned not to flip them off—there's an obscure Tumblr page out there of photos of me giving the middle finger.

"Can you leave us alone?" Danny asks. "We're having a family dinner."

"Make her say 'It's not fair.'"

"I don't want to get the manager," my mother says, faith in the system full as ever.

The girl snickers and points to the zucchini. "Still eating your veggies!"

"Can you be a human being?" I'm startled to hear my father speak. He's always held back, waited for others to speak first—my mother usually, sometimes Danny or me—and the condemning tone of his voice is one he uses only rarely at home and never with strangers. It is the voice of utter disappointment, of expectations savagely unmet. He is speaking, I fear, to me.

"Whatever," she says and flips her hair for relish, "I got all y'all." She saunters away, phone in hand.

"I'm sorry," I mutter when I can sit back up. The dragon's severed head is on my plate. Somehow, our chef was unruffled by the interruption.

We eat in silence a moment, a collective attempt at radical ignoring, when the chef whistles, spreads oil on the cooktop, and begins a rapid dice of a chicken cutlet.

"That's amazing." Danny keeps saying this to resurrect the night. "We should get one of these things," is his other remark, exchanging approving nods with the father of the boy in the Che shirt. Danny lets out a whoop every time the chef flips his spatula and the chef, getting the impression from Danny's enthusiasm that this is a table wishing to party, starts flickering the light above the grill like a strobe. The heat from the grill, the pervasive onion smell, the pulsing light and the wine are combining to make me nauseous but the courses keep coming. Shrimp, salmon, chicken, steak—I'm not a vegetarian but I'm disturbed when a mound of carcasses accrues at the edge of my plate, globby bits and pink fly-wing tails.

"Do you want some dumplings?" my mother asks my father, her head in the menu. "Let's get some dumplings."

"I don't want any." My father answers while he watches the chef entertain some children at the other end of the table by making a shrimp crawl across the edge of the grill.

"You might want some," my mother says. "I'll just get some. We can always take them home."

"If you want dumplings just order them. You don't have to pretend they're for me."

"Do you remember we came here when I turned sixteen?" Danny is looking to me, but speaking loud enough that he clearly wants everyone else to join.

"That was really fun," I lie. "Don't we have a picture of us with the red hats?"

"I'll just get one order," my mother says as though it's a confession. "And why don't you get a drink? It's a celebration."

"I feel fine," my father says, and from my seat on the other side of him I can imagine his eyes flitting to the second martini glass beside my mom's dinner plate. "It looks like you're the one who needs to unwind."

My mother blows out a long breath. "The chancellor called an emergency budget meeting for Friday. Essentially, I need to justify why we should keep the lab open. This is your job on the line," she turns to my father. "I don't know how you can be so nonchalant."

"Maybe it's fate," he mutters.

"*I'm* fate," my mother says. "Alpha and omega, right here."

My father looks at her a moment and, somehow, his face softens. "Don't put so much on your shoulders. You're going to make the right decisions."

But these encouraging words do nothing to quell the flames now jumping inside her eyes. "Don't minimize. You always do that. You have no idea how this pressure feels." My father tries to put his hand on her arm but she shrugs him off, and I'm relieved when the chef begins constructing the onion volcano.

"Here it comes," Danny says rubbing his hands together, and I'm both baffled he could derive joy from such cheap pyrotechnics and envious that his amusement comes at so little cost. After dousing the onion with something from a squeeze bottle steam shoots out of the opening and the chef shines a red flashlight over it, presumably to remind us the steam is meant to be lava.

"No fire?" Danny cries, sounding wounded to the core.

"Nah, we don't do that anymore." The chef shrugs, putting the flashlight back in his pocket. "Some dude in LA caught fire or something."

"That blows," Danny says, and I know he's not referring to the tragedy of being set on fire by a hibachi stunt.

We decline dessert, the check is paid, and everyone gets to their feet. The wine is in my head and I stumble a little standing up. The boy in the Che shirt catches my elbow before I can twist my ankle.

"Mona?" he asks. "From Foothills? It's Gil. We had AP chemistry together."

Fantastic—my family's dysfunction is on full display at a Japanese steakhouse and someone I know from high school got a front row seat. "Yeah, I remember you," I say, though I don't really. "Didn't you start a video game club, or something?"

"Lords of the Underworld. How have you been?"

"Um, good. Really good. It's my dad's birthday so we're out here. Celebrating."

"Yeah," he says, bending closer and lowering his voice, "my parents love this place but it's super lame, right? And I've been a vegetarian for years but they conveniently always forget when I'm home, so I've basically had zucchini for dinner."

I'm struggling to recollect Gil. A nerd like me, we orbited the same circles—concert violinists, Dungeons & Dragons players, closet bulimics and Adderall abusers—but our paths never crossed in any meaningful way. His body is monochromatic with skin and hair the color of oatmeal. Inoffensive is the word that comes to mind. Like cinnamon potpourri.

"What are you doing now?" he asks. "Are you working?"

I clear my throat. "I'm, uh, looking at a lot of different options right now. I'm interviewing for an equity trading position that looks pretty promising. What about you?"

"Stanford Law," he says and I nod my head, imagining the Che shirt is required uniform in Northern California. "I'm going to be a patent attorney. To give back, you know?"

To give back? Okay, sure. "Are you on break or something?"

"Yeah, just for the week. Why don't you give me your number? We can hang out."

He won't call, but I give him my number anyway. I skip a goodbye hug with my parents since we're going to see each other at home in eighteen minutes, but as I'm heading to my car Danny calls for me to stop.

"Well, that was a nightmare," he says.

"Wouldn't you be upset about turning fifty-eight?" I ask.

"You don't think they'll really shut down the lab, do you?"

"Maybe the school would have more money for research if they didn't spend it all on sports."

"That's not helpful."

"That's kind of my thing, not being helpful."

"I wish you wouldn't make a joke out of everything."

"That's kind of my thing, too."

Danny blows a long breath out through his nose.

The wine makes me honest. "I told you to stop babysitting us— them, I mean. They're gonna do what they do whether you fuss about it or not."

"Yeah," Danny says shaking his head. "I wish I could be as above-it-all as you are."

"It's a gift."

Danny, apparently having had enough of my deflections, puts his hands up and walks away.

"Sorry!" I shout after him, and I mean it, but he won't turn around and I don't have the energy to chase him through the parking lot. He's used to my sarcasm, my refusal to discuss things earnestly. I know he organized this dinner to try and make a family moment, but like all his attempts at cohesion, it failed. When I was a kid being driven across the city from one résumé-builder to another, Danny mostly stayed home with our father, who'd usually put on the television rather than actively parent. So, Danny was raised largely by the Tanners, the Seavers, the Conners, and the Keatons. He gets these perfect TV moments in his head, gets us out and arranges everyone like the portrait in the opening credits of *Family Ties*, and then can't understand why we won't stand still, why we turn and face the other direction, why the image disintegrates the moment he's composed it. I'm sorry that he erects his failure in this way, but I'm not sure if his untarnished hope is any healthier than my cynicism. They're probably both illusions.

When Danny drives off, I don't leave the parking lot right away. Through my windshield the sky is cloudless. I find Orion and the Big

Dipper, the only two constellations I can identify. I remember taking a field trip to a planetarium once and hearing a lecture about the scale of the solar system. If the sun could fit in the palm of your hand, Pluto would still be six football fields away. I remember this and I get angry. If the universe is so limitless, why do we all feel trapped?

Chapter 3: Everything's a nail to a hammer.

When Alexander the Great had finally conquered the known world, supposedly he wept because he couldn't imagine what he'd do with the rest of his life. I'm not comparing being valedictorian to the conquest of the Persian Empire (although I'd like to see any Macedonian king run a multiple linear regression in SAS), but sometimes I wonder if I'd react any differently. To think that a man who studied with Aristotle could be incapable of enjoying his own success, could value nothing but the fight. Is there something addictive about achievement? Once you've summited Mount Everest, does everywhere else seem flat?

The terminal point
of freedom

The evening news is a scab I can't stop picking. Every night I watch, knowing I'll come away worse, seeing the strings that currently bind the country—greed and lassitude and short-sightedness—pulled tighter and twine rounder the collective ankles. And yet some Pollyanna part of me wants to believe everything will be alright, that one night I'll turn on the news and the president will say he's starting a public works program, or that Congress has banned predatory lending, that the credit rating agencies will no longer be allowed to offer positive bond ratings in exchange for cash, that banks will care about climate change, that corporations will pay more than an effective tax rate of two percent, that CEOs will refuse to accept compensation three hundred times what their average workers receive, that marginal tax rates will be restored to the low nineties, that wage gains will equal productivity, that I'll never have to hear another paste-faced old man simper through the myth that a rising tide lifts all boats. This is ironic, I'm aware, given that I want to work for the very robber barons who'd sell their own mothers for a Chateau Lafitte and a foursome at Augusta. But it's precisely because it's my chosen vocation that I care, that I can see the way things could be, and wish. And I have hope, just a scrap, though night by night the light dims.

And tonight is the same. The drought is spreading. Food prices will rise by five percent. One channel recaps Senate hearings on lead and melamine poisoning cases connected to Bannerman offshoots and their Chinese manufacturers. A line of grade-school children file into the chambers in their Sunday suits and recount how they were sickened by lead-laced candy at a church party. The children are followed by a weary group holding forth posters of dogs. Eleven people tearfully recount finding their beloveds limp in the laundry room or the porch, blood creeping out open mouths and pink noses.

An older brunette, who looks as though she would have relished the chance to electrocute strangers in the Milgram experiments, cuts in to the Senate hearing to announce the Attorney General of New York has filed charges of accounting fraud against Bannerman executives. Bannerman Global: world's largest company, a textbook example of the majesty of the leveraged buyout. At its peak, the company tentacles extended to a spray cheese manufacturing plant in Alabama, software development offices in Oregon and California, a pantyhose mill in Ecuador, and dozens of power plants along the East Coast. They made instant coffee and microwavable brownies, they owned oil pipelines that spanned South America, their Viva Vegas resort was the first casino with a great white shark swimming inside the lobby ceiling. Of course, these subsidiaries were spit in the ocean compared to their Financial Services operation on Wall Street. They owned one percent of the world's total wealth. They weren't a company; they were a goddamn economic system.

I switch channels. On this network they're interviewing three financial journalists each writing a different book about Bannerman's demise. They gab happily at a round table, with steaming mugs of coffee and a plate of flakey croissants, as though they discuss Oscar fashion instead of picking apart the still-warm corpse of a giant that crushed a billion people when it fell.

I'm feeling low and have my fingers on my pencil case when my phone rings. It's Gil, calling as promised. I almost don't pick up. I look from da Vinci to my phone and back again, but curiosity wins.

"Was it always this hot?" he asks.

"It's unusually bad this year. Lucky you're only here for break."

"Well, I'm here, like you said. You want to get coffee?"

Is this a date? Do men and women hang out platonically? Not in my experience. He is only here a week. I look at da Vinci again and his eyebrows seem to go up like, Sure, go on and get you some.

"Sure," I say. "Yes. Thank you."

"Awesome. I'll pick you up in twenty."

Now, I'm not a virgin—there was the Portuguese guy from my freshman composition class, and Josh, the praetor of the Latin Study Group. I can still remember the oily, scabrous feeling of his back acne under my fingers—ora pro me! But I have limited experience with boys. And if we define boy-*friend* as someone with whom you share an emotional and physical bond lasting longer than two episodes of primetime television then no, in the strictest conventional sense of the word, I have never had one.

And now that I think of it, dating is like a job search, isn't it? There's a ritual entreaty, a seduction, a mating dance, a presentation of the old gaudy feathers or engorged buttocks or whatever you consider your greatest personal attribute, and then, if you're lucky and the other party is aroused, consummation. It's just a bit of a sham that to feed and shelter ourselves, and find an occupation that fulfills us enough that we don't bash our heads against rocks or bring rocks to crash upon the heads of others, we enact much the same choreography as magpies in mating season.

Twenty minutes gives me just enough time to brush my teeth, shave my armpits, change clothes three times, and put on mascara. I don't know if budding romance has ever been derailed by stubbly legs, but I'll have to take my chances.

Gil picks me up in his mother's station wagon and apologizes several times for driving a gas-guzzler. Seeing him again, I'm reminded why I don't remember him from high school. He's wearing a grey t-shirt and cargo shorts, the uniform of someone who will go unnoticed, and his features are so ordinary it occurs to me he'd make a great serial killer—no one would ever remember his face. Still, he's educated and willing to buy me coffee. My threshold for boyfriend material is at an all-time low.

We recount the few classmates on whom there is any news to report: this one's married, this one's back from Afghanistan, this one drank half a bottle of Jim Beam and split his car on a telephone pole. A few years ago we'd all trod across the same stage, secure in the belief we'd achieve our dreams or at least live long enough to try. Five years, I suppose, is plenty of time for everything to fall apart.

"You look really nice tonight," he says as we crest a hill, and I'm glad he's facing the road so he can't see my face redden. I *am* on a date!

We stop in an older neighborhood on the south side of town. I get out of the car and see a giant plaster bull, its horns strung with white lights, greeting us at the entrance to a seventies-era strip mall. We pass the bull and park between a bingo parlor and a Cash 'n Go. Hidden in shadows, almost invisible in the yellow glare of the overhead lights, is a small, plain sign that reads, 'bean /bēn/'.

"This place is weird," Gil says, "but they have the best coffee."

"He looks familiar," I say, pointing to the bull. Its face is oddly human with stern, wide-set eyes and a firm chin, making me think it had been modeled after someone.

"It used to be over at Magic Carpet Golf. Remember the putt-putt place on East Speedway?"

"Oh my God, yes." A long-discarded memory resurfaces from the summer after sixth grade. We'd been in Puerto Peñasco to see the dolphins and visit my dad's cousins. I came back to the States with a furious sunburn and a Selena t-shirt. I'd only been back a few days but already the ironed-on gold foil letters had started to peel. I was wearing the shirt when we came to play putt-putt. I was licking a chocolate soft serve and coughing every time Danny took a shot. And I couldn't play because I was limping. I was limping? Why was I limping?

Gil puts his hand on my shoulder and his fingers are cold and reptilian. I jump and bark, "Don't touch me!" before I turn around and see Gil is standing there in the sallow light looking concerned. Something flared inside me like a distant explosion but now when I look for it it's gone, only smoke that fades as I try to see what's behind it. I look at the bull and now his face is menacing. I don't like being under his gaze and I turn away, though I can still feel him behind me, watching.

"I'm sorry," I say, over and over. And when I tell Gil I don't know what came over me, I mean it.

His face relaxes and he accepts my apology, and we walk into the coffee shop in silence. The interior is as sparsely decorated as its sign, and only somewhat better lit. The tables and chairs appear to all be made of aluminum and patrons sit slouched over their laptops looking uncomfortable. Behind a counter made of reclaimed pallets scowls a teenager with blue hair beneath a chalkboard on which is written, 'Coffee $5.'

"Two please." Gil hands the girl his debit card.

"Five dollars for coffee," I say, loud enough that the teenager pauses her pour-over to sniff.

"I know," Gil says, sheepish, "but it'll be the best coffee you've ever had. I swear."

Coffees in hand, we navigate the metal furniture and find one love seat upholstered in what appears to be vintage Ronald McDonald sheets. For a moment we sit in silence, knees touching, listening to Fleet Foxes strumming through speakers over our heads. I'm calming down after my performance outside, trying to focus on the matter of being on a date. But what do people talk about on dates? War crimes are on the rise in the Sudan, the Euro is crashing, horse starvation rates are through the roof—I can think of a dozen things to talk about but none seem conducive to getting him to tongue kiss me.

"Oh man," Gil says, yawning, "it's good to be back home. I've already been to Beyond Bread four times. The weather's brutal here but I missed the food. The burritos in California are weak."

"You miss Tucson? How could anyone miss a place with an annual rodeo parade?"

"I love it here," he says. "Parking's easy, everyone's super laid back. Palo Alto's kind of a pressure cooker, even when you're not in school. And you don't want to know how much my rent is. Don't you like it here?"

"Not after twenty-three years, no." I sip my coffee, savoring the burn on my tongue. And I have to admit, it is superb.

"So where would you move, if you could go anywhere?"

"I don't know. Boston? New York? Literally anywhere that isn't Arizona."

"It's cold up there. I went to Cornell," and he points to a faded script on his t-shirt that reads, 'Ithaca is gorges.'

"My parents work at U of A," I say. "Short of getting a full ride to Harvard there was no notion of me going somewhere else."

"The northeast is overrated. It was so cold in the winter my nose hairs would freeze."

"Frozen nose hair sounds like heaven compared to burning your leg on your seat belt."

"And remember metal slides? Remember how badly you'd get burned if you went to recess in shorts?"

"It's like playground designers wanted us to get permanently disfigured before we reached puberty." This is good, right? Conversation is moving.

"You said you're interviewing for a job—what was it? Financial analyst?"

"Equity trader."

He nods, and I'm pleased by how this information seems to impress him.

"Yeah, I had a job at Bannerman after graduation but that kinda fell through."

"I saw the video," he says and he looks at the ground.

I blow out a big breath. I'm going to be sixty and going on dates and guys are going to say, "Yeah, I saw the video…"

"It's super shitty how that blew up," he says. "All those people on the internet are full of crap. Anyone would have had the same reaction in the moment."

"I guess I can be thankful it's not a sex tape, though I think there'd be more money in it for me if it was."

"Well, here's hoping," Gil says, and we touch paper cups. "So, you're still going for something at an investment bank?"

"Yeah. It's a good job, I can do it in pretty much any city, the money's obviously great, it's intellectually challenging, you know…all that."

"There aren't a lot of women in finance, I'm guessing. Like you said in the video, it's an old boys club. I guess I'm curious why you're drawn to it. It doesn't have the best reputation, especially now."

"Well, it's never going to *not* be an old boys club if women self-select out of it. And, I don't know. There's something I almost admire about the power those guys wield. I think that's what attracts me to it. It's exactly the old boys club element of it that I like. You know, getting access to something you're not supposed to have access to. I think maybe I want to be an old boy. Turning yourself into a Big Swinging Dick is kind of the apotheosis of the American Dream. There's a reason music videos always show these guys throwing wads of cash up into the air on a yacht or in a strip club, and it's because that's how you know you've made it, when you've really reached the top in this country, when you can be outrageously and publicly careless. F. Scott Fitzgerald used careless as an insult, but I actually think carelessness is what most people in America strive for. It's the terminal point of freedom."

Gil's eyebrows go up and up until he laughs. "That's astoundingly cynical. You do sound exactly like a business school graduate. But carelessness won't make you happy. More than anything people want to be happy."

I cock my head and, reminding myself this is likely a date, try to smile more. "Yeah, but no one knows how to do that. Carelessness looks like happiness, at least on the outside, and I don't know if most people can tell the difference. Did you ever see *Gone with the Wind*? At one point, Scarlett O'Hara says, 'I want to be so rich I can tell everyone to go to the devil.' Well, me too."

He rotates the coffee cup in his hands, piecing together a counter-argument. "But aren't you conflating careless and carefree? I buy that people want to be care*free*, but not that they want to be care*less*."

"No, I'm not," I say, shaking my head. "Those guys at the top of Goldman and J.P. Morgan, they answer to no one and no one can touch them. You think any of those Bannerman executives are going to jail? This isn't Enron. Right now, people want jobs more than they want rich assholes to go to jail. With so much cleanup to do in the economy, no one's going to bother chasing after some book cooking that literally everyone else was doing, too. I'd like to be that untouchable someday. I'd like to not have to answer to anyone. I think it's impossible given that I have a vagina, but yeah, when I say I want to be careless I mean exactly that. I want to care less, and I think a lot of other people would like that privilege, too."

He leans back and looks at me like I've given him some new information and now he's reappraising me. "You want to be one of those people making it rain in a strip club?"

I laugh. "When you say it like that it sounds vulgar. No, I want to be happy, obviously, but I think that comes with having a job you like and being good at it, but always striving for more. Take my parents:

they're not happy. For my dad I think it's because he hasn't achieved what he wanted in his career, and for my mom I think it's because that's *all* she did."

"I think you have to do something that's meaningful, too. That's why I want to go into patent law. It's an exciting time to get into intellectual property." I must be making a face because he laughs and says, "No really. I want to work with start-ups and small businesses and people of color especially, because the big tech companies can be old boys clubs too. If no one stops them, they'll steal everything that's not nailed down. Even when things are patented, they still try to snatch bites when no one's looking. Take your dad—if he invented some new drug and didn't have a good lawyer behind him, anyone could come and steal his idea."

"He works for a university, so there'd be no such thing as his own drug."

"I know but still, I'm saying that people of color get taken advantage of all the time."

I don't like the insinuation that my dad is some gullible immigrant— he was born in Flagstaff for Chrissakes. I get the feeling Gil wants me to congratulate him for his moral excellence. I won't.

"I'm sure you'll be a good lawyer," I say, not entirely intending it as a compliment.

We've both finished our coffee. His knee is still touching mine, so hot it warms the entire left side of my body. I'm about to suggest we say goodnight when Gil clears his throat and says, "I have a bottle of vodka in my car. You want to get out of here?"

I'm not entirely sold on the idea of spending more time with the patent avenger, but it is nice being out of the house, doing some light verbal sparring. And free vodka never hurt anyone.

In a few minutes we're driving up Campbell back into the foothills, past my old elementary school, through a subdivision, and eventually pull into a parking lot at the top of a hill, the city glittering below.

Tucson passed an ordinance in the seventies banning light pollution and from up here we get the benefit of two views: the nighttime cityscape in blues and oranges, and the sky, vast and starry, a homogeneous array of twinkling white lights bounded only by the mountains. We get out of the car and sit on a bench. I've already sat down when I notice someone's helpfully graffitied the seat with the words, 'I had sex on this bench,' complete with arrows.

"I used to take swim lessons at this club," Gil says, indicating a building behind us. "I remember coming up here with Rakesh Joshi one time in eighth grade," and he pours Gatorade and vodka into cups and hands one to me. "We built a potato gun and somehow Rakesh shot it through the window of this BMW. Shit, we rode home so fast. I can't believe we never got busted."

"Well, I got up to my own shenanigans," I say. "One time I was at Circle K and I dropped a Peach Snapple on the floor. I didn't even pay for it. I just walked out."

Gil laughs. "The thug life chose you, huh?" he says.

I sip my drink, but it isn't nearly strong enough.

"So, what happens if you don't get this job?" Gil asks. "Are you looking at anything else?"

I finish the rest of my drink in one gulp. Gil hands me the vodka and Gatorade and this time I mix them in a proportion more to my liking. "I just feel like promises were made." I say. I know his question is innocent, but I start to get heated, "that if we worked hard, and got good test scores, and followed all the rules, we could skate past the pitfalls that waited to catch everyone else. You spend a lifetime absorbing that message, that there's this path to success and all you have to do is follow it, and so when you get to the other side and find out there's this big, black hole where all the jobs used to be, it's…disheartening. You know? Bannerman only took fifty analysts and they picked me." I still have the message in my inbox. You'd think it would be too painful to see the truncated sentence, "We are pleased to inform you…" seared into my eyeballs every time I check my email, but I think if I keep reading it, one day I'll feel in my heart how close I got.

My second drink is gone.

"That sucks," is all he says and I nod. That's the most accurate assessment I've been able to come up with. "You're smart; you'll find something."

You'll find something. Optimism is a cheap sentiment—it's the only opinion we're never allowed to question.

We're quiet a moment before Gil asks, "Have you ever fired a gun?"

I cock my head. "Come again?"

"I bet you haven't," he says, and I can see his eyes brighten under a streetlamp. "Come with me. You're gonna shoot a cactus."

From the trunk of his mom's car he produces a rifle case, a lantern, and a box of cartridges he shakes in my face like a rattle. I tell him I find it disturbing that these items were preloaded in the car and all he says is, "Arizona, baby."

We walk to the far side of the parking lot, Gil clanking the shells in his hand with the ease of someone jingling change in his pocket. By the entrance to the building is an ornamental rock display around a cluster of tall saguaros, their arms raised to receive us, unaware they're about to be pumped full of lead. Gil walks into the display, stepping around chollas and ocotillos, and pulls a baseball cap out of his back pocket and places it on an arm of the tallest saguaro. Then he takes the rifle out of its case and readies the gun quick as a grunt fresh from boot camp. He points the barrel at the cactus grove, looks through the scope and, satisfied, hands it to me butt first.

"You must be joking," I say, holding my third vodka and Gatorade with both hands so I won't have to touch the gun.

"It's easy," he says. "You hold it like this," and he takes the cup from my hand and places the butt up against my right shoulder. "Don't lock your knees, just relax. Put your hip out a little like this, and make sure you're putting most of your weight on your front foot." He steps back and appraises my posture. "It's perfect," he says. "You're a natural."

"Do you know how many years I spent in Model UN arguing for a global assault weapons ban? This feels fundamentally wrong." Though as I speak, I have to admit there is a certain thrill to holding the gun, its metallic heft in my arms awakening a subterranean hunter instinct that could warm to the notion of lying in wait for a fat quail. "Aren't you a vegetarian? Why do you even own a gun?"

"Will it make you feel better if we eat the cactus after we shoot it? Okay, now look through the scope and make sure the barrel is lined up over your elbow. Focus on the cap. Then take a deep breath, let it out, and pull the trigger."

I look through the scope and can just make out a Subaru logo stitched on the baseball cap. Gil covers his ears and gives me the thumbs up. I suppose, in the realm of possible things that could go wrong on a first date, drunkenly shooting myself in the foot might not be in the top ten. I train my eye on the largest star in the logo, breathe in and exhale while trying to stand dead still, and squeeze the trigger.

"Ow, goddammit!" I yelp, my shoulder throbbing from a recoil that felt like being slugged with a golf club. When my ears stop ringing, I hear what sounds like a fire alarm clanging somewhere inside the building.

"What did you do?" Gil exclaims, his eyes wide in surprise and joy.

"I didn't hit the cactus?" My voice has risen an octave in panic. "Where did the thingy go?"

Gil jogs around the side of the cactus. "Judging by this," and he holds up a mangled bag of Cracker Jacks, "I'd say you hit the snack stand."

My heart is thudding and I have a gut, illogical impulse to wipe my handprints off the gun with my tank top. "What do we do? Are the cops going to come?"

Gil takes the gun, laughing. "Calm down, Lee Harvey Oswald. I think Tucson PD has bigger problems than going after the Cracker Jack killer."

"Should I leave a note?"

"Not unless you want to pay a $5,000 fine."

"Ok," I say, eager to flee the scene but reluctant to leave such destruction in my wake. I start to hurry back to Gil's car but halfway there I stop and tell him to wait. I fish twenty dollars out of my purse, my gas allowance for the week, climb back through the chollas and ocotillos that scrape my bare legs, and stand on tiptoe to reach the Subaru hat. I tuck the twenty inside the band and put it back on the cactus and then jog across the parking lot to Gil, my conscience a hair lighter.

"You're kind of unethical for a future lawyer," I say later when we're stopped at a red light.

"Could be," he says, nodding and looking out ahead like he's weighing the accusation.

He pulls the car up in front of my house, excusing himself from walking me to the door with the claim that he doesn't want to wake my parents.

"Thanks for the drinks," I say, not sure whether the situation demands I offer him my cheek or my hand, but he resolves the dilemma by licking his lips and leaning in for a kiss that tastes of Gatorade and, inexplicably, picante sauce. This is not fun, and yet I sit here hostage to some internalized sexism that I repay him for the night, allowing his slobber to spread south to my chin and north to the bridge between my nostrils. I'm trying to close my mouth with the hope he'll close his a little too, but bringing my lips together only seems to make his widen and I see I'll have to somehow jerk my face free, as Gil is now attempting to pull my lips fully into his mouth. I put one hand on the door handle, hoping he'll take the hint. But instead Gil advances past the Maginot Line of my collarbone and begins twisting my left nipple through my bra in the manner of someone attempting to open a safe. My reach in the front seat is limited but I manage to work his hand away from my breast with my left elbow, only to have him attempt the same maneuver with his other hand.

"Okay," I say, done being polite and pulling away and wiping my very wet mouth with the back of my hand, "I should go."

"We had a good time tonight," he says. "I obviously can't get into anything long-term,"—as if!—"but I feel like you were throwing me some signs with all that stuff about strip clubs."

I open my mouth but I'm so gobsmacked I can't speak.

"And seeing you shoot was super hot." He unzips his pants and indicates the erection straining at his BVDs.

"Oh," I say, unable to stop my face from wrinkling with some disgust, "I should go."

"Come on."

"I have to get up early."

"*Come on.*"

Now that I look at him in the low light his eyes have a sort of vacant, bovine quality that was maybe always there. "I'm going inside now."

"Fucking tease," he mutters and zips his shorts and restarts the car.

I scramble out of my seat before he takes off and I have to roll out the passenger door. "Asshole," I say before I slam the door. "And FYI, having a savior complex doesn't qualify as 'giving back!'"

I stand at the doorway under the yellow porch light and watch his taillights dissolve into pinpricks before disappearing around a corner. Falsus in uno, falsus in omnibus—false in one matter, false in all. In my bedroom I wince changing into my pajamas. I'm going to have a massive bruise on my shoulder.

In bed I can still see the bull's eyes and I can still feel the heat of whatever compelled me to jump when Gil touched my shoulder. And reliving both makes me angry enough that I'm balling my fists under the comforter and kicking the top sheet away from my toes. I shouldn't have gone out, I should have pushed Gil away, I should have gotten out of the car before he kissed me, I shouldn't have said any of those things about strip clubs, I should have turned down the vodka, I should have more self-respect than to let drooling asshats think they can do what they want to me, I—I—

I fall asleep and the bull follows me even there. His horns are missing and I spend the dream searching for them, pulling open drawers, turning out closets, running room to room in a tumble-down house. Hard as I look, they never turn up.

One of those salad girls

The email for a follow-up interview with Phoenix X is curt:

> Slammed w/ meetings. No time to meet @ office. I'll be @
> Big Barn BBQ @ noon on Tuesday. Come prepared.

—Duck Ford

After a quick eye roll at the name Duck, I pump my fist in the air, righteous vindication lighting up my blood for three entire seconds. Then I remember the barren silence of Phoenix X, the pall of survivor's guilt on Jenny Nosek's face. No, that's not your problem. This could be a good job. This *will* be a good job. And I cover my ears to keep from hearing a small, solemn voice struggling up my ear to whisper an insistent, Yet.

This news was met with predictable reactions from the parentals: My father nodded and said, "If that's what you want." My mother hugged me and then handed me an apartment finder magazine.

In the car on the way to the interview I'm shaking. Nothing less than my worth as a human being lays on the scale as I park in front of the red and white barn-cum-rib joint. I try to remember Laura Horn's words, and I force myself to smile as I straighten my skirt and recheck the résumés and transcripts inside my leather portfolio. A great person gets a great job. Great job begets great person. Great person is to great job as great is great is...

Unpretentious is a kind way to describe this restaurant. Peanut shells crunch beneath my high heels and the lone waitress is wearing cow-print bell-bottoms. I see in dismay I am the only one here. I'm shown to a booth where I check my teeth four times for lingering poppy seeds from breakfast and read my notes until Ford arrives. At twelve sharp, the door bangs open and in he strides. Silhouetted in the doorway, he's no duck. At six feet tall he's a brutish horse with a fresh-shaved, palfrey jaw and a swimmer's bullocky shoulders. He grunts hello and shakes my hand with a vigorousness all out of proportion for a meeting conducted under a plaster bust of a long-lashed lady cow.

"I do all my interviews here," he says. "You can tell a lot about a person by what they eat." He pauses and gives me a hard look. "Are you one of those salad girls?"

I freeze, the grimy, plastic-coated menu still in my hands. This is the first interview question and I'm guessing the right answer is no.

"I'm gonna get a turkey burger."

He snorts and I worry he considers turkey a vegetable. When the waitress comes, he shakes her hand, calls her by name, and orders a full rack of ribs and three sides. "And a large Diet Pepsi and tell Julio I want the ice crushed, thank you, Colleen." He places the menu in the waitress's dirty hands and looks back at me, finally letting out a breath and a low-toned, hrmm.

"Where are you from? What's your background? What have you done so far with yourself?"

It's my turn to let out a breath. The questions fly so fast my instinct is to pull out a pen and write them down so I don't miss anything, but betraying any kind of weakness now would be fatal. I hit all the highlights, the GPA, the awards. I begin my tale about Bannerman and he stops me. "I saw the video," he says and blows his nose with a napkin and then drops it on the floor. "Do you do that a lot? The crying?" He asks this with some disgust as though it were an embarrassing medical condition.

"First time," I lie with confidence, "and it won't happen again."

"Tell me what you know about arbitrage." His eyes make an obvious detour to my chest before finding mine again. I'm unfazed.

"Arbitrage is when you exploit a price difference between two markets. If a stock is listed in Market A for a dollar and in Market B it's ninety-nine cents, you buy at ninety-nine and sell at a dollar. You do that a few million times a day and you're making money." I open my portfolio and take out my résumé, robin's egg blue to suggest loyalty. "I can show you here—"

"Don't need that," he says and sloshes around the ice in his Styrofoam cup. "A bunch of marketing bullshit. I live by these," and he indicates his eyes, "and by these," and he points into his lap and, I assume, to his testicles. He's pushing me, trying to see whether he can provoke a reaction. I'm not stupid enough to fall for that. I make my face a stone and stare back at him, waiting for him to continue. "You want to put together a counter-cyclical portfolio. Tell me what's in it."

"Well, I'd start with dollar stores, public utilities—"

"Obvious. Best small cap stocks."

"Uh, Hansen, Green Mountain Coffee—"

"You saw that on CNN."

The food arrives, thank God, and interrupts this examination. Ford tears a rib from the rack, dunks it in a cup of baked beans, and mouths half the bone. The expression of rapture on his face is so profound it embarrasses me, as do the tearing and chewing noises and little utterances of pleasure, soft moans and irrepressible grunts that give me an all-too-clear soundtrack of what Mrs. Ford hears on special

Friday nights. The rib bones, cleaned and sucked dry, are discarded in a red plastic basket. I look down at some orange grease congealing beneath my turkey burger and my appetite is miles afar, but I suppress the nausea and, seeing an opportunity where his mouth is momentarily too full to ask me a question, try to wrest the wheel from his hulk hands and steer a while myself.

"Phoenix X executes, what, five million trades a day?"

"Ten," he says around a mouth of baked beans.

"I saw you own your own stock exchange as well. That would cut down on latency, though, in a recession I'd have to imagine trade volume is down." He snorts. "I am planning on getting my Series 7 license, I'm versed in risk management, economic capital analysis, and I'm confident that, even in a down market, I can make your investors a lot of money."

Out of Ford erupts a stentorian belch. "You in favor of the bailout?" he asks, grabbing a hank of cornbread and sweeping meat drippings into a puddle in the middle of his plate before sponging the cornbread through the pool and chasing it with more Diet Pepsi.

I clear my throat and detest how delicate the sound is. The government announced that morning they're bailing out Bannerman to the tune of $700 billion, and all I could think about was this boy I knew from high school who drove his brand new Mercedes into a swimming pool, only to show up a few weeks later with another, like the first one didn't even happen. I try cautious honesty.

"I think it runs the risk of creating a moral hazard. Government meddling in the free market should, in my opinion, be avoided."

"Wrong. You know what would happen if there was no bailout? A shitshow, that's what."

"You don't think it rewards bad behavior?"

Ford gives a vigorous shake of his large head. "No such thing. Every man acts in his own best interest. And you know what you end up with when everyone's doing that? An efficient market. Everything running as it should. There's no bad or good. There's an order to it. Everything is exactly as it should be."

Oh good, he's a philosopher. "But that's not, uh…" I start to argue and change my mind. "What's the difference between a pigeon and a stock broker? A pigeon can still make a deposit on a Porsche."

If he found my joke funny, he makes no indication. I feel pretty good, though. I think I've demonstrated I'm knowledgeable, capable, eager, tough, and perhaps just good looking enough that Ford might be motivated to hire me if only to chase the fantasy we could one day screw.

I'm summoning the courage to ask another question when he squints one milk-blue eye and starts talking again. "Mireles—you're Spanish then? You don't look Spanish. You could pass, if you wanted to. You could pass for all white."

"Thank you." The words are out and gone because I have to say something and I have to have this job and because I don't know how a person could possibly respond to a statement like that without climbing high on a soapbox and extemporizing before an audience that wouldn't hear anything anyway and would only grow hostile and more committed to their ignorance. I loathe myself for this and loathe him the same for putting me in this impossible spot. My smile falters but never breaks. Great person, great job. Everything is great, great, great.

"Sss—so you guys aren't still using Black-Scholes in your modeling, right?" I'm trying to find again my footing in this interview when I feel a presence behind me and look up to see a sleazy, cheaply good-looking fortyish man in a suit skulking.

"I'm sorry to interrupt," the man says, extending his hand to Ford. "I couldn't help but overhear—are you talking about Phoenix X? I used to play golf with Tandy Shultz. How's that asshole?"

"Excuse me," I say, my voice hot and righteous, "we're in the middle of an interview." I turn back to Ford and make a face to say, Can you believe this guy?

But Ford is ignoring me. He's leaned far over the table and shakes the man's hand. And in a move taken from the dictionary definition of cojones, the man plops himself down next to me, nearly sitting in my lap until I inch over, then pulls a French fry off my plate and introduces himself as Brian.

"I could tell this was a job interview," he says, eating another fry and ignoring the drop-mouthed horror on my face. "And you were doing pretty good," he says throwing me an unctuous wink, "but I had to step in when I heard you say you don't have your Series 7. I worked at TradeBoost for ten years. Just got 'downsized,'" and here he uses air quotes and pantomimes masturbation in a sophomoric bid for comedy. And it works! Ford chuckles and throws another bone on the pile. "And I'll tell you you're leaving money on the table if you don't have a Hadoop cluster. This business is all about speed." And he raps his pink knuckles on the red gingham oilcloth to reinforce this twenty-four-carat insight. "You gotta spend money to make money."

"Yes sir," Ford says, thick lips around his straw.

"'Spend money to make money'? Use platitudes much?" I face Ford and speak to him, hoping to demonstrate I do not take Brian or his Hadoop clusters seriously. "I've just spent four years reading the latest research in quantitative analytics. This business is all about using the best methodology. I'm ready to take what I've learned from theoretical to practical application."

"Theoretical what?" Now Brian's making a can-you-believe-this-guy face at Ford and he whistles to the waitress to bring them a couple of beers. "I don't have a fancy degree," he says. "I don't read *Harvard Business Review*, but I know what I know. I've been in the game a long time and I can smell bullshit from a mile away."

"Are you calling me bullshit?" I ask, furious in equal parts with Brian for hijacking my interview and with Ford for allowing it. "This," and I gesture to Brian drawing my plate by inches nearer, "is bullshit. You can't just interrupt someone's job interview and smirk about how much you know 'the game.' It's unprofessional. You'd know that if you *did* read *Harvard Business Review*."

"Sweetheart," Brian says, "I was clearing thirty K a month when you were pouring tea for your dollies."

Ford and Brian laugh and then Ford sighs and folds his hands together. "This is dirty work," he says, settling his face into a long frown. "It isn't a business for egghead girls." The waitress delivers two ice-cold Budweisers and Ford stops her and takes her hand between his. Her purple lips spread and orange foundation cakes in the creases around her mouth. "Colleen here would be more qualified than you are. You can read books and get good grades but if you aren't born with a nose for blood forget about it."

He must see my face coloring pink to red to purple, because he puts his hands up in a defensive pose. "Now listen, I'm doing you a favor. I could hire you. You'd work a few years. Maybe you'd get burned out or maybe you wouldn't and you'd stick around ten years, twenty, long enough to get your pretty fingernails nice and dirty. But sooner or later you'd wake up—and this I promise you—you'd wake up one day and say, What the hell did I waste my life for? You're a what-do-they-call it? A square, a square—"

"Square peg," Brian answers, and I could deck him.

"I looked you up online," Ford says. "That's how I found your video. I found a bunch of paintings you did. Honey, this is a business for people who don't make things, who don't create value, who don't give a shit about pointing at something and saying, 'Look here. I did this.' I'm telling you, for your own good, this isn't it."

"Oh my God," I say, no longer able to contain my incredulity. "You two are the most sexist, racist, ageist, shitty people I've ever met. I hope you get hit by a bus!"

Ford clears his throat and Brian takes a sip of beer. Ford flicks his eyes from me to the door and I realize, five minutes later than everyone else at the table, the interview is over and it's time for me to go. I pick up my purse, my leather portfolio, and stand. Brian reaches for another fry but I snatch the plate away before he can get more of what's mine and dump it in a nearby trashcan.

"You're a pretty girl," Brian calls out, "you should smile more."

"Get fucked!" I shout before the barn door slams behind me.

* * *

An hour later I find myself sitting cross-legged on my parents' front lawn, my suit jacket crumpled on the ground, and a bucket of fried chicken between my legs. I crack open a beer and tear into a drumstick and try to think if I could have handled the interview differently. No, the game was rigged; there was no way I was ever going to get that job. And if I see Brian again, I'm gonna tolchock his ass.

It's the middle of the afternoon, everyone I know is at work or at school, but I need someone to tell me there's hope, there's a reason I should get off the grass and not just lie here and wait for the ants to devour me.

I try my father. He picks up on the second ring: "You wouldn't want to work for those people anyway. Maybe it's time to give up on those sorts of jobs."

I scroll past the number marked, Mom, move on to Ashley: "That sucks, but I can't talk now. The cooler went out in the cheese aisle and we have to get all the parmesan wheels stored before they start sweating."

Paulette doesn't answer: "I can't come to the phone right now. Until then may the Lord bless you and keep you!"

Out of desperation or boredom or both I call my brother. He answers on the seventh ring with a prolonged, "Whaaaat?"

"I didn't get the job," I wail into the phone. "I'm sitting in the front yard eating fried chicken. Help."

There are scraping sounds and muffled voices in conference on Danny's end. After a long time, he finally says, "Ok. I will let you come to my house and partake of my weed but all who enter must pay the toll."

"What do you want?"

"We want fried chicken. Bring a bucket of wings and I'll smoke you up."

* * *

I haven't been in Danny's frat house in a year and once I'm at the front door and the tripartite odors of stale beer, Axe Body Spray, and insecurity masquerading as machismo hit me, I remember what an icky place it is. But the promise of impending relief, an ability to blot out the present and alter my mind so I can fast-forward to some future where things are better, is enough to push me in. The place is quiet, most of the brothers are still in class. I leave the dim, wood-paneled living room and follow the wide staircase up three floors to what my brother has deemed the Presidential Suite, and find Danny and several of his friends in various states of repose, window shades drawn and a Bob Marley playlist blaring from a laptop. They rush at the chicken like starving, caged animals; in two minutes the wings are nothing but bones.

I'm sitting on a wooden chair (I refuse to sit on anything upholstered in this house) jiggling my foot up and down, trying to be as patient as I can, until I can't contain my lust anymore. I pack my brother's bong, rub down the mouthpiece with hand sanitizer, light the bowl, and inhale until I'm woozy. Somewhere heavenward I hear a choir of angels singing Handel. I take another hit and the familiar burn fills up my lungs and I hold it in, in, in until the smoke rushes out of me in a coughing spasm that leaves me warm and nostalgic. This is what I missed. This is what I needed—nirvana in the Chi house.

I must look exalted, as Danny takes the bong and says, "Calm down. It's not that good."

My whole body is rushing sideways as though on a carousel and I have to grip a table to steady myself. I'm self-conscious, I know I look ridiculous, but the thought makes me giggle and giggle until soon I'm howling and eventually everyone else joins in. After a while, the laughter subsides and the room stills and somewhere I think there's a Victorian-era photograph of an opium den that captures the current mood in the bedroom exactly.

Two brothers are in spirited debate over whether a person could die from eating batteries, and I encourage them to try it and find out, while another complains loudly about how many fake IDs he's had confiscated. "The bouncer at Dirtbag's has it in for me—I swear!" Danny is sitting at his desk trying to beat box along with *No Woman, No Cry* while trimming his toenails, and I've spent what feels like an hour leaning my head on the wall, replaying storylines from *The Babysitters Club*. And for the first time in months the listlessness doesn't hurt, I don't feel like I should be somewhere else, doing something more productive. This is the first guilt-free afternoon I've had in months. I feel so…normal. Is it the pot or am I drawing comfort in having broken out of my solitude, even among people I'd affectionately call mouth-breathers? I have the uncontroversial epiphany that unemployment would feel gobs better if I was high all day.

The weed is making me sleepy so I close my eyes and something on my periphery stirs. It's an edge of something round, something dark grey, something… It's clearer, closer, creeping my way with slow but definite progress. It's the texture from my nightmare, following me into my waking life. I jerk without a sound and open my eyes and everything in the bedroom is the same. No one notices me. I'm not doing this, I tell myself. I'm going to enjoy myself. I can choose to do that, can't I?

The day tapers, brothers leave and others arrive. I'm coming down myself and decide I should probably go, too. I'm looking for my keys when Danny asks, "Do you feel any better? You came in here all feisty. I thought you were gonna pick a fight."

"Yeah. I mean, no. I don't know. The guy at the interview told me I wasn't cut out for working in finance. Like, not intellectually. I think he meant I didn't have the right personality. He called me a square peg."

"That's just one person's opinion. I bet everybody successful has some story of some douchebag who told them they weren't cut out for the thing they ended up doing really well."

I bite my lip and shake my head. "I was angry at the time but now when I try to think of working there, I just get depressed thinking about spending all day punching buttons, making fractions of a cent, all of which go into someone else's bank account." I press my fingers to my temples and try not to look at the stains scattered like rose petals over my brother's grey carpet. "Am I an idiot now if I decide I don't want to work in finance? Like, what does that even mean? That I just threw away my entire college education?"

"I don't think it's that big of a deal. I think a lot of people change their minds. You could start painting again."

"I should get a job painting?"

"No, that's not what I'm saying. But you're not exactly starving on the street. You can take some time to like, figure everything out. Maybe losing the job at Bannerman was a good thing. Maybe everything is going to work out for the best. You don't have a job. It's not like you're dying."

"It feels like I'm dying."

"No, it doesn't."

"Yes, it does. It feels like there's something wrong inside me, like I have a brain tumor or something. I get so angry sometimes I can barely hold it together. Even before Bannerman, a long time before, I felt like I had something inside me, like this mean little seed eating me up with sharp teeth. It feels like if I could kick and scream enough it would be happy and leave me alone."

"I don't know what to tell you, dude. Meditate or smoke more weed or get a prescription, but you've gotta get that shit under control. We just threw out a brother because he was punching the walls and starting fights with everyone. It broke my heart, but that shit's contagious. It spreads."

I bite my lip harder. I hate to admit it but I guess being a fraternity president means you have to have some sensitivity to the human condition.

"Are you gonna take that telemarketing job?"

"No," I say, resolute. "I know I can do better. Someone has to hire me. I can't be unemployed forever, right?"

"It's just a job. Shit, I worked at Domino's that one summer before senior year. That was the funnest job I've ever had because Samberg was with me, and Jayvon, and Shady Pete. Like, everything doesn't have to be life and death, all serious all the time. Sometimes you just have to say, Fuck it."

"Wow, you should make bumper stickers."

"That's my advice: Fuck it."

I thank him for the pep talk and the weed and I leave, now too aware, in my polyester blouse and heels, of how much I look like a bank teller. The house is noisier now, with rap music wafting out of open doors and curses from brothers watching basketball in the den. I'm invisible, happily, maybe regrettably, not a girl any of them want to bang, and I slip outside without a glance my way.

When I get home my parents are already retired to their separate chambers, a cold half pizza open on the dining room table. I pile slices onto a paper towel and tiptoe to my room when my mother's voice deploys from the darkened hallway, "Why did I find chicken bones in the front yard?"

"I didn't get the job."

A long sigh. She emerges from the den and there's eyeliner under her eyes like she's been crying. "Your father told me."

"But before you lecture me, I was never going to get it. The interviewer was a complete douchebag."

"If they brought you in for an interview that means there was a chance."

"Nope, not this time. I think the interviewer brought me in so he could enact some weird fantasy where he eats ribs and destroys someone's dreams."

"Well I had five hours of budget meetings," she says. "I guess we *both* had bad days."

"Are you waiting for me to say sorry? Because you're looking at me like this was my fault."

"I don't expect you to apologize but I don't think you see my side in this. Do you know how many hours I spent ferrying you from one activity to another? How much money we spent on math camp and art classes and hotel rooms for the spelling bees and—"

I chew on my tongue, any transcendence from earlier evaporated.

"—held my career back for years. I could have been Dean—"

I stand there but it doesn't matter if I'm there or not. She's exorcising demons tonight. I see light under the door of my father's study and while she scolds, I watch to see if it'll grow with the opening door, if it'll extinguish, or if it'll stay right where it is, steady and quiet on the other side. I watch for a long time. The light never changes.

Don't flush your life away

"**M**artin," my mom fires from the table, "you need to wear a tie tonight. The State Senator is coming."

"Yes, mí amor," my father answers while refilling his coffee mug. I'm toasting a bagel and I look over and his eyes have this faraway look like he's on a hot air balloon, like he's already kissed everyone goodbye.

"And don't wear the green pants," she adds, thumbs hammering her phone. My God, she's even multitasked nagging.

"What's going on tonight?" I ask, interested only in case there's free food for moi.

"Donor appreciation dinner," my mother answers on her way out of the kitchen.

And as soon as she leaves the room a brigade of cleaning women marches through the kitchen with buckets and purple gloves, and I startle at their sudden appearance. "It's here?"

"I emailed you three weeks ago!" she shouts from some other part of the house.

I sit down at the table next to Danny. He's here to do laundry and is wearing, without irony, a Reagan/Bush '84 baseball cap and I have to restrain myself from swatting it off his head.

"Sounds like a fun night," Danny says to our dad but, coffee cup in hand, Dad is already stalking to his office and a second later we hear the door slam.

"What's their problem?" Danny asks.

Instead of answering I put my head on the table and stare out the patio door. Another sunny day.

"Hey, check this out." Danny turns his laptop toward me. "Because of that thing last May the university is making all the houses do a community service project. It's total horseshit but we can't graduate if we don't do something, so help me pick a charity."

I snort. 'That thing last May' was a little more than a 'thing.' Some Betas jacked up on cocaine and Red Bull had gotten into it with a few townies at a bar and, like gentlemen, they stuffed billiard balls into socks and started cracking skulls. No one died, miraculously, but the university was sufficiently disgusted, so they put the entire Greek system on probation. The Greeks just about died from the injustice of it all, and my brother cursed God for letting it happen the year he made chapter President. "Can't you start a fund for aspiring models who want bigger boobs?" I ask without raising my head from the table.

"Nah," he says, turning the laptop back to him, "I already asked if that would count and Dean Alvarez said no. It has to be legit. I should give the money to Mom and Dad's lab," he says with a laugh. "How pissed would you be if I was the golden child for once?"

I snort again. As a popular kid born to a family of nerds, short of accidentally curing cancer by combining tequila, mint gum, and Polo Sport cologne, there's nothing Danny could do to outshine me.

Every few seconds his computer makes a sound like a drop of water hitting an empty sink. After the fifteenth ping, I can't take anymore.

"What's that noise?" I demand. "Turn it off."

"That's Samberg," Danny says without looking up from the screen. "He wants to know if you're bringing Ashley tonight."

"If I'm bringing her where?"

"Oh yeah. We're having a pimps and hoes party. And you're coming and Samberg wants you to bring Ashley. He's gonna ask her if she'll get back with him."

"Thanks, but I'll pass."

"Come on, don't be like that. You never hung out at the house when you were in school. That's just rude."

"I'll think about it," I say.

"Don't think," Danny says. "That's your problem. Just do it. And bring Ashley."

"I'm not coming."

Danny tilts his head back and looks at the ceiling. "You are coming, because Mom gave me a hundred bucks to get you out of the house."

"Jesus Christ!" I scream, finally raising my head off the table. "Are you serious?"

"Yeah. So, if you come, I'll give you twenty."

"You give me fifty or I don't budge."

"Fine," he says, "but you have to bring Ashley. And," he adds, taking a look at my hair held aloft with a Chip Clip, "you should probably take a shower."

"I'm not dressing like a ho."

"Fantastic," he says with sarcasm.

I've had two cups of coffee but, with an entire day stretching Sahara-like before me I go back to my room for more sleep. Before I get back into bed, I stub my toe on my desk and yelp in pain. This is obviously a premonition that today will only get worse.

* * *

That afternoon, caterers descend on our kitchen like a colony of bees, and workers in black aprons clang steaming pans and shout things like, "Hot behind!" My mother supervises the front of house—floral deliveries, furniture rearrangement, making sure my father doesn't wear the tie with the Erlenmeyer flasks on it—eventually banishing Danny, my father, and me to the backyard where we can no longer annoy her or unfluff the pillows. The three of us stand under an orange copse for shade as the sun breaks across the yard one last time. After hours of cajoling, Danny wore me down enough to dress somewhat in theme—black skirt, fishnets, pink rouge so thick I could win a part in a Robert Palmer video—while Danny's costume consists of having clipped a bowtie to the front of his polo shirt. I look at the three of us slumped in the waning light and wonder if my mother wouldn't prefer we took my father to the party, too.

Danny produces a pint of Jack Daniels from the pocket of his shorts and my father and I take grateful swigs, no one remarking on the annoyances binding us here in the yard.

"Mona," my father says and clears his throat, "you don't have any marijuana, right?"

Danny bursts out laughing.

"Um, no," I say, trying to understand why a man who claimed he spent the seventies 'getting high on Miles Davis' would be asking me for drugs. "Weren't you on that campus drug task force a few years ago?" I ask. "They hung those horrible posters in all the bathroom stalls that said, 'Don't flush your life away.'"

My father straightens his tie and looks sheepish. "The bathroom stalls were my idea," he says. "The average person spends over a hundred minutes a week on the commode."

"This party's not going to be that bad," my brother says, trying to cheer up my father. "They've got a buttload of porterhouses."

"I'm not worried about the food," my dad says and wipes his forehead with a handkerchief. We wait for him to continue but my mother pokes her head out of the patio door and asks when Danny and I are leaving.

"Why do you want me out of the house?" I ask, hurt but also secretly glad I won't have to spend the night sequestered in my room or worse, forced to watch my mother preside over another dinner party where she sermonizes about the beneficent power of public sector research.

She closes her eyes and brings her hands together, and I feel like she's trying to impress upon me how much of a burden it is to be my mother. "I want tonight to be nice. No snarky comments, no speeches about how universally screwed your generation is. This is a nice party for people who give a lot of money to the school. They don't need to be glared down by Arizona's most dissatisfied customer."

"So, I don't get to have feelings," I say. "Good talk. Thanks."

"No," my mother shakes her head, "you can have all the feelings you want. Out of the house."

My father puts his head down and wishes Danny and me a good evening before joining my mother in the house. I take the bottle from Danny, finish the Jack, and straighten my stockings. As we walk past the patio doors, I catch my reflection in the glass. You're a traitor to your gender, the reflection says. And you're still not going to make out with anyone tonight. Degrading myself seems pointless now.

Ashley picks us up in her aging Mercedes, music reverberating down my parents' quiet street making the neighbor's dog bark like the goddamn Germans are invading. Inside the car, Ashley's drumming her hands and nodding her head along with the radio. When I'm in my seat, she turns down the music and faces my brother and me and her words tumble out all at once:

"Ohmigod I have the best news. I GOT A JOB! Can you believe it? It's this hip little graphic design firm downtown. I sent them my portfolio and they loved me! The director even wants to buy one of my paintings. I'm dying. I start in a week. Isn't it the best news ever?"

A thick sadness drops down on me like wet wool. My tongue is heavy and my thoughts slow. Ashley did it. She got her dream job. I'm supposed to be happy for her, but it takes all my acting skills to force my mouth up into a smile. I have to take surreptitious deep breaths after I congratulate her. In an ugly, shamefaced way, it was good to know neither of us had achieved any modicum of success after graduation, reassuring to have someone else down in the muck with me. We were together, boats against the current, sisters in mediocrity. Maybe I even relied on her to fare worse than me, that I would always win in comparison. Jesus, what a thing to admit. Now I'm a remnant, one of the unlucky seven-percenters who still don't have a job all these months after graduation. In a month the number will have dwindled further. How long until I'm all alone?

"That's great, Ashley," Danny says from the backseat. "Proud of you," and he squeezes her shoulder.

There's a pause and I realize they're both waiting for me to say something, and so I try ignore the big lump now glued to the back of my throat and, coughing, say with too little inflection, "Tremendous. It's fantastic."

"So, this is gonna sound stupid," Ashley continues, pulling out of my parents' neighborhood, "but I tried this thing called a vision board and I honestly think it got me the job. Mona, you should try it. You put up pictures of the things you want and concentrate on them and it creates this wave of energy that alters the course of your life. There's, like, science behind it."

I roll my eyes so hard I think they're stuck. I can see Orion through her moonroof. There are at least three things wrong with what she just said. At least. Thankfully, Danny has no problem listening to pseudoscience and he takes over the conversation.

It should have been me. The words bullet around my brain so loud I'm sure the others can hear them. I watch Ashley, her hands aflutter while she speaks, and feel like I want to roll out the speeding car and run back to my house and my pencil case. Danny's said something funny. Ashley arches her back while she laughs, a trick she learned after getting new breasts. I can't help but think—*know*—that Ashley's flirtatiousness, her easy way with men, has won her the job. I don't even want the job at Phoenix X and yet I think of Ford and the unctuous Brian, and wonder if things would have been different if I'd loosened one button, if I'd giggled and reached a porcelain hand across the table, licked my lips and made my eyes sparkle when asked about the bailout. Then I'd be the one with the good news. I'd be the one whose life was finally figured out. I look down at my fishnets and it's all too perfect that we're going to a party to make believe we're prostitutes.

I watch Ashley, the ease with which she parts her lips and fills her eyes with laughter, how she uses her charm as a cocoon inside which she assures her companion he's the only person in the world. No, I never could have done it. It would have been a knife at my chest, the blade hitting skin every time I laughed at another offensive joke, every time someone like Brian would look me up and down and let me know exactly what I was worth. But who would be holding the knife there—Ford or me?

There's a lull in the conversation and I realize Ashley has asked me a question and sits waiting for a response. Say something, dummy! Be positive! Whatever you do don't tell her about the knife. "That's great!" I say, stabbing frantically for something sincere to tell my best friend. My voice pitches up weirdly at the end. "Do you have any gum?"

At the frat house we're greeted as celebrities. The president's sister and her hot friend. Inside the door a throng of girls dressed as naughty nurses rush at Danny, and he's carried off by the stream. The music is so loud I can feel the bass in my eyeballs. It's barely nine o'clock and the floor is already slick with beer. The other girls at the party have apparently never heard the phrase, "Leave something to the imagination." By the time I've crossed the living room I feel old, and fat, and my feet hurt, and somehow my hands are covered in glitter. Who still wears glitter?

"Beer me," I say to the guy working the keg, and I drain my lukewarm Coors before he's finished filling his next cup. Wasted, from the Latin, vastus: empty and unoccupied like my cup, my wallet, my pin-pricked heart. Synonyms for unoccupied include derelict and uninhabitable. In an hour or so I want to be derelict as a plastic bag buffeted by the wind, now here then there, caught open on a branch, then summersaulting through a parking lot and moving, always moving, impossible to catch. And why would anyone chase after a torn bag anyway?

"So, what did your brother say about Joel?" Ashley asks as I start my second beer. "Did I hear he's moving to Europe?"

Joel Samberg has been my brother's best friend since elementary. I don't know where he and Ashley met, or how, but he is the maypole around which she pivots, even though her hands might be full of colored streamers belonging to any number of other gentlemen. That is until they break up, and break up, and break up. Which they do, seemingly, according to the phases of the moon. If he and Ashley are reconciling tonight, I can guarantee I'll have the pleasure of listening to Ashley debate, for an hour, whether *this time* Samberg's sincere when he says he loves her. And I don't know if I have it in me to be a nice person tonight.

"I don't know," I say, watching two girls in bunny ears bend down to drink vodka out of a lopsided ice sculpture. "He doesn't share his plans with me."

Ashley takes a Jell-O shot from a passing tray and squeezes it into her mouth, making sure all the while she has the eye of some goon with a barbed wire tattoo encircling his bicep. "I don't know what to do. I like Joel—he's so nice to me—but I don't want to be tied down. What should I do?"

She's not looking at me at all. Her words are directed my way but her body is now pointed toward several bros, all in vaguely racist pimp-like costumes—feathered hats, loud suits, gold chains with pendants shaped like pistols—and I'm actually looking forward to finding Samberg, handing her off, and facing the party alone. "You should probably have more anonymous sex," I say. "That'll fix everything."

She gives me a look. "You're such a prude," she says, and I can tell she's teasing me because she wants to steer away from a conflict. With her back against the wall she'll come with her claws out, but it takes a few punches first. "You're coming to my sister's engagement party, right?" she asks, gripping my arm. "She is turning into such a beast. Now she and my mom decided I need to highlight my hair. You have to come. I need someone normal there."

Ashley prattles through the next four songs, all of which seem to be about bodily fluids. The songs come with their own hand gestures that everyone at the party has memorized and it's surreal watching a roomful of people mime ejaculation in unison.

Why can't I be happy? What the hell is wrong with me? I want another beer. And quiet.

I'm pulling her through rooms, searching for Samberg or my brother, anyone who can distract me from the fist of jealousy squeezing my stomach. I find them on a third-floor balcony, smoking cigars and playing cards with a few brothers and their girlfriends.

We're given a friendly welcome and are invited to join their game, something called Circle of Death. Samberg and Ashley find a corner and she perches on his knee while he whispers things that make her giggle. I glance at them again after a few minutes and he's looking at her with such tenderness and admiration I'm lost for a word to describe my feelings: something in between boiling envy and syrupy joy on her behalf.

I need a boyfriend. Like now.

"What do you want?" I look up and Danny's standing over me, waiting. I don't have an answer. I don't know the context of the question but, literally whatever it is, I don't have an answer.

"The keg beer downstairs is skunked," Danny says, taking the red cup out of my hand. "Do you want a forty or do you want me to get you a mixed drink?"

I say I'll take a forty. I've seen enough rap videos to know what a forty is, but when it's in my hand, all those sloshing ounces seem frighteningly endless. This could get ugly.

"Gimme a cigarette," I say to the gentleman on my left. His zebra-print fedora is cocked over one ear and I feel I have to lean far into his personal space to make myself heard. But as I lean over, I forget gravity exists and have to grab hold of his crushed velvet jacket to keep from toppling. He catches me before my head smacks the arm of his Adirondack chair and flashes a wide, forgiving smile. "I love you," I say, and wish I was close enough to kiss him.

Why am I asking for a cigarette? I've never smoked one before but I figure I can learn as I go. I put it in my mouth and light the end, and can't understand why I've suddenly got bits of char-tasting tobacco all over my tongue. I smack myself on the forehead. Duh! I put the wrong end in my mouth. There is much guffawing. Ashley gives me a disapproving look and I telepathically inform her no one, least of all her, is going to judge me.

I request a second cigarette and allow my friend in the fedora to light this one for me. I cough for what feels like a long time as the smoke floods my capillaries and gives me a rush that causes me to grip the sides of my chair. This is the high point, the rollercoaster at its zenith. Now, the ride will plunge four hundred hair-raising feet.

We've switched games. This one's called Fuck the Dealer, or Asshole...I can't keep up. I have a lot of cards in my hand and when it's my turn I decide which card to play by imagining personalities for the numbers and then seeing which one seems the most fun. This method doesn't work though, and the other players keep shouting at me to "Just play a two!" I catch Ashley's eye again. The look she's giving me isn't disgust, it isn't disdain, it's straight up pity, and I'm moved to shout at her over the jeers for the guy who won the card game that she can wipe that smug look off her fat face.

The balcony is silent, or as silent as it can be with dance music shuddering through the beams. Oh boy, I said it out loud. Okay, no turning back.

"What did you say?" Ashley rises from her seat. She heard me. Bitch is just trying to be all dramatic.

"Which part didn't you hear?" I ask. "Smug or fat?"

She smooths down her hair and closes her eyes. I'm dying to know what she's going to say under the glare of a dozen male gazes. "You're drunk," she begins, "and you look very stupid, and I have class, so I'm not going to stoop to your level right now." She tries to give me a withering smile but can only manage a grimace. I can see what's coming next, the sensation the same as an oncoming panic attack. The twin lights of the train bore at me, eyes growing larger and more condemning, seeing all the way to the soot-black bits of my soul.

"Class," I snort. "You gave that bartender from Chili's a blowjob on the hood of his Neon. That was a real Jackie Kennedy move right there."

Samberg is holding Ashley's shoulders and whispering in her ear as her lower lip begins to tremble, and Danny shouts across the table for me to knock it off. But I can't. Or won't. For once the razor's turned away from me.

"And that time you banged the sound guy from Riverdance? And he promised you tickets and then you went to the box office and he never gave them your name? Where do you find these people?"

Ashley's crying now. Samberg's alternating between consoling her and shouting profanities at me. Three naughty nurses have formed a wall around her and are giving me shank eyes.

"I'm sorry I called you fat," I say. "I should have said, occasionally overweight and at-your-convenience. Has Samberg seen your pillow collection?" Nail in the coffin. I know it. I'm a terrible person. We're not going to recover from this.

I feel an arm jerk me up out of my seat and it's Danny dragging me through a dark corridor to his room. He slams the door and I stand, arms crossed, feet planted, the giddiness from my performance ebbing, slinking back to the lonely table of my inner monologue.

His room is cleaner than I remembered. I catch a whiff of eucalyptus.

"What's wrong with you?" he demands. "Why would you say that?"

I'm about to answer, about to say the world craps on everyone and Ashley's turn came up tonight, but he cuts me off.

"You're turning into a real bitch. I get you're pissed off you don't have a job, and you think nothing ever goes your way, whatever woe-is-me story you tell yourself all day long, but half your problem is you. And me, Mom, Dad, everyone is sick of it. Your own mother paid to have you out of the house so you wouldn't embarrass her. Tonight is the first time you've showered in what, a week?"

It couldn't have been that long. The last time I washed my hair, Oprah had that exposé on botulism, so it must've been…shit.

"And you're so full of yourself. Do you ever think about anyone else? I bet you know who was on *Conan* last night, but can you tell me when was the last time you saw Mom and Dad kiss?"

George Lopez was on *Conan* last night.

"I used to wish I was like you," he says. "Do you know what it was like growing up surrounded by all your awards? Mom and Dad came to my soccer games, and they made sure I had enough tutors, but I never got one-fucking-tenth the attention you did. Your 4.0. Your full scholarship. And what are you now? Huh? What are you now?" He swipes his hand across his desk and a stack of papers takes flight. Neither of us moves. "I'm glad I'm dumb," he says. "I'd rather be happy than smart."

He ends his spiel by taking out his phone and firing out a text to someone, probably Samberg. I realize I've made things awkward between them. I'm about to respond, say something in my defense or apologize. I'm drunk and slow, I can't collect my words and assemble something he'd like to hear, but Danny holds up his hand to silence me. He puts the phone back in his pocket and shakes his head. "Take the telemarketing job," he says. "And stop being a bitch. And apologize to Ashley. Hand me my keys. I'm taking you home."

I throw up on the way back. Danny is patient as I lean into a ditch in front of a Wal-Mart and let the horrible night expel from my body. I'm meek and avoid eye contact as he drops me off in the driveway. I raise one hand in a half wave as he pulls away but I can't tell if he returns the gesture. When his car rounds the corner I'm alone and wishing I could be marooned on an island where at the very worst I'd hurl insults at the macaws.

In the house, I head straight to the kitchen. I'll be ferociously ill in the morning unless I have a sandwich and some juice. The scent of charred steak still hangs in the air and wine glasses beaded with water stand upended in the drying rack. I'm smearing peanut butter on bread when I hear the staccato clatter of a suitcase rolling over tiles. My father is pulling a large Samsonite behind him and heading for the garage.

"How was dinner?" I ask, trying not to slur or spill as I gulp the last of the orange juice straight from the carton. "Are you going out of town?"

My father's tie hangs askew and he has the look of someone emerged from the rubble of a protracted siege, weary and afraid. Far down the street a car alarm starts. "I'm going to be gone for a while. Do you think you can help your mom put the garbage cans out?"

"Where are you going?" My father travels to conferences at least once a month, but this doesn't feel like a little jaunt to San Diego.

"Well, tell her." My mother appears in the dining room holding a goblet containing a hand's breadth of red wine. "He applied for another job," she says, before he can speak. "In *Pennsylvania*," and she stamps on the name like it's a cockroach. "He didn't have the courage to tell me, either. I had to hear about it from Dean Alvarez. Concealing it from your wife *and* boss—bravo," and she feigns a hand clap.

"Don't make this ugly."

"I didn't speak to my parents for *ten years*. For this? For *this*?"

"What do you mean?" I'm slow to catch on. I need them to spell it out.

My mother, unflinching, says clean as surgical steel, "We're separating."

The word, once out, echoes cartoonishly off the walls. I can see it hanging in midair above the granite countertop and inflated with a bicycle pump until the bubble letters reach the ceiling and my parents and I are squeezed out against the appliances.

"They collect the cans before six on Monday," my father says, leaning in for a clumsy hug, "so you need to put them out on Sunday night."

I feel the beginnings of a migraine pulsing behind my right eye. The foul forty is working its way through my digestive system. I want to give them hugs, words of affirmation or condolence, something a loving daughter might do, but instead I keep my eyes down, my arms wooden, and pretend I am not here, that I'm that empty plastic bag, that I'm already gone. I have a thought, a needle jabbing the soft flesh around my belly, that my parents were living in wedded bliss until I returned home, the prodigal daughter seeding angst and despair in the once fertile ground of a happy home. I want to rewind, go back to breakfast or last year or first grade: there has to be a butterfly I can step on to make everything in the future turn out okay.

"You didn't take the job, right? It was just an interview. It's like you're giving up." I say all this through the corner of my mouth. If I open it all the way I'll fall apart, everything will come tumbling out.

"I don't need your opinions," my mother says giving me a hard look through red eyes. "This is entirely out of your purview."

"She's allowed to speak," my father says.

"You do not tell me what to do." My mother gestures with her glass, red wine sloshing over the rim. I'm scared. I see my mother, hard, calculated, ready to hurt someone because she can. I see me, barely an hour ago. My parents say nothing else. I guess everything was said before I came home.

"So, what now?" I ask, searching for order in the carnage.

"I'm going to a hotel. I'll call you tomorrow."

"And don't tell your brother," my mother says. "I'll call him in the morning."

"That's it?" I say, trying to stall Dad's exit. "I just got home."

"Please," he says, the tired fear still in his eyes, "help your mother out." Then he takes his keys off the hook in the kitchen as if it was as easy as going to the grocery store. A minute later there's a long, loud grind as the garage door closes and he's gone.

My mother stretches her arms out. I don't want it. But I stiffly inch my body closer until her powdered cheek is mashed against mine and I can feel the frailty of her bones, the looseness of her aging skin. She asks if I had a good time at the party and I nod, barely able to stitch the night's events into one evening. The hug gets more awkward the longer I don't pull away. I don't want this; I don't want to feign comfort from her. But I don't move until she lets me. She squeezes me again and then lets me go, and her eyes look as though she sees the rescue boat and it's going the wrong way.

In my bathroom I throw up again. With my head in the toilet, the images of Ashley and my father fight for primacy in my mind. I brush my teeth and my stomach drops. Danny. This is going to break Danny.

I pull my laptop into bed with me. In my last moments of lucid thinking before I fall, grimly, into a drunk, dead-sleep, I compose an e-mail to my mother's friend, Belinda, and tell her I'd be delighted to interview for the telemarketing position. "Thrilled at this opportunity." I proofread it three times, and the letters don't stop swirling. I pull the blanket over my face and fall asleep, trying to find an answer to the question growing stronger with every drum of my heart, pounding behind my closed eyes:

What.

Is.

Wrong.

With.

Me?

Rocky Point

Chapter 4: Pinche pecas.

I refuse to call it Rocky Point. I use the Spanish name, Puerto Peñasco, though honestly, I don't know why I care. I'm pledging linguistic fealty to a tourist trap built three hours south of Tucson, so that spring breakers could get alcohol poisoning a little closer to home than Cancún.

We went all the time when I was a kid, and when it was just the four of us, I loved the town, loved seeing the dolphins and drinking apple soda and collecting the little plastic wrestler figurines to fight in their wooden arena with the red string ropes. I painted a lot of pictures of it when I was a kid—the sombrero vendors on the beach, painted guitars spilling from a market stall, my mom squeezing lime over a shrimp cocktail.

But some years we'd meet my dad's cousin, Noni, who would come up from Hermosillo with her three boys, Mando, Javi, and Manuel. They were older than Danny and me and mostly ignored us, immersed always in whatever amusement they'd brought for the long weekend—X-Men comics at first, then Gameboys, and finally flip phones and Hilfiger cologne. They spoke flawless English at meals with my parents, but as soon as the grownups were away, their speech devolved into a rapid slur of Spanish slang and cusses that largely excluded Danny and me. The only thing they said clearly and for my benefit was pecas, freckles, which is what they called me instead of Mona. Pinche Pecas, they'd say when I tattled on them for smoking or listening to rap music with bad words in it. I hated the way they said the word, a barb that somehow managed to hold inside it their chauvinistic derision for a little girl, and the concomitant resentment that they had to pay base respects as I was still family. You could hear the sneer on their lips, could almost feel the rough hands on the small of your back, the inevitable shove coming from behind.

Pinche Pecas pops up sometimes now in my brain unbidden. Pinche Pecas when I do something stupid like scrape my car on a pole at the gas station and Pinche Pecas when I'm holding too many bags of groceries and a jar of mayonnaise shatters in the parking lot, and Pinche Pecas when I burn my forehead with the straightening iron and Pinche Pecas when I don't notice the light is red and I try to cross the street and Pinche Pecas when I wake up and Pinche Pecas at night and pinche and pinche and pinche and pinche and...

* * *

Two weeks after the party, I'm back at Job Seekers and for some reason, one corner of the church annex is taken over with Christmas decorations: paper candy canes, a spindly fake tree with sagging strings of white lights, an enormous banner that commands, 'Keep CHRIST in Christmas!'

This is my last day at Job Seekers, and it does feel a little like Christmas, the end of one thing and maybe the beginning of something better. I've come to say goodbye and wish everyone well and I'm surprised that I'm feeling nostalgic. I might actually miss Paulette's relentless enthusiasm, Randy's folksy cheer, even Chasen's tongue ring, which I can hear rapping the backs of his teeth as I take the seat next to him. Maybe not the tongue ring. But I'll miss the camaraderie of shared experience, everyone down in the dirt, our little company knit together by the insanity of performing the same action over and over, each time praying for a different outcome.

I won't miss the food: I turn around and see a rectangle of mild cheddar sweating on a paper plate and I shudder imagining the greasy fingers that unsheathed it.

Paulette is flustered when she arrives. She upsets her travel mug and has to spend several minutes toweling off her binder. She says nothing, however, and we begin as we usually do, checking in on everyone's progress.

Paulette's agitation is not contagious, as Dara stands and shows a wide, contented smile to the room like she knows a happy secret. "Well, I just came to say goodbye…because I got a job!" And here she runs in place a little and the room breaks out into applause and a few cheers. "I'm working over at Galaxy Nails in Armory Park. Annnnd, I found out last week," she says, looking down and coyly putting one finger to her cheek, "I'm pregnant." More applause. Paulette crosses the room and squeezes her. Chasen puts two fingers in his mouth and whistles until my ears hurt. "So be sure to come get your nails done," she says. "I'm gonna need a lot of diapers."

Randy stands next. "Well, this isn't about a job but my band is doing a gig out at the Silver Dollar Saloon next weekend. Some blues, some Tull. Should be a good show. Y'all come out and see us if you're free."

Chasen is next. He's wearing a shirt with a mailman on it, captioned, 'I have a huge package!' He shares that he's gotten a promotion to weekend cashier and winks at me when he adds he's also been given keys to the glass case where they keep the premium liquor.

When it's my turn, I stand and the room stares back. Keep CHRIST in Christmas! "I have some good news, too," I begin. Paulette looks up at me, eyes brimming with hope, and I wish I had better news for her than how I'll be making minimum wage at a call center. "I got a job so…thanks." Another round of applause. Paulette gets up from her chair again and holds me close in a tearful hug and this time I don't try to squirm away even though her hair keeps getting sucked up my nose.

"What's the job?" Randy wants to know.

"Telemarketing," I say, my face coloring. For all my pride and posturing I feel foolish to have come back to the group with nothing more to show than a job a robot could do. And their joy on my behalf only makes me feel worse, guilty that I've judged myself as better than them all these months when in reality I'm no more deserving of a plum job than I am of gilded wings. "And it's full time," I say, "so this will be my last day here."

"Full time?" Chasen asks. "You get bennies? You're lucky as fuck." Paulette narrows her eyes at him until he says, "Excuse my French."

I hadn't thought about it like that. Living with two doctors—well, one doctor now—I suppose I'd taken my health care for granted.

"We're all so happy for you," Paulette says. She dabs her eyes with a tissue and blows her nose and I think she's not crying solely out of joy for Dara and me. "You might have noticed the room is a little more crowded today," she says, indicating the Christmas decorations. "The church will be undergoing renovations and they're going to use this room for storage." She clears her throat. "What this means, unfortunately, is that this will be our last meeting. I'm so sorry I didn't tell you sooner but I just got the news this morning. I'm heartbroken because I love seeing you every week, but I'm thrilled some of you are moving on and I hope I've given you the skills to go forward and achieve your dreams. Thank you all so much for this opportunity and I hope everyone will have a blessed day."

I queue up to give Paulette a parting hug. "What are you going to do?" I ask. I know she'd been paid by the church to run the workshops, only a pittance, but a steady check all the same.

"I'm going to pray on it," she says with resolve, "and then it's back to the job boards." She takes my hand between hers. "I'm so, so proud of you. You have so many gifts. One day you're going to be very pleased when you realize what they are." I don't know what she means but I let her hug me again and I leave the church dazed and wounded, wondering why both my families have to break up.

Back at my house I'm restless. It's my last Friday of freedom, my final empty weekday before I start my job on Monday. I feel the pressure of impending captivity, like I should make the day memorable. My mother gave me some money to buy work clothes, but something about going to the mall by myself in search of cotton-poly separates makes me depressed.

I obviously can't call Ashley. I haven't spoken to her or Danny since the party in enactment of the exile I've decided to suffer for the rest of time. It's better, I've reasoned, to sequester myself, to spare everyone my dragon-spume. Ashley and I both hold a secret. If she knew mine, if she blurted it at a party, treated my confidence with so little care as I did hers, I know I wouldn't have it in me to forgive. It would be too much. I want to spare her the agony of even having to try. Danny I'll have to see at holidays and funerals but Ashley can forget me, find new friends, glide unburdened into the golden tomorrow where me and my knife can't follow.

It shocked me how easily I accepted solitude and how quickly I've adjusted to the narrow parameters of my new life. For the first few days I'd find some stupid video and pick up my phone, typing out the text before my memory could catch up and arrest my thumbs. But I don't find myself reaching anymore. Withdrawing has got to have its spiritual benefits. I'm sure ascetics didn't freeze to death on mountaintops for nothing. When I was in college everybody had these Bob Marley posters up in their dorm rooms that said, 'Man is a universe within himself.' Well, I'm a universe now, I guess.

I'm not completely alone. My mother's here, as well as the ghost of my father. The Monday morning after my dad moved out, she went into the lab and eighty-sixed his entire team. It was easy to justify—it was a low-probability project, something about flashing lights into people's eyes to try to dampen the effects of dementia. And depending on how you looked at it, terminating the project either looked outrageously impartial or the most scandalous thing that ever happened in a gerontology lab. But cuts had to be made and she was the boss. My dad apparently absorbed the decision with his usual slow resignation, and then turned around and accepted a temporary teaching position in New Zealand. It all happened so quickly; my anger towards my father for leaving soon morphed into anger towards my mother for firing his team and then doubled back on my father for giving up and fleeing the country. I don't believe their separation is the shock of the century but they've been so mild and composed their entire lives, never prone to dish throwing or making scenes, that to have this drama play out publicly and faster than milk curdles has been so disorienting I think we're all privately still waiting for our eyes to stop spinning in our heads.

My father came home briefly to get his universal adaptor before his flight. "I took the call center job," I said. "Maybe by the end of summer I can move out."

"That's great," he said, crossing my room to hug me. Then there was an uncomfortable silence, both of us staring at the carpet. This was a breakup for us, too.

"When you were interviewing at Bannerman," he finally said, studying the white eggshell surface of the door jamb, "and you went to New York by yourself, how did you feel when you walked out of the hotel lobby onto the street?"

I gave a little shrug. "Nervous, I guess. A little overwhelmed."

He took in a breath and I felt like he was looking for a different answer. "Maybe excited, too? Like, you were in a new place where no one knew you. Like you're invisible, but not in a lonely way. In a way that you're free? Where you can do anything. That's what I want. That feeling of waking up in a hotel room in a strange place and, for a few hours at least, of having nobody that you need to be."

"It sounds like you don't want to be tied down." I didn't finish the sentence with, *to us.*

"It doesn't get any easier," he said, "to know what you want. I'm almost sixty and I'm still struggling with it. And it doesn't get any easier to know what's the right thing to do, either." He looked down at me and his face seemed full of regret. "I don't envy you having your whole life to live."

Now he exists in the suit he saves for weddings and funerals, hung in drycleaner plastic in the front closet, and three cans of sardines are stacked in the pantry, and the rose bush is un-weeded and wild along the back fence. I feel his absence but it's no more painful than a hole left behind by a fallen tooth. The wound knows how to close, the skin will knit itself. For the first few days the tongue wants to probe the hole, but after that it adjusts to the new landscape, the mystery fading into a hard, little scar.

My mother wears three faces: anger, triumph, and blind terror. Anger is when she drives her car straight into the plastic trash cans and later can't find the tweezers and screams "Fuck!" so loud I see a neighbor pick up his head as he passes by with his beagle. Triumph is the night she comes home with hair the burgundy of cherry cough syrup and new blood-colored lipstick, when she says she will embrace this opportunity to remake herself into a better, more fearless woman. And terror is when she sees the reality before her of dating in her fifties, bending to the calloused minds of strange men for the first time in decades. She accepted one hasty date with a widowed anthropology professor and came back within the hour pale and almost trembling, saying he spent the entire thirty minutes complaining about the high price of coffins.

Despite how much she's put me through, I feel sorry for her, marooned after twenty-four years. I am angry, at both of them, as well as afraid my being around the house brought out the worst in everyone, and made gangrenous whatever wound in their marriage was already festering. But I just haven't had the time or space to make sense of anything.

The night of the party it was like the world split, like there was an earthquake and my mother and I ended up on one side of a canyon, with everyone else on the other. And anyhow she cycles through her emotions at such a fast clip it's honestly not worth my trouble to take anything she says or does seriously. We're roommates now, and as part of my overall effort to be a better human being, I tell her she looks nice, I remember to take the chicken out to thaw, I sit with her while on television she watches yuppies rehab their Craftsman bungalows.

~~I'm unemployed,~~ I've never had a boyfriend, I live with my ~~parents~~ mother in the most boring town on the planet, and I hate myself.

It's the middle of the day but I open a beer. My last lunchtime beer. I think about the long months of unemployment and feel I squandered my time. I should have taken a road trip or lost ten pounds. New job, blue job. Three days before I'm due in the office and it feels like an ending, not a beginning. When I was a kid, I wanted to see the future in my mother's day-planner, pleased it could be parceled out in neat little squares. I can see the future now and it's a grey concrete wall, a break room lit by a flickering bulb, a stained toilet in a women's room that always smells like bleach, and the tedious march of time across my twenties. It's a job, it's a job. I should be grateful. Lucky as fuck. I feel like I've surrendered, like I prostrated myself before my enemy and he cut off my head to set an example.

I bring the beer to my room but don't drink it. My hand closes around the desk drawer handle and I feel an anticipatory calm, maybe what junkies experience when they see the needle, when they can feel the sharp point before it even punctures the vein.

Mona Lisa's right arm is giving me problems. How do you recreate shadows on skin? I worry sometimes I'll be seventy and still cutting, that I'll be forced to earn my bread traveling the country with Lobster Boy and the Wolf Man. The Incredible Scarred Woman. Shows every fifteen minutes. See her injuries live and in color. Some people have rubber band collections, some restore vintage cars, and I'm forging an Italian masterpiece on my thigh. We all have our thing.

When it's over, I repack the case, place it carefully in my drawer, and wash my leg with antibacterial soap.

I feel restored just enough to face the mall and buy a bunch of pinstripe pants. I pour the beer down the kitchen sink and get my purse. The air conditioner hums and the house is so still I feel like I could lie down and feel the earth turning. I won't miss these afternoons alone. Isolation is a dangerous privilege to a girl with a razor.

Here's to you, here's to me

Whoever decided to house the 'Sunshine Phone Bank' at 53½ East Diablo Road was a real bastard. For one thing, that address doesn't exist according to my mother's GPS, Google Maps, or any person I could find working at a gas station. And East Diablo Road isn't actually a road in the sense that it connects one place with another, it's a circle, and depending on which part of the circle you're driving through, you can be at 53 North Diablo Road, 53 South Diablo Road, 53 West Diablo Road, or 53 East Diablo Road. Congratulations, city planners of Tucson: You are worthless.

But the fun doesn't end there. The building isn't visible from the street. It's not even *on* the street. It's behind an RV showroom and a self-storage facility, and you have to drive into their shared driveway, pull around the rows of Thor and Winnebago trailers, NOW WITH A FREE TOW HITCH! and into what looks like a blind alley, before you notice a sign, no larger than a sheet of paper, reading, 'Sunshine Phone Bank'. I was an hour late on my first day because of that nonsense. Harry Potter had an easier time figuring out how to walk through a wall at King's Cross.

The name, Sunshine, must have been chosen for its irony since the building is windowless, everything inside it is grey, and the only sun you'll ever see is when the janitor wheels the trash through the back door every afternoon and a brief burst of light hits the copy machine. It's cold, too. I've spent my entire life inside air-conditioned buildings, but there's something wrong with the thermostat when your hand goes numb from using your computer mouse too long. And the break room is worse than I thought: there are *two* flickering bulbs, and I spend my lunch hour waiting to see if they'll synchronize.

The best thing I can say about my job is that I don't find it morally objectionable. Sunshine is paid to solicit donations on behalf of thousands of charities, too small and understaffed to make calls for themselves. The charities all have vague names like The Eugenia P. Gettis Foundation for Advancement, the Lucky Lindy House, or the Abbott's Booby Defense Fund. The other callers and I sit in our icy, fluorescent cavern for eight hours a day and robo-dial strangers, begging for money to buy eyeglasses for Columbian orphans in Kenosha, Wisconsin, or to update the library at the Polka Museum in Ennis, Texas. It's boring, it feels pointless, and the pay is terrible. I love adulthood.

And it turns out my mom's friend, Belinda, isn't really an active owner. I kinda figured she'd hook me up, that I'd come in as a management trainee, cut some costs, innovate, throw around business school buzzwords like vertical alignment and paradigm shift, and in a year or so they'd hand over everything to me. But I soon learned not only does Belinda have a minority ownership, she's in the process of selling her stake. So, I was brought in as an Operator, one of the bottom feeders of the company. Above the Operators are the Team Leaders, then an Assistant Manager, and finally, Skip Ramirez, the General Manager. What contortions must a man perform to survive life with a name like Skip?

It's a small company. There are probably three dozen Operators, mostly people in their 20s and 30s, all wearing the same polo shirt/ khaki pants combination and a numb expression in their eyes. My first day, I was led around the room by my Team Leader, Nadine, a blonde woman in her mid-thirties with what I can only describe as 'shelf butt' and a gold pentagram pendant dangling around her neck. She caught me staring at the necklace and said, "Yes, I'm Wiccan. No, I probably won't cast a spell on you. If you want to come to a coven meeting, let me know. We're always happy to welcome newbs."

All the Operators sit in high-walled cubicles that preclude conversation, looking wistfully at the clock above the receptionist's desk, or seeing who's approaching your desk before they're right on top of you. The high walls would also encourage lengthy wanking sessions or naps, were it not for the monitoring software installed on our computers that alerts a manager when someone has stopped making calls. Big Brother, how are you today? My desk is placed back a bit from the others so, apart from mandatory team meetings, I spend most of my time alone on the phone. Alone, save for an animated yellow smiley face that bounces up and down on the lower corner of our monitor all day, reminding us to smile. When I was in business school, I wrote florid essays on employee engagement, the importance of getting people to "buy in." Living it, however, has made me realize there's a special place in hell for management gurus.

Today I'm making calls for the San Jose Puppet Theatre. Next up I've got Steven "Suli" Hooper and his wife, Bitzie: contributors since 1998, last donation, $30. As the phone rings I have no choice but to stare at the smiley face. Rule #1: Smile! Only six more hours until I can go home.

An elderly woman answers the phone with great hesitation. "Hello?"

"Good morning! May I please speak with Bitzie?" Rule #2: Always ask for the person who answers the phone.

"This is."

"Good morning, Bitzie. My name is Mona and I'm calling on behalf of the San Jose Puppet Theatre. Could I have a minute of your time to speak about your contribution?"

Bitzie shuffles around on her end of the line. Rule #3: No pressure. Give them time.

"The what? Speak up!"

"The San Jose Puppet Theatre," I repeat. We get paid hourly, regardless of how many names we get through, but I still hate to spend too much time on any one call. I have this fantasy that one day I'll make so many calls, the computer will run out of names for me and I can go home early.

"I'm ninety-three years old," she says. I wait, clenching my teeth to prevent me from answering, "Your point?"

"They're seeking contributions for their new performance space, Bitzie. This year shows include, Rock n' Roll Mother Goose, Shakespeare and the Samurais, Zombie Pillow Fight, and their annual Peter and the Wolf production, featuring musical accompaniment by Huey Lewis and the News." Rule #4: Stick to the script, however hysterically insane it may sound.

"I don't vote anymore. I'm sorry, I can't answer any of your questions," she says.

"That's okay, Bitzie. Might there be a better time to reach you?"

"You too, dear. Goodbye."

The animated smiley face does a backflip and looks at me with indefatigable joy and something that, in his pixilated countenance, I take to be scorn. Up yours, smiley face.

I feel someone behind me and turn around to find Skip with a clipboard.

"Good morning," he says, and clicks his pen a few times. "How are you settling in?"

"I'm fine," I say, dropping the pen I was holding and then banging my head on the underside of my desk stooping to retrieve it. "I think I'm getting the hang of it."

"Do you mind if I listen in while you make a call?"

Like I have a choice. "Be my guest," I say.

He pulls up a chair and sits close. He's wearing cologne—it reminds me of tennis balls fresh from the can—and I can count the strands of grey scattered throughout the hair above his left ear as he pulls on a headset. "Remember," he says, "what's rule number one?"

"Smile," I say, refusing an actual smile until absolutely necessary.

Next I've got Aaron Harris, last donation, $20. Aaron answers the phone and it sounds like he's in a hurricane. "Hello?" he screams.

"Good morning, Aaron. My name is Mona and I'm calling on behalf of the San Jose Puppet Theatre. Could I have a minute of your time to speak about your contribution?"

"Make it fast," he says. "I'm surfing." I roll my eyes before I can stop myself. Skip is looking right at me but gives no sign that he disapproves.

"Okay, well your last donation was $20. Would you consider increasing that by five dollars? They're seeking funds for their new performance space. Upcoming shows include Peter and the Wolf with music by Huey Lewis and the News."

"Yeah," he says. "Put me down for $25, and send me the bill." He hangs up before I can thank him or verify his address. Just as well. Only fifteen minutes until lunch.

"That was great," Skip says, taking off the headset and smiling. His teeth are so perfect I wonder if he models dental veneers on weekends. "You were courteous, enthusiastic—that's the attitude I want with every call." I'm waiting for him to leave so I can clock out and eat my turkey sandwich, but he leans back in his chair and rests the clipboard on my desk. "That puppet show sounds pretty nice, huh?"

"I guess," I say. "If you like Huey Lewis."

"Oh, he's great," Skip says without irony. "I saw him at Casino Del Sol. Great show, great show. What kind of music do you like?" he asks, and I swear he winks at me. Oh my God, is he flirting with me? Well this is an interesting development. I'm horrified and intrigued in one beat. I scan him up and down and decide, if it came down to it, I guess I'd bang him. He's not that old. No wedding ring. And he's in seemingly good shape—no visible gut, no overgrown fingernails, no peek-a-boo back hair—and his eyes are a striking cornflower blue offset by a smooth, dark complexion. He could even be handsome if you could get over having to scream, "Oh, Skip!" during intercourse.

"I like Madonna," I say, reaching for an artist I'm sure he's familiar with.

"Oh," he says, and his eyes crinkle at the corners, "I see." He brings his hand up and, for a second, I think he's going to put it on my knee. I flash on hundreds of PSAs and Lifetime movies about sexual harassment in the workplace and arm myself with retaliatory speeches while simultaneously picturing us doing it on the executive desk in his office. "Okay," he says, putting his hand on the arm of his chair and pushing himself to standing. "Keep it up," and he shines his fulgent teeth once more before going back to his office. Hmm. Tomorrow I'm definitely wearing a skirt.

* * *

Two single career gals, my mom and I have been working through the frozen entrée section of Trader Joe's. The food is better at Ashley's store, but I won't risk an accidental run-in. We've taken to watching cable news during dinner, letting the TV fill the air. The stock market rallied today following passage of a massive spending bill and meanwhile Keith Olbermann can't stop giggling when he uses the word, tea-bagger, to describe the people protesting outside the Capitol. My mother changes the channel and Anderson Cooper is talking about the president's new dog. Commercial for energy pills. Commercial for headache spray. Commercial for another TV show purporting to show the *real* victims of the Recession, in this case, luxury carmakers. An infographic posits Republican contenders for the 2012 election. Horse starvation rates are through the roof.

I have so many questions. I want to know what it feels like to have decades of love and companionship ripped away. Does it feel like an amputation? A sudden severance and a lingering sensation that something vital is not there? Or is it like weight loss—the feelings melt so slowly you can't see it, until one morning you wake up and realize you've shed a whole person? But I shove forkfuls of chicken tamales in my mouth and swallow the questions down, too afraid that if I ask what happened, my fears about my part in their split will go from a hunch to a fact.

But my mother, in a moment of Anderson Cooper-induced calm, says, "Your father called me today," and stirs her Chana masala.

I swallow. Okay, are we doing this now? "What did he say?"

She blows out a long sigh. "He's lucky I answered the phone. You have no idea how many emails I have in my Draft folder right now, these long diatribes without punctuation where I spill out every thought that's popped into my head since he left. He has no feelings. That's what I've concluded. How else can you explain someone who throws years and years of work out the window, like it was nothing? What was it all for, then? Huh?"

She looks at me, but thankfully doesn't wait for me to say anything. "And on the phone, he was so normal, like he was just calling to say hello, like just a regular trip overseas. The university's got him staying with another professor who keeps a pot-bellied pig for a pet. The pig ate your father's lecture notes the first day of class and nearly made off with his passport. I refrained from making a joke about how many pigs are now living in that house."

This is the most she's said about the separation so far. I'm torn between holding my breath to not disturb her, and hurling my empty dinner-tray at the wall for a distraction and a quick get-away.

She keeps going. "He's lonely, though. I know it. He didn't say he was but I know he's sitting in that strange house wondering why he did what he did. And he apologized again about interviewing for that other job, but that's not even what makes me upset. I'm not even that upset he kept it a secret. I mean, I'm not blind. I could see he wasn't happy at the lab. I don't begrudge him wanting to see what else is out there—not that *I'd* ever move. I was hurt that he never consulted me, never asked, never told me what he was thinking. And it hurt me more that I had to find out from someone else what was going on in my own house. But…the waste of the years we spent together? If it was all for nothing. All the sacrifice and everything—if you don't make it to the end, what was it all for?" She lets the question hang there over the glass coffee table, before she sniffs and says, "But I know he regrets it. I know he wishes he was back here. I could just sense it over the phone."

"What are you saying? You think he's going to come back?"

She chews a few seconds and the reflection of the television dances in her eyes. "He's been unhappy for a long time," she says. "I encouraged him to go to therapy but he wouldn't do it. And to be honest, when I cut his team he put on a good show for our colleagues, but I think secretly he was relieved. He wanted an excuse to get out of there." She doesn't take her eyes off the screen but she nods her head slowly. "But he's going to come back. We're all we've got."

I remember my father's face the day before he flew to New Zealand, how sorry he was for not knowing what he really wanted all these years. My mother's optimism is unfounded. I know it is. But she needs the belief to sustain her through whatever comes next, so I don't contradict her. We all tell ourselves stories to survive.

* * *

Five o'clock on a Friday: Are there any sweeter words? I've completed my first full week on the job, I've thrust my half-eaten turkey sandwich into my purse, my keys are in my hand, and as I near the door I can almost feel the sun's embrace around my stiff, frozen body.

Skip's at the door wishing everyone a good weekend. I put my head down, not wanting to make eye contact until I'm close, and when my eyes meet his I'm struck again by the unexpected contrast between his skin and his eyes, a lazuline blue like something Titian would have painted. He says goodbye with a practiced smile and I nod and try to make my mouth do something flirtatious but work-appropriate.

"Is that your car?" I ask, pointing out the door to an electric blue BMW I'd seen parked in the same spot all week.

"Isn't she beautiful?" he asks with the kind of reverence usually reserved for a baby or beloved horse. "I wanted to treat myself after my divorce."

Rich *and* divorced. I bet he takes his dates to Ruth's Chris. "Oh, I didn't realize—"

"Three years now."

"Okay," I say, unsure what to say next, "well, have a good weekend."

"You too, Mona."

And as I move past, I feel a warm, gentle hand squeeze my shoulder. I startle and get a delicious chill that starts on my scalp and spreads across my upper body. I don't turn around, possessing a vague notion that, if this is a game I want to play, I should play hard to get. Inside my car I rub my hands together. Ohmigod, ohmigod, ohmigod. I think he likes me.

I'm carried on a current of endorphins almost all the way home. The Friday traffic is already snarled on First Avenue when an ambulance screeches past, practically on the sidewalk. I settle back in my seat, this looks like it's going to take a while, and in all the noise of sirens and horns I don't notice my phone ringing—it's Danny. I catch the call before it goes to voicemail and steel myself for any number of uncomfortable topics.

My finger shakes as I push the speakerphone button. My mother said Danny took the separation hard, missing classes the first few days and spending hours in the gym. I knew this call was coming, but I hadn't had the courage to make it myself. Of all of us living on fictions, Danny may be the most dependent.

"You at home?" he asks. He sounds deflated, a tire in need of a patch.

"Not yet." My lane has stopped moving and I'm trying to merge left but there's a Lexus edging me out.

"Mom came to the house today," he says. "She brought sandwiches and we just sat on my bed eating. It was super awkward."

"She said you missed a bunch of classes. Are you doing better now?"

I glare at the Lexus driver as he throws his hands up like he can't help being a jerk.

"It sucks," he says. "I didn't even know how to feel, at first. Now I think they're both being selfish."

"Mom thinks Dad is coming back. She says he's lonely."

"Well," Danny sounds reluctant, "probably not after shit-canning his team. Do you...feel bad?" he asks after a pause.

"About what?" I'm trapped. I see a split-second opportunity to overtake the jerk and I take it, swinging my front tire into a two-foot wide gap between the Lexus and a garbage truck.

"Any of it. Fighting with Ashley, fighting with me, fighting with... everyone."

Everyone. He means Mom and Dad. He's implying I broke them up. At least that's what I hear. "Of course I'm sorry," I say, trying in vain to shield my eyes from the sun glaring off a piece of chrome jutting from the garbage truck. "I don't want to hurt anyone. Come on."

Lexus Guy is freaking out. He's hollering and gesturing and throwing me the middle finger, so I extend my own bad finger and knit my brows over the ugliest expression I can make as horns chorus around us.

"I'm not saying it's all your fault," Danny says. "I'm not, Mona. Really. I just think there's a lot of negativity going around."

Unbelievable. The Lexus is trying to get in front of me again. My car is fifteen years old; does he really want to tussle with someone whose car can't lose value? He's maneuvered his car left and is trying to push me out again, get one car length ahead and arrive at his destination a nanosecond faster. I slam my fist on the horn but he won't give in, so I inch, inch forward, creeping until my front bumper is just resting against his car. Ha. Your move.

"I just don't know why she had to axe his whole team," Danny says. "You don't think that was extreme?"

"Mom told me she thinks Dad was relieved. She said he wanted a way out."

"But that's his whole life."

"What if he didn't like his whole life?"

"Jesus, Mona." Danny sighs. "Let's get a drink later."

I really don't want to. I'm still living inside my self-imposed exile, and I don't think I'm ready for prime time. But I can't find a compelling argument for staying home. One more night of watching home renovation shows with my mom—Will Craig and JoAnn choose the light brown granite or the beige? Find out after the commercial break!—and I may have to swear off TV altogether.

"Fine," I say. "But you're driving."

"Okay."

We hang up. There's a gap now between Lexus Guy and a red pickup. I move my car as close to the gap as I can, but then, out of nowhere, I sneeze—a bellowing, full body eruption out of the deepest reaches of my respiratory system. And as my head is turned Lexus Guy barrels around me and up the street, throwing out a triumphant middle finger for me to enjoy as he escapes the congestion. I honk my horn a few times, weakly protesting my defeat, and watch the concrete city shimmering in the late afternoon heat.

* * *

When Danny picks me up, we head south. I stipulated that university bars are off limits. I don't need to run into any college acquaintances and have to explain why I'm neither living in New York nor making millions. Plus, running into any pimps or hoes who witnessed my explosion at the frat house is the last thing I think either of us need. Danny tries to pique my interest in several places, establishments I rule out for being too trendy, too expensive, too noisy, or too full of douchebags. We approach a place called The Silver Dollar Saloon and the building looks charmless and forlorn so I say, "There. That one. Let's go there."

Situated next to a row of bathroom fixture warehouses, The Silver Dollar Saloon is a long, low concrete building lit by a moth-riddled blue light. Danny's 4Runner is conspicuous amongst dirty pickups and sagging junkers, and my feet slip on the loose gravel as I exit the car. From the parking lot I can already hear the high-pitched deedle-dee of someone playing blues guitar and I fear I have chosen unwisely.

It's freezing inside. My arms prickle with goose bumps and I try to pull my sleeves down. The air is thick with stale smoke and the sweet and sour stench of cheap beer. Danny and I are possibly the only people under forty, and definitely the only people with reliable dental coverage. A woman with a greasy ponytail and a sunburned face tends the bar, handing Danny our drinks in between wipes of her nose with the tattooed back of her hand.

"This place is gross," Danny says, staring at a man in a denim vest who squeezes between us to ask the bartender for quarters to play Big Buck Hunter.

"One drink," I say, refusing to admit I agree with him.

We take the only seats left, in front of the stage, and watch the band. A man in a bolo tie steps forward holding a flute and I realize with a groan it's Randy from Job Seekers. Goddamn my luck—he's gonna think I came here to support his band. The other instruments drop out, save the drummer, and Randy jerks into motion with his solo. He takes large breaths in between runs, and at times it sounds as though he's growling into the instrument. The music is jarring. It's rock and roll, and the melody would sound fine coming out of a guitar or a saxophone, but I keep waiting for a line of rats to appear and follow Randy off the stage and out the door. His face shines under the lights, he's sweating liberally, and I'm afraid he's going to pass out. The whole interlude feels far too effete for such a grimy crowd but the audience roars when he finishes, standing up and whistling, and Randy accepts the adulation with a half bow before stepping back and taking up a bass guitar. I try to turn sideways in my chair and hide my face but it's too late. Randy's spotted me and grins, flaunting a gappy smile.

"Flute solo," Danny says with disbelief. "I'm really glad you made us come to this skeeze-hole."

I shrug, not wanting Randy to see me add to Danny's disinterest.

"Hey, check this out," he says, thrusting his phone at me. I look down and see a website cluttered with photos of my brother and his fraternity planting a tree, reading books in the library, loading groceries into a car while an old lady beams with appreciation, and rooting for the Wildcats at a football game. It takes me a moment to realize it's a donation portal for the Daniel Mireles Fund with a ticker, flashing red, showing more than seventeen thousand dollars has been raised thus far. I blink several times and rub my eyes, positive my vision is bleary after a long day staring at a computer. Nope. $17,322.50. And as I stare, the page refreshes and another hundred-dollar donation comes in. $17,422.50.

"What the hell is this?" I ask.

"I told you about it," he says. "I have to do a community service project to graduate, so I started a charity. Pretty sweet, right?"

I read through the page but can't glean anything about what the money will fund. I ask Danny but he's cagy. "You'll find out soon," he grins. "I don't wanna spoil the surprise."

"If I find out you're raising money for some Newt Gingrich-sponsored Super PAC on fighting climate change legislation, I'm gonna punch you in the mouth," I say.

"It's epic," he assures me, taking back his phone.

After Randy's set finishes, he comes down off the stage and heads straight for me. Danny's in the bathroom and I'm all alone, forced to make small talk.

"You came!" he shouts. "What did you think?"

"It was good," I say. "Very…energetic."

"Thanks," he says, beaming. "I've been ride or die for Tull since junior high." He rolls up one sleeve of his shirt and shows me his tattoo.

"Cool," I say, craning my neck toward the bathroom. "Well, I think we're gonna leave in a minute."

"Really?" he asks, looking disappointed. "A couple of us are going out back to smoke a jay, if you're interested."

I perk up immediately. "Yes," I say. "I *am* interested."

I text Danny that I'm going outside and follow Randy out a back door where we find the drummer and the lead guitarist leaning on a wall near the dumpster, the familiar orange smolder of a joint hovering in the darkness. The drummer, a man with long sideburns who introduces himself as Boss, hands me the joint and I inhale, thanking God and everything holy my job doesn't mandate drug tests.

"More, please," I say, receiving laughs.

"I knew you weren't that stuck up," Randy says after a few quiet moments of toke, toke, pass.

"Huh?" I say.

"You seem kinda, I don't know, unfriendly sometimes. But I knew you were a cool chick."

"I am cool," I say, fighting an inclination to lie down on the asphalt. "I'm cool!" I shout to the parking lot.

The back door opens and Danny pokes his head out. He looks behind him and nods before coming down the steps and I stop laughing. I have a weird feeling suddenly that something is going to happen that I'm not going to like.

Ashley steps out after Danny, her wedge heels precarious as she teeters down the narrow concrete steps. She looks good—she always looks good—and I realize, seeing her here scowling with one foot thrust out before her in a defensive posture, how much she must value our friendship that she would want to reconcile, and how undeserving I am of the opportunity.

"You're a cunt," Ashley says. Well, I guess she's here to fight, not forgive. That's fair. Randy offers her a hit, and she glares him down. "The only reason I'm here is because Danny begged me—promised me you were *dying* to apologize to me—and here you are smoking pot and yukking it up next to a dumpster." She pauses a moment and adds, "Seems about the right place for you."

"Huh, hi." I stammer, already impossibly high and unprepared. "It's nice to see you."

"Do you have something to say to me, Mona?"

"Oh jeez, I wasn't expecting—How are you?" Ut sementem feceris ita metes—As you sow shit, so shall that shit come back to thrash you in public.

"Do you have something to say to me, Mona?"

"I'm sorry," I say, trapped on all sides by five sets of eyes. And then the words spill out, and I'm angry with myself because I haven't practiced, that I didn't have the foresight to memorize something containing everything I feel, knowing this apology could be better. But even unprepared, I know everything I say is true and the words stream together like a flood unleashed, heavy and fast. "I'm really, really, really sorry. I'm disgusted about what I said. There's no excuse. I'd never forgive me if I was you. I was drunk and I was upset about your new job—not that those are excuses—but I took your trust and your confidence and I threw them in the garbage and it was the worst thing I ever did. I don't deserve you as a friend and I don't expect you to forgive me or even ever speak to me again, but for what little, little it's worth, I am, from the bottom of my heart, sorry. For everything."

Ashley leans closer and speaks in a gruff whisper. "In front of all those guys, and Joel? You completely humiliated me. And yourself. Joel's super pissed. You should apologize to him, too."

"I know. If you want, I'll call Joel and apologize. I just don't want there to be this acrimony. I was horrible—mean and horrible for no reason." And then, though I don't expect the plea to be of any use, I can't help myself. "Please don't hate me." The last words come out almost in a squeak as my throat clenches and my jaw aches from how tightly I'm holding myself together. "I'm so sorry."

And then I realize something horrible: Ashley might not take me back. A possibility that seems more certain as I take in her barren eyes, her square shoulders. My isolation for the last few weeks had been my choice, justified by telling myself I was saving Danny and Ashley *from* myself. And now it's so obvious that what I'd said was a kindness on my part was more selfishness, a bitter fact I can taste in the bile edging up my throat. That Ashley might dump me on her terms was something I hadn't foreseen. In my selfish exile I'd envisioned her flitting through her perfect life unburdened from bearing the weight of my friendship. I never considered I was only compounding the injury I'd caused her with my distance. It makes me incredibly and unforgivably stupid. "Please don't hate me," I repeat, my voice desperate, short, and weak. "Please."

"You can be really oblivious," and her voice is back to normal volume. "I know you think you have all these witty observations about life but I don't think you spend any time with your eyes all the way open. I feel sorry for you."

I look at the gravel and take my medicine.

"Do you believe all those things you said?"

"No," I say, shaking my head. My vision is blurring. The tears burn hot trails down my red cheeks. "No, of course not. Like I said, I was drunk, and I was jealous of your new job, and I messed everything up because I'm a mess and a fucking moron."

"Because I can't be friends with you if you think those things about me. You sounded like my sister," she says and pulls her cardigan closed over her chest.

"I'm sorry," I say. "I'll do anything. Please."

I remember a comment Ashley made at the end of freshman year. We were sitting on her bed watching a May-December reality TV couple exchange vows when Ashley turned to me and said, "I just realized something. We're going to be in each other's weddings!" I never thought I would ever be in someone's wedding. But Ashley's cheerful assumption, her faith that our friendship would last through college, through our twenties, and into the fuzzy unknown of wedding registries, close of escrow, and gender reveal parties was one of the sweetest things anyone had ever said to me. I've held onto it ever since, a little gem from the future I get to close in the palm of my hand.

"Please," I say again.

"Well," she looks at Danny, "I suppose I can try to forgive you. You can buy me a drink. Or a lot of drinks. I heard about your new job. And thank you for your apology." My head snaps up. Forgiveness? For me? She almost smiles, "Even though I had to corner you for it."

"I know! I shouldn't have made you—"

Danny steps between us. Ashley's eyes have softened. We keep looking at each other around my brother. I hope she knows what I was going to say.

"Okay," Danny says, clapping an arm around me and the other around Ashley. "Everyone's good now, right?" He looks to Ashley. She hesitates, but nods. He looks to me and I do the same, still waiting for the carpet to be pulled back out from under me. Still not believing I deserve Ashley again. "Tequila shots," he says, and motions to Randy and his bandmates to join.

Inside the bar we crowd together and hold our shot glasses high. I'm cautiously festive, watching Ashley for cues on how much to laugh, how much enthusiasm I can show. On the other side of the circle I meet Ashley's eyes. She looks weary and my stomach twists knowing I did that.

Danny recites a toast popular with the brothers at his house and, to his credit, it's gauchely poetic:

"Here's to you, here's to me: friends forever we'll always be. But if by chance we disagree, well fuck you and here's to me!"

Chapter 5: Mystification.

During finals week, U of A always had a fair in the student union where you could get cotton candy and free massages and henna tattoos. My senior year they had a tarot card reader and, I don't advertise this, but I was curious and I sat down.

She pulled out three cards: 5 of Wands, The Lovers, and The Universe. At the time I was so convinced about the impermeable brightness of my own future that I didn't really listen to her warnings about strife and stagnation. Even now I won't admit to her having any abilities beyond performing the bland parlor trick of telling graduating seniors they're going to encounter challenges along the way. But I do remember she paid particular attention to The Lovers, and how she emphasized the importance of love in my life, and how opening the heart to help would eventually open it to love.

"Each of us is half a person," she said. "Only through love can we find unity." I don't know about all that, but the world is a different color when you stop being alone.

Sunk costs

A few days later, I'm with Ashley at a café in an upscale mall built to look like, I don't know, a pueblo? A hacienda? Apparently, people now want to hear birds and fountains while they shop for designer dog carriers.

Ashley's on her second mojito. Her mother, Crystal, is on her way and Ashley looks like she's about to receive a colonoscopy. I haven't told her about my parents yet, too afraid to burst the bubble of rekindled friendship we've blissfully floated in since the Saloon. We have a few minutes and I decide I might as well tell her about the separation, distract her so she doesn't sit here obsessing about whether she wore the wrong shoes. But what am I supposed to say? That my parents have just thrown their marriage and my father's career into the fire? That they dissolved twenty-four years of reasonably good coexistence in a matter of hours? How about that I partly blame myself? And that I'm now being forced to evaluate everything I know about life, career, love, and permanence? Are you even allowed to talk about anything important in a mall café?

"So, my parents are separating," I say, stuffing a wad of complimentary bread into my mouth after dropping the bomb.

Ashley responds automatically, as though I'd caught her in the middle of a thought. "You're so lucky." Then, catching herself, "Sorry. I didn't mean that. That's terrible. I'm so sorry." She covers my hand with hers a moment. "What happened?"

"Well, my dad apparently interviewed for another job in Pennsylvania and didn't tell my mom about it. She heard what he did from a colleague, freaked out, and they decided to separate. Then my mom fired his entire team under the guise of budget cuts—as you do—" Ashley nods and waves her hand in a 'but of course' motion, "though she thinks he actually wanted her to do that so he could be free, or something. I kind of think so, too. Now he's in New Zealand for a month and Danny thinks I'm partly responsible for the whole thing because, well, just because of how I am."

Ashley gives me a sympathetic look. "You did not break up your parents. You're extremely hard to live with, but if your dad was secretly going to out-of-state job interviews, they were headed that way for a long time."

How does she have the capacity to be so kind? "You think so?"

"Remember the New Year's party when I said it was weird your parents didn't kiss at midnight? And the time your dad took us bowling and I told you he was flirting with the hot dog lady? Plus, your mom is—was—his boss. How could that not make things weird? And as for her firing his team, I mean, it sounds like maybe that *was* what he wanted. Maybe he was just too scared to admit it."

I'm looking at her over the rim of my wine glass, remembering mornings I'd found my father stretched out on the couch in his study, glasses fogging under his nose. Or resentful utterances under my mother's breath about being the only one who ever drove Danny and me to meets and practices. Maybe the fairytale beginnings of their marriage, love besting hate, lent them an aura of forever love that wasn't matched in their daily life. Maybe the pressure grew too big for them. Maybe I never understood the story at all. Maybe I definitely needed Ashley back. There's a reason eyewitness testimonies are supposed to be more reliable from someone uninvolved in the crime, right?

"Your mom and my mom are kind of alike," Ashley says. "They have such high expectations—with your mom she wants you to get a fancy job so she can justify all the time she spent driving you around and padding your résumé, and with my mom she wants me to be pretty and rich so she can justify all the years she spent climbing up the social ladder. It's like they want to be paid back. What do you call it? A return on their investment. Why can't they just be glad they tried their best and hope we don't join a cult?"

"I think you're right," I say. "And I think what's driving my mom crazy is that she feels like it was all for nothing. Investing in me and being married to my dad. She's so fixated on this idea that she wasted years of her life, I think she'd take my dad back in a second if he came home and apologized. In fact, I think she's counting on it. There's this principle you learn in economics called 'the sunk cost fallacy.' It's about how you shouldn't throw good money after bad. Like, no matter how much you invested in something, no matter if you spent ten years developing a technology or blew through millions of dollars, if it's not working you just have to walk away. You're never going to spend enough to make it successful. Just eat the loss and move on. And that's what my mom's doing right now—honoring sunk costs."

"I need to remember that," Ashley says. "The next time my mom gets on my case about using cheap eyeliner I'm going to tell her I'm a lost cause and she needs to stop honoring sunk costs. Ugh, well, I hope your dad figures out what he wants to do while he's away. And who knows? Maybe the distance will be good for him and he'll come back. Meanwhile my parents are so inseparable and co-dependent they're like conjoined twins. The only reason my mom's coming down here today is because my dad's playing golf in Alabama. Then when they're apart all they do is call and text about the most mundane crap—I guarantee you my mom'll send my dad a picture of the menu when she gets here, just to show him how cheap the crab cakes are."

I missed Ashley. I feel badly, selfishly, that this fact hits me while we're talking about my parents. But it's true.

"Speak of the devil," I say, indicating Crystal coming towards our table. Ashley's mother is smiling, or at least making her best approximation: her mouth is stretched wide, but the top half of her face refuses to participate and her nose wrinkles slightly and her eyes dart around the room almost in fear, almost as though she sees danger in the wilting irises at the hostess stand, in the overflowing bins of dirty dishes outside the kitchen door.

She and Ashley hold each other at the arms and touch cheeks, both sides, because I'm sure Crystal thinks this greeting makes them look très distingué. She goes through the same pantomime with me and then sits down and asks the waiter for a Perrier at room temperature.

"Well, when did Tucson get a nice mall?" she asks.

"Right after we got indoor plumbing," I say. Ashley kicks me and I stuff bread into my mouth to hold my tongue. She shuffles in her seat, pretends to fix her top, and I think she's looking down so her mom can't see she's smiling.

"Mona," Crystal says, eyeing me over her menu, her blonde hair white hot in the late afternoon sun, "are you seeing anyone? With your personality I'm stunned you don't have ten boyfriends."

"As a matter of fact," I say, trying to mimic the bared teeth of my aggressor, "there might be someone."

"For serious?" Ashley asks, mouth agape.

"For serious," I smile. "He's a little older and we work together so…we'll see."

"I hope he's not your manager," Crystal says. "That's beyond tacky." And she excuses herself to the 'powder room.'

I adjust my legs under the table. I usually shrug off Crystal, but this comment snags me.

"Is he your boss?" Ashley asks once her mother is gone.

"Well, yeah," I say. "I don't see what the big deal is."

"It might not be a big deal," Ashley says, "but don't you think it's a little weird your dad just moved out and suddenly you're seeing an older guy?"

Now my mouth drops. "You're sick," I say, wagging a breadstick at her. "Really sick."

Ashley's mother returns and mercifully the conversation turns away from me. Ashley buzzes about double happinesses: she spent a weekend with Samberg in Sedona and bought a new car with her new paycheck.

"My job's going really well," Ashley says, cutting her salad into tinier and tinier bites. "I got to design the posters for Tucson Beer Week so I built a cactus out of beer cans and photographed it. They came out super cute. I never thought I'd get paid to do stuff like that, but here I am. It's so cool."

I feel an attack of jealousy bubble up in my stomach. Don't do this again. She's your best friend. You're happy for her.

"Well, Ashley," Crystal says, laying her fork down next to her untouched meal, "why didn't you use your sister for your little ads? You know she's been having a hard time booking jobs in this recession. You need to do what you can to help her out."

I've never met Ashley's sister but I've seen photos. She's a low-level model who poses sometimes for lifestyle magazines in Scottsdale. Her biggest coup was a billboard off of I-10—she was reclined in a bubble bath holding a glass of champagne to advertise one of the casinos near Phoenix, and the tagline was something like, "Catch the excitement." Except someone got up there with a can of spray paint and changed the tagline to read, "Catch the clap," and it took a few days for the billboard people to take it down. Ashley drove out and took a photo of it herself, and she said she was outraged on her sister's behalf, but that didn't stop her from showing the picture to everyone for months.

"Next time, okay, Mom?" Ashley sighs.

The rest of the meal moves in this fashion—Ashley making overtures and Crystal responding with criticisms or comparisons to her other daughter, and me, unable to retreat down a bottle of wine because of drunk driving laws, forced to sit mostly sober for the whole charade.

"Ashley says you're still looking for a job, Mona."

I pull in a long breath. Crystal has some sadistic talent for finding the thing you don't want to talk about and dragging it into the center of the room.

"I am. I took a job at a call center, just temporarily, but I'm still hoping something better comes along."

"Well you're not going to find anything down here. Tucson is not exactly a place where things happen."

"Yes, it's no Snotsdale," I say.

"Oh, that's good," she says with sarcasm. "I've never heard that before." Crystal gives Ashley a blistering look and I decide to make peace.

"Okay, I'm sorry," I say. "Yes, I'm aware it would be better if I lived in a bigger city, it's just not possible for me right now. But…thank you for the advice." Why was that so hard to say?

"Did you know, when Ashley's father was starting out, he bankrupted the company three times? And this was the early eighties—anyone with a pulse could make money in Arizona real estate. *I* was the one who turned him around. And *I* was the one who saved him from losing everything in all the savings and loan craziness. I was a flight attendant when we met, and by the time I was finished with him he was one of the biggest developers in the state."

I only nod, unprepared for whatever this is—chastisement or motivational speech or prolonged gloat.

"If you really wanted a job," she continues, "you'd go out and make one instead of moping around a call center waiting for stars to fall from the sky. Everyone wants to get rich but no one wants to put in the effort. I used to get pinched blue by drunk oilmen and now no one can build a doghouse in Scottsdale without coming through me."

"Are you suggesting I marry well?"

"I'm suggesting you get off your butt and use what God gave you." And after a quick appraisal up and down says, "Which I'm assuming is your intelligence."

She's blunt. Respect, Crystal.

"Ashley, hold the menu up to the light," she says, putting on her readers and squinting down at her phone. "I want your father to see the price on those crab cakes."

The waiter comes and we all decline dessert, Ashley and her mother for obvious caloric reasons and me because I want to beat it back to my house and the relative comfort of my own dysfunctional family.

In the car I'm thinking about Crystal's words to get out there and make something happen, and I'm thinking about sunk costs. There are good reasons people can't walk away, chiefly that they just don't want to stop believing that tomorrow everything could turn around. I've stopped applying for new jobs, partly because I'm tired when I get home from Sunshine, partly because there's been a fucking lot going on, but mostly because I just don't want to. I'm trying to remember why I decided to major in finance in the first place, and all I can recall is that I knew I was good at math, and I didn't want to work in a university. No child has ever raised their hand on career day and said they want to be a bond analyst. I don't recall ever being fired up about learning how to calculate net present value. I think, like Crystal said, if I really wanted to make something happen, if I woke up every morning in a fever to reverse my fortunes my damn self, I would. And if I'm going to be rational, if I can accept the wasted time and admit to myself that mistakes were made, maybe I can wipe the dust off my hands and walk away. Free.

I find my mom reading on the couch in the den, the news humming in the background and a small, brown lump on top of her feet. I get closer and two bat-like ears emerge out of the brown, joined by a nose and two rows of glistening teeth.

"Yapyapyapyapyapyapyap!"

"Shhh," my mom says, stroking the dog on its head. "This is Mona. She's my other baby." And she picks up the animal and nuzzles her nose into its neck. "Mona, come meet Pepper."

"You got a dog?" I approach, my palm out so he can smell me, but he begins to emit a mean little growl that's soon bigger than his whole body. I back up and the dog resumes his position on my mother's feet, keeping his eyes on me. I look closer and notice he has an underbite, giving him an expectant, pleading expression like he can always smell sausages somewhere. Between the teeth and the ears and a rod-thin tail hastily thumping the remote control, this dog is ugly. "What is it?" I ask.

"A chiweenie," my mom says, beaming into the animal's face.

I raise my eyebrows, indicating she needs to say more.

"A Chihuahua and a weenie dog," she says. "A chiweenie. Isn't he the cutest thing you've ever seen?"

It looks like a less cuddly Gollum, but I keep my mouth shut. "So, you just thought, 'I'm gonna buy a dog today?'"

"Well, I'd thought about it before. When you kids moved out it was so quiet around here." She glances behind her at my father's study. "Now you've got a job, so it won't be long until you move out. It'll be nice to have someone happy to see me when I get home from work."

"I'm happy when you come home from work—I don't know how to cook."

"Very funny."

"This is acturience," I say smugly. "It's the impulse to act because you feel dissatisfied. In other words, acting out. I read about it in a paper on seniors who divorce. I just psychoanalyzed you." I put out my palm. "That'll be three hundred dollars."

"*Seniors* who divorce? There's no need for that kind of language. And it's a dog, Mona. If you want to think it's a midlife crisis, be my guest."

"Well, I'm not taking that thing for walks."

"Did you donate to Danny's charity yet?"

"No, and about that—what is it? I looked all over the website and I couldn't figure out what they're planning to do with the money. You know, he's raised almost twenty grand."

"Twenty-five as of this afternoon."

"Jesus! Where's it all going?"

She says she has no idea and then adds that she gave a thousand dollars.

"And what if he's using it to film a porno?"

"I trust him," she says, scratching Pepper under his chin. I look at her beaming contentment down on the dog and decide that this is the moment, that I'm never going to get answers unless I demand them. Amped up with warring confusion and clarity after dinner with Ashley and Crystal, I'm ready. Thunderdome, here we go.

"Why are you so easy on Danny and so hard on me? Is it because you're trying to recoup some investment?"

"I'm not."

"Yes, you are."

"Now how do you expect me to answer that?" she asks, turning around to look at me with indignation. "Do you want me to say I have higher expectations for you because your grades have always been higher? Yes, I put a lot of time into helping you realize your potential but I'm not trying to 'recoup my investment.' You make it so transactional. I was trying to give you tools to survive. And I'm proud of you. If you don't know that then maybe I don't do a good job of showing it. But I am."

"Thanks," and I'm surprised how good it feels to hear, that I'd needed to feel the words wrapping around me.

"I think that sometimes I take my frustrations out on you instead of where they should have been going all these years."

"Dad?"

She nods. "I hate cooking. Did you know that? I haaaate it. I hate laundry, I hate remembering doctor's appointments, I hate school carpools, I hate sweeping crumbs off the dining room floor after every meal. I hate all of it. But your father, for all his other good qualities, never helped out with that stuff. I tried, in the beginning, to get him to pitch in, but it was a different time back then and we were both raised in houses where the woman did everything, and besides, there are only so many times you can ask someone to wash the dishes before you just get fed up and do it yourself. And after a while I stopped complaining because that just makes everything more ugly and—It's just all compromise. That's it."

"That's a lot of resentment, though, building up all those years. Like, what's the point?"

"Marriage is a lot bigger than who does the dishes. Your father always supported my career. He never stood in my way or got jealous that I was rising instead of him. And he might not have driven you around but he was always available for you kids. He read to you and your brother every night when you were little. And he's a good man. He's honorable."

She pauses and looks left and right as though giving herself permission to say more. "I got pregnant with you after our third date."

My eyes grow wide and she doesn't say anything for a few seconds, letting that bombshell sink in.

"I never wanted you to think that you weren't wanted. It was just…a big surprise. I was a graduate student; he was a first-year postdoc. I think we had a few hundred dollars between us. Once I'd made up my mind that I was going to…go through with the pregnancy, I told him that he could walk away. That I wouldn't blame him." She shakes her head. "I didn't even know his middle name. He thought about it for a while. Those were the longest two weeks of my life, I can tell you. And then he came into the lab one morning with a gold band and asked me to marry him. It was the single greatest day of my life.

"And I think about all we went through at the beginning. The fights with my parents—who were just as angry that they'd sunk all this money into graduate school only for me to wind up pregnant as they were that I'd gotten knocked up by 'some gardener's kid' as they called your father. And I think about your father tutoring high school students for extra money, and how I'd type reports with one hand while you or your brother slept on my shoulder, and the ugly little holes we used to live in until we could finally afford this house. I just can't—I can't walk away from all that. That's my whole life."

She covers her mouth with her hand and I give her a tissue, put my arm around her shoulder, and sit while she cries silently and nuzzles the dog. And I do it because I want to, because neither of us wants to feel alone.

I always struggled in my economics classes to get past the fundamental assumption that people have rational preferences. That always seemed like crap to me. A lot of the time people have highly irrational preferences for perfectly rational reasons. Maybe honoring sunk costs is the right thing to do sometimes. Maybe irrational belief in the future is one of the best things about being human.

I scratch the dog under his chin and the dishwasher groans and begins a new cycle. Tucson sleeps and on the other side of the globe I imagine my father is wrestling his breakfast away from a hungry pig, and if anything good comes from all this, it may be my mother and I here, now, together, at last.

Do you believe in soulmates?

I haven't had sex in three years. It's not a big deal, I wouldn't say it interferes with work. Sometimes I sit on the phone with old ladies as they wax poetic about why it's important to fund the spotted owl preserve, and I imagine being bent over my office chair by Skip, or Ricky Gervais, or all the male cast members of *Gossip Girl*. But like I said: not a big deal.

So being an intelligent young woman, I decide to solve this problem the same way I've learned to solve every problem: hours of painstaking research. I swiped an armload of women's magazines from Ashley's apartment, and for a week I poured over every lurid article: "Ten Ways to Make Him Want You," "One Move That Will Have Him Begging for More," and "Give Him What He Wants: Our Sexperts Tell All!" I studied their tips on body language ("Lean in close when you're speaking to your crush. Wear a low-cut shirt and give him a peek of the ladies!"), flirting ("Try to touch him as much as possible. Your hand on his knee makes him feel sexy!"), makeup ("Release your inner porn star! Kaitlyn Kittens shares her tips on how to get your eyes bedroom ready!"), sex ("Stroke his…ego! Tell him how hot he is while you're doin' the nasty."), and I even read their health advice ("Want perkier boobs? Stand up straight! Better posture can make your bust look bangin'!").

At the end of my studies I feel fun and fearless and also fat—I make a mental note to get on a juice cleanse, whatever that is. I head out of the house this morning ready to snare Skip with my charms, lure him spider-like between my legs.

I'm wearing my first push-up bra and I've stuffed myself into a skirt at least one size too small. My vision is blurry. I got a lot of liquid eyeliner in my eyes this morning and I can feel the rest of it leeching into my corneas. I bought new perfume, something called Promiscuous Pink, and I'm leaving a cloud behind me that smells like cotton candy. After I got the job at Bannerman, I celebrated by buying a pair of designer snakeskin boots, my one piece of tangible evidence that I had a cush job, but until today I never found an occasion to wear them. Squeezing them up over my calves, they were a little tighter than I remembered. And a little higher. Teetering through the parking lot to Sunshine I think I may have been a tad ambitious about my ability to walk in six-inch heels, but I *do* look like Catwoman and I have no spare shoes, so I'll endure.

I feel like a hooker and I can hardly breathe. Being a woman is exhausting.

When I get into the office Skip is in a darkened hallway with his clipboard, his body lit by the neon glow of the soda machine. I reach for my coin purse hoping I can drag out the purchase of a soda long enough to make meaningful contact.

"Good morning, Mona," Skip says. "You look lovely today."

I giggle. ("Smile! It makes him feel appreciated.") "Thanks. Did you have a good weekend?"

"Yeah," he says, putting down the clipboard. "I went mountain biking with my daughter. Beautiful weather on Saturday. How about you?"

I'm spending a long time dropping quarters in the machine and selecting my drink. I bend almost all the way over, partly to force him to look at my butt, partly because my eyes are watering so much, I can't see the options at the bottom of the machine. Finally, I make my selection and bounce back to standing, almost toppling over in the asinine shoes. "I went sunbathing," I lie. ("A picture's worth a thousand words. Get him to envision you naked!")

"Oh," he says, and his face falls. He puts his hand on my shoulder and bends close. My heart speeds up at his touch and I congratulate myself for a plan well-executed. Yes, I would love to make out in the parking lot. "You shouldn't go sunbathing," he says. "Skin cancer is terrible."

Now it's my face that falls as he walks away. He takes several steps before turning around to ask, "Do you smell cotton candy?"

* * *

I'm not getting any better at using liquid eyeliner—today it looks like I've smeared my eyes with crude oil. I've got blisters on all ten of my toes and I've lost feeling on the left side of my body from being pressed into clothes that are too small. I soldier on, however, determined to get a date even if I have to reverse the progress of feminism in the process.

I've spent the week inventing excuses to go into Skip's office—I came in so many times to ask about timesheets he must think I'm slow—and by Friday I can't find any more. I tried leaning on his desk, dropping pens on the floor, touching his arm while I spoke, complimenting his eyes—I'm now pretty sure he didn't know the meaning of the word 'azure,'—but nothing sparked a definitive response. It was always the same genial demeanor, the same is-he-flirting-or-isn't-he ambiguity. Maybe my mother is right: Women would rule the world if they didn't spend so much time parsing conversations with attractive men for hidden meanings. Maybe when he pokes his head into the cubicle this morning to tell me there are bagels in the conference room, he's just trying to tell me someone brought breakfast.

I slouch into the room, nodding politely to the others as I grab a bagel. People are milling so I nibble my food and watch. Skip's got one hand against a wall, chatting with Nadine, her pentagram necklace now joined by earrings shaped like howling coyotes. She says something that makes him laugh and he falls against her for dramatic effect and I realize, beyond a doubt, he is not interested in me and I've spent the week chasing a phantom. He's a close talker, you utter twit. He's a friendly guy who enjoys speaking to people, and I'm so unused to niceness I mistook it for romantic attraction.

I walk back to my cubicle doing a mental facepalm and work through lunch, now self-conscious about my revealing outfit. Late in the afternoon I go to the soda machine, relieved to find the hall empty when I get there. I've just swallowed the bubblesweet first sip when Skip rounds the corner and heads my way. On a reflex I pull up the neckline of my shirt and feel foolish.

"I'm glad I caught you," he says and looks over his shoulder. "I wanted to ask you something," and I brace myself for what is sure to be a request that I put in overtime. "What are you doing tomorrow night?"

"I don't know," I say.

"Well, I wanted to know if you'd like to have dinner with me."

My heart stops. The magazines were right! "Yeah, I'm free," I say with a noncommittal shrug. "Dinner sounds fun. Thanks."

"Tremendous," he says. "Do you like steak? There's a place you're gonna love. Pick you up at seven?"

"Awesome," I say. "Seven."

"Great."

"Great."

I'm back in my cubicle and have completed a victory lap around my desk chair when I remember the big, scarlet flaw in all this: What if I get exactly what I want out of this date? And what the hell am I going to do about my scars?

* * *

At five thirty on Saturday I open a bottle of wine, pour a stiff glass, and swing my closet wide open. Mercifully I'm the only one home. My brother's on campus and my mother took Pepper to some playgroup for dogs. I can only imagine introducing Skip to my mother and having her sniff with derision when she finds out he went to Arizona State.

I thumb through my hangers, hoping for inspiration. I like clothes, I really do. I occasionally read fashion magazines and I can always point out why someone has been put in the "Yikes!" section on the back page. But when it comes to dressing for an event, I'm paralyzed. Staring at the offerings in my closet I can't see anything sexy, flattering, or current. I pull out a cornflower blue dress with ruching up the sides and it looks too "late-90s homecoming dance." A black and white jersey dress with long sleeves screams "daughter of a televangelist." And a gold and white strapless bustier number plainly says "new money mafia princess."

I look down and see I've finished my first glass of wine but I have almost an hour before Skip comes, so I tell myself I can have another. Drink in hand, I face my closet again.

I laid awake for hours last night, terrifying myself with visions of Skip's hand reaching up my leg and his fingers tracing the perimeters of my horrible secret, him pulling back my skirt and my sick predilection being laid bare for his blue, blue eyes. It's possible on a subconscious level I've been pushing possible boyfriends away so I won't have to have this problem. I want to push these thoughts away too, so I put on a pair of jeans and focus on finding a shirt.

I spend what feels like hours, trying things on and holding things up, different permutations of layered tops, tops with accessories, shirts tucked in, belted, unbuttoned, sleeves up or down, and I get so worked up the second glass of wine disappears and I'm left blinking at the red-tinged bottom of the cup. Finally, I put on one shirt I don't despise, one that clings to my waist and flatters my bustline. But it seems too modest for such an auspicious night and I tell myself, now armed with a new, wine-backed sense of purpose, I should improvise.

So, in my lightly inebriated state, I take off the shirt and lay it on the floor. I eyeball about where I think my cleavage hits, and start cutting. It's more or less even. I trim a little more here and a little more here, and fold it over to make sure the sides match. Success! Sewing is easy. I try it on and can tell, before I've got my arms through, it's beyond trashy. It's so low cut they may refuse me service at the restaurant. But I look with dismay at the other things hanging in my closet and decide to make it work. Bibamus, moriendum est: Let us drink, Seneca said, for we must die.

Okay, now what? I'm running out of time and I haven't begun my hair or makeup. "Ugh!" I scream and throw a scarf around my neck, strategically draping it over my exposed bosom and praying I don't flash my ratty, six-year-old Wal-Mart bra at Skip all evening, and that the temperature in Tucson spontaneously drops forty degrees. Lord, give me strong air-conditioning tonight.

The wine bottle is sitting on the bathroom counter when I start pulling makeup out of drawers. Fuck it, I think, and pour another.

Tonight is the night I will conquer liquid eyeliner. I get out the little black tube and hold my hand steady, steady, trying to aim the point into the inner corner of my eyelid. It's hard to do this with my eyes open, though, so I close them and let the tip slide across. When I open them it's bad: teardrops of jet black smattered all over my eyelid and nowhere near the lash line. My phone dings and it's Skip telling me he's five minutes away. Crap! I don't have time to redo anything so I grab grey eye shadow and start caking it on, hoping to cover up the eyeliner mess. My hands are shaking from either nerves or wine and I'm dropping flecks of grey everywhere, so I sigh and rub shadow over and under and all around until I look like a very tired raccoon. I calm my nerves by chugging the rest of the wine and chasing it with toothpaste, lest Skip think I have a drinking problem. My hair is whatever, I have a zit on my shoulder, and I can't find my lip-gloss. Time's up. This is it. I'm ready.

Skip's at my front door holding a half-dozen red roses and wearing a sleek buttoned shirt and dark jeans. Fastidious, I would say. *Pulcher est*. Out of the fluorescent lights and dingy carpet at Sunshine he looks like an attractive, successful man, someone to turn heads at a barbecue. And he smells exquisite, like roses and leather.

I'm dizzy from the excitement and the heat and the wine, and I'd just like to sit in his car and direct the air vents at my armpits. He holds open the door of the BMW and I slowly, *gracefully* sit down. I decided to wear the lucky boots and now I'm careful to neither tip over from the heels, which seem to have grown taller with the wine, nor spill my breasts out all over the dash. Skip gets in and starts the car and Dave Matthews Band fills the air. I hope he hasn't put this music on for my benefit. Dave Matthews is what would happen if beer pong became a person.

I try to ignore the bad vibes coming out of the stereo, though, and focus on the positive. Skip could be rich. Maybe he'd let me move into his house and I could stay home and watch cartoons instead of killing myself all day on the phone. Maybe we'd fall in love and get married and have a honeymoon in Prague and I could drink absinthe until I hallucinated.

Oh shit, he's talking. Pay attention!

"So that's when Donna and I split up," he says. "I couldn't look her in the eye anymore after that. You know?"

"Yeah," I say, clawing at my subconscious to tell me what's been going on for the last five minutes. Nada. "So, um, are you from Tucson?"

I get a weird look. "No, I'm from Phoenix, remember?"

"Yeah, of course. Sorry," I say and stab around for some other subject that won't expose my poor listening. "Um, I like your car. Matches your eyes."

"Thanks," he says, and his skin crinkles when he smiles. For an instant I panic, flashing on liver spots and arthritic fingers, old man underwear and a medicine cabinet full of ointments. Relax, I tell myself. He's not that old. I'm sure he doesn't have a daughter my age.

"I have a daughter about your age," he says, and he's facing the road so he can't see me wince. "She's always after me to let her drive it, but she's too irresponsible."

The steakhouse Skip has chosen is in an upscale shopping center, and everything inside feels like a corporate façade. It all looks nice— the art deco chairs and the calla lilies and the soft, recessed lighting— but there's an unspoken meanness, a frugality of character penetrating everything from the bleached tablecloths to the frozen smiles on the servers.

Skip orders our cocktails, vodka tonic for him, vodka cranberry for me, and I try to loosen up and enjoy being young, desired, and out on the town.

"Don't you want to take off your scarf?" he asks.

"No," I say, a little too loud, and adjust it without sneaking too many looks down at my shirt.

"You look beautiful tonight," he says.

I say thank you and follow his eyes as they scan the menu and I admire the smooth, dark skin on his fingers absently tracing a pattern on the outside of his water glass. I think his nails are manicured. This relationship could work.

The bread comes and I cram it in, trying to soak up the wine and vodka sloshing around my bloodstream. I recall reading that men don't like it when women eat too much on a date, but I decide Skip would be more grossed out by my barf in his dinner salad.

We chat. I learn he's a Catholic Republican but that he "considered buying a hybrid." He's lactose intolerant and worries that eating too much soy will make him grow breasts, he bikes through the foothills on the weekends to clear his head (because being a call center manager must confront him with such weighty moral dilemmas as to necessitate grueling physical exertion and temporary removal from society, *eye roll*), and his favorite movie is *Saving Private Ryan*.

I tell him I majored in finance, I visited the Vatican with my family in the ninth grade, I try not to exercise if I can help it, I won't eat mayonnaise under any circumstance, and my favorite movie is *The Big Lebowski* (my carnal desires be damned, I almost walk out of the restaurant when he says, "Lebowski—I just didn't get it.")

I'm concentrating hard on not acting drunk. I keep my voice measured, I fold my hands in my lap to stop from gesturing too wildly while I speak, and I keep bathroom breaks to a minimum lest I stumble in my heels and embarrass us both. There's no reason to tell him I drank a whole bottle of wine before coming out. He might be alarmed. Other things I leave out: cutting and assorted compulsive behaviors, my obsession with Laura Horn, the fact that most of my pajamas have cats on them, my parents' impending divorce, and my ability to recite the first hundred lines of the *Aeneid* in perfect Latin. I've said so little, in fact, about who I really am, I'm starting to understand why people say dating is hard. I'd rather stay celibate than admit any of that stuff to someone I'm trying to sleep with.

We finish dinner and as I'm now filled with twelve ounces of porterhouse and a baked potato, my reeling drunkenness has dulled to a pleasant buzz. I agree to go to a club.

I've never been to a club. Ashley got me out to Senior Sunday at this or that dive bar a couple of times, but a stinky college bar with a trough in the men's room and a prize for drinking the sludge off the floor mats is a little different than a club with valet parking and table service. We get inside and I'm frozen, paralyzed in sensory overload. Between the postmodern light sculptures snaking the walls and the thirty-foot high projections of Anime characters pulsing to the music, the seven-foot-tall girls with breasts so perky they practically boing out of their necks, I can hardly believe I'm still in Tucson.

I totter over to a plastic couch and sit while Skip orders drinks. I look at him, speaking to a waitress who could easily be a runway model, and feel sorry for him, at how out of place he must feel in this temple of youth. He'd probably rather be at home with a craft beer and a Tom Clancy novel but, owing to my age, he's decided to brave the club scene because he thinks that's what the kids are doing.

"Screwdriver," he says, handing me a glass. "Let's toast to a perfect first date."

I take a sip and decide to be bold. I lean over to wrap my arms around his neck and kiss him, but I misjudge my distance and fall against him, spilling some of my drink down his back. He jumps and I straighten, embarrassed but undeterred.

"Why don't we dance?" he asks after sponging off his back, and I agree, eager for another opportunity to kiss.

But like Leonidas betrayed at Thermopylae, circumstances on the dance floor are not to my advantage. My feet are treasonous in their leather casings, swollen and feeling as though they're run through by metal spikes. Two short girls keep bumping into me, and worst of all, Skip is a dancer beyond all expectation. I don't think I'm bad at dancing—I've faked my way through plenty of weddings—but I've seen enough televised dancing competitions to know when someone has real talent. Skip is graceful, confident, and sexy. Other girls are watching him sway his hips and hold my waist while I use every screeching bone in my feet to stop from falling, stepping on him, or doing permanent damage to my metatarsals. Though there's an obvious thrill to being out with someone other girls want, I feel less in control of the night than I did ten minutes before. If I don't go home with him, he could likely get any number of girls to take my place.

My scarf is beginning to dampen at my neck, and I want Skip's attention focused on me and not the gathering horde so I take it off, seducing him with my eyes while I do it, and could almost cry from how good the fresh air feels on my skin.

"You're a great dancer," I shout.

"Thanks! I've been coming here almost every weekend since the divorce. You have to put yourself out there, you know? My soulmate could be anyone, so I have to be open to meeting her anywhere. Do you believe in soulmates?"

"Totally!" I totally don't, but I don't see that it matters for this conversation.

"I'm looking for someone kind and funny. Someone with good morals. You might say it's hard to meet women with good morals in a club, but it's easier to get to know someone here than in church."

I'm feeling pretty loose now, the alcohol having produced its intended effect, and I decide I'll try execute a shoulder shimmy, a move my sober self would never attempt. I start shaking my shoulders and jiggling my chest and trying to synchronize my gyrations to the beat, and Skip's eyebrows go up and he motions to my chest. A nipple has escaped! My shirt is completely below the top of my bra and my left nipple has worked its way free and is now peeking out at the other dancers. If I was sober, I would call a cab, go home, quit my job, and maybe move to Canada for good measure. But I'm decidedly not sober, so I pop the little darling back in and laugh it off, hoping Skip will find the whole thing playfully erotic.

Skip goes to the bathroom, so I collapse on the plastic couch again and try deep breathing to get through the pain in my feet, now spread up the entirety of my legs and into my lower back. When he returns, he asks if I'm ready to leave and I say yes, demure and respectable as a governor's wife, though on the inside I'm performing cartwheels and compiling lists of sex moves gleaned from Ashley's magazines.

In the car I arch my back and cross my legs and purse my lips in a pose I'd describe as, sexalicious.

"Is your back hurting you?" Skip asks. "You look uncomfortable."

"I'm fine," I say, straightening up. Don't be obvious! "So, where do you live?" I ask.

"I'm over by Sabino Canyon," he says. "It's peaceful out there. I'll bring you by sometime. You'd love it."

"Why don't we stop by now? For a nightcap?"

He turns to me and looks pained. I'm confused. I thought men were perpetually dying to have sex. An economist would say that to maximize utility it's better to be open rather than playing hideous games all night with neither party getting what they want. No, I stand by what I said.

"Okay," he says slowly. "We can stop by, but…" He trails off. It's so late they've turned off most of the traffic signals and we fly through all the blinking yellows. Dave Matthews is still on in the background. I could swear it's the same song from before, though all these upbeat saxophone pieces sound the same to me.

I move my hand to the stereo to find a song that doesn't make me cringe, but Skip reaches out and blocks the controls and I throw my hands up in mock surrender.

"I'm sorry," he says, but doesn't move his hand. "I always keep this record on in the car." I give him a look, but he's facing the road.

Skip lives way out in the hinterlands. I see a lot of For Sale signs as we approach. His subdivision must have been one of the last ones built during the housing boom. We pull up to a sprawling ranch on the edge of civilization and I'm relieved to see old Skipper is doing quite well for himself.

The house is immaculate and appointed in the Southwestern décor inherent to most Arizonan homes. I sit without being invited and take off my boots and socks; the feel of the wool rug on my toes is sublime. I want to dig my feet into the rough fibers, massaging out all the sweat and tension and blisters built up over the last five hours, but I satisfy myself with furtive swipes of the balls of my feet over the low pile surface. I may never get off this couch. I accept another cocktail, and a coaster, and wait for things to get steamy.

I wait a long time. Skip excuses himself and disappears into the back of the house and I spend ten minutes on the couch watching the fronds of a potted palm flutter in the breeze of the air conditioner. I'm in so much pain I'm pretty sure I can no longer walk without assistance. I may spend the night just to avoid having to stand up again.

When Skip finally returns, he apologizes, gives no explanation for his absence, and sits down next to me. For a few minutes the only sound comes from the ice clinking in our glasses as we sip, desperate for something to fill the silence. I know I should make the first move, make him feel desired, but I'm reluctant, now afraid I can't go through with the deed, that I don't even want to.

I clear my throat, about to ask him the provenance of a large painting above the mantle of a shirtless cowboy about to lasso a bull, when he puts his hand on my knee and leans in for a kiss.

It's a strange practice, kissing. The exchange of body fluids results in a flood of oxytocin, chemically binding you to your partner and creating a biological imperative towards monogamy. Each tongue thrust and caress urges you closer to nature's goal of propagation, every strand of DNA in your body screaming at you to tear your clothes off and get busy. And yet. Kissing Skip feels empty, like making out with the back of my own hand when I was thirteen.

That's not to say there's no sensation. His hands are soft. As he sweeps them across the small of my back and runs them up and through my hair a cascade of chills crashes down my skin. Every nerve ending is electrified by the touch of his hands and his mouth on my neck, my ear, and my chest. But still, despite all the magazine propaganda about how much I should be enjoying casual sex, about seizing the world by the testicles, here on this couch, making out with my boss, I feel silly. And alone.

And afraid. Skip's hand is on my Mona Lisa thigh and through my jeans I can feel my secret pulsing, a tell-tale heart beating a confession through stretch denim. My heart rate quickens and I start to sweat and Skip's oblivious, no doubt sure I'm lightly panting with sexual desire.

Our shirts come off. We lie back on the couch and the cold leather is welcome against my clammy skin. Fortunately, Skip isn't enthusiastic about eye contact, otherwise I fear he'd see the machinations at work in my head as I try to plot a way off this couch. I could fall off, I think, and kill the mood with clumsiness. I jerk sideways a bit to see if rolling over is an option, but Skip is spread starfish across me. I could say I have to barf. I've been drinking all night—it's totally plausible. But as if sensing my thoughts, Skip initiates a prolonged kiss that prevents normal breathing, much less talking.

I'm really panicking now. He's going to see my scars and be so horrified he'll pour bleach in his eyes and then burn the couch we're lying on to rid himself of my very DNA. And worse, he'll fire me. My last effort, I think, is to be so bad at making out that he aborts the whole endeavor. I tug on his chest hair. He winces but continues sucking on my neck. I start to hum the *Star-Spangled Banner*. But instead of pulling back and asking me why I'm suddenly patriotic, he hums along! His hand cupped around one of my breasts and my hand gliding down the smooth skin around his spine, we hum the entire national anthem and lose no sexual momentum in the process.

I've given up trying to fight the inevitable. I am repulsive and public scorn is the only punishment befitting my crime. When Skip fires me I'll get a job as a hotel maid, laundering soiled sheets and fishing used condoms out of clogged toilets. I'll start smoking Virginia Slims and I'll go to boat shows to meet men. I'll have a cat named Booger and when I die, Booger will sit on my corpse and mew until a neighbor kicks in the door of my trailer and finds me ensconced in a recliner, my mouth ajar and crushed Cheetos plaited into my hair.

I'm okay with what I'm about to do as long as I have a plan.

I undo the top button of my jeans, ready to face the most awkward five minutes of my life, when Skip pulls away and sits up. He swallows the rest of his drink in one gulp before facing me again. "I'm sorry," he says, looking down at his hands. "I'm not comfortable doing this.

You're beautiful," and he takes my hand in his and tries to force a smile. "I'm just not…" He clears his throat and tries again. "I'm not, uh…"

I pull on my shirt, thanking God and the spaghetti monster for my reprieve, and decide to save Skip the embarrassment and finish his sentence for him. "You don't want to date a co-worker," I say, and I hold his hand and smile to show him I'm not disappointed, pretending the reason is that I too value our relative positions at the phone bank enough not to jeopardize them with one night of tawdry sex. He'll never know I'm doing internal backflips. However much I may have wanted sex, I cannot thank him enough for not letting me actually go through with it. "I think it's for the best," I say.

He sighs and gives me a genuine smile now.

Shoes in hand and trying not to grin, I follow Skip to his car. As I get in, he takes one of my boots by the heel and asks, "Are these Dolce and Gabbana?"

Rule 34

The Monday following our date, Skip calls everyone into the conference room for an all-hands. I hug the doorframe and, while he's speaking and assiduously avoiding eye contact with me, all I can think is, *Your tongue was inside my ear!*

I tune out as he lists company achievements and reminders about timesheets, and I'm about to edge my way out and back to my desk when he claps his hands together and announces the real reason he's assembled us: The office is getting rearranged. Operators will sit clustered around their Team Leaders, and the cubicles will be taken down to promote teamwork and whatever. Everyone mumbles, and I suspect the timing of this move has less to do with operational efficiency and more to do with the fact that in the current set-up, Skip can see my desk from his office.

As the meeting concludes, large men appear and start breaking down the cubicles and moving them out of the room. They come back in and arrange all the desks in pairs. Our computers and personal effects are left on the floor—untangling cords and hauling dusty monitors to their new homes is our job for the day. I scoop up my red and blue U of A mug and a novelty paperclip holder shaped like a hard-boiled egg and head across the room to see where I'll be sitting.

"We want the Operators to function more as a team, like the Navy SEALs," Skip says as we stand around waiting to be told what to do. "This new arrangement will allow you to share information and learn from one another." He accidentally catches my eye and pales. "And Nadine's going to take it from here." Skip ducks out, eyes on the floor, and almost flattens a plastic ficus.

My Team Leader, Nadine, jiggles up to the front of the room, smiles, and clasps her hands like she's about to begin a cheer. "This is going to be great, guys," she says, nodding to reassure us that moving to the other side of the room will, in fact, make our lives better. "From now on, Sunshine is invoking the buddy system. Everyone gets a desk-mate. If you have a problem, you and your buddy are going to work through it together. You'll be mentors and friends, and you'll encourage each other to get money for some great causes. I'm passing around a seating chart, so if you'll all have a look…"

There's my desk, right next to the bathroom. Well that's nice. Who's my buddy? Duncan Moore. Which one is he? Tall Guy or Pimple Guy? He's not Machete Tattoo Guy—I'm pretty sure his name is Alex. Oh shit, here comes Pimple Guy. It must be him. But Pimple Guy walks past me and starts speaking to someone else. I get a tap on the shoulder and turn around to see Tall Guy smiling down at me.

"Hi," he says. "I think you're my buddy."

"Hi," I say, pulling my head back to look up at him. He's about my age, at least a foot taller than me, with light brown hair, messy but business casual. His eyes are a watery brown, he's probably a stoner. No tan—practically a political statement in Arizona—and plenty of freckles. His most prominent characteristic, aside from being a Sasquatch, is his giant, beaklike nose. From this angle, I can see right into it.

"Are you looking up my nose?" he asks.

I blush and look down. "No. My name's Mona."

"Yeah," he says, smiling, "I know. We've met a few times before. Your first day, you were complaining about how hard it was to find the office and I told you the directions are right on the company's website. And another time you were banging your head on the desk and when I asked you what was wrong you said, 'existential crisis.' Plus, we're on the same team, and there aren't that many of us, so it's not hard to learn everyone's name."

"Jeez," I say. "Next you're going to tell me you gave me your kidney and I never even sent flowers."

"No," he says, still smiling, "I'm sure you'd send flowers."

After the IT staff plugs everything in, Duncan and I sit at our terminals, facing each other, and put on our headsets. It's strange sitting like this. It's like the worst dinner ever, but instead of speaking to each other, we're always on the phone and the food never comes.

Immediately I can see there's going to be a problem if Duncan doesn't stop tapping his pen on the desk as he speaks. "Hello, Mrs. Jones." Tap, tap, tap. "Oh, three-hundred? That's very generous." Tap, tap, tap. "Can you read the last four digits again?" Tap, tap, tap. "Ha ha, no I haven't heard the one about the twelve-inch pianist." Tap, tap, tap. After fifteen minutes of this I'd like to tap, tap, tap my skull with a crowbar.

I clear my throat as he finishes a call. "Duncan, can you please stop tapping your pen? It's distracting."

"Oh? Am I tapping my pen? I'm sorry."

It's quiet a minute while we both wait to be connected to another donor.

"Say, Mona," he says, "while we're on the subject of distractions, can you stop scratching your leg? It's shaking the desk." He smiles, and I can't tell if he's being passive aggressive or if he's teasing me. I'm not amused. I want the next six hours to go by so I can go home, sit in a bubble bath, and fantasize about firefighters.

"My leg itches. What do you want me to do? Sit here in agony?"

"You could ignore it."

"So could you."

"Hm," he says, and begins speaking to a woman about a homeless shelter in Orlando. Then out of the corner of my eye I see his hand, the tapping hand, twitching up and down as though he's tapping a pen against the desk. Ugh! This is worse than the actual tapping. He's trying to antagonize me and I can't focus with his hand waggling all over my periphery. I've got to say something.

"Duncan," I say when he gets off the phone, "what are you doing with your hand over there?"

"Oh this?" he asks, continuing his pantomime. "I'm pretending to tap my pen."

"Can you stop?" I ask. "It's awful."

"No," he says. "But thanks for asking." His cheerful tone only makes me angrier, and I get up and walk around the room for a minute, afraid I'll scream. Buddy system, buddy system. We're supposed to be buddies.

I get back in my seat and take a moment to stretch, hoping the improved blood flow will make me a nicer person for the remaining fifteen minutes before lunch. I roll my neck, align my back, hold my arms above my head and move them from left to right in a graceful arc. I straighten my legs out before me to relieve the tension in my thighs, and can feel some of the stress from the morning exiting my body and releasing into the atmosphere like dust.

"Mona," Duncan says, interrupting my bliss, "can you move your feet? You're kinda crowding me."

"My feet are where they need to be," I say, and advance them a little further, defending my territory regardless of whether I actually want it.

"I'm tall," he says, as though this gives him some right to more than his share of under-desk space.

"I'm not moving," and I dial in to my next call. I'm saving songbirds today. But as I begin speaking with an older gentleman about the threat posed to starlings by urban sprawl, I start to move backward in my rolling chair. What the hell? I look under the desk and Duncan's sneakered feet are pressed up against mine and he's pushing me away from my desk and out of my staked terrain.

Stop it, I mouth, shanking him with my eyes. But he ignores me and twirls a lock of hair around his finger and looks contentedly up at the ceiling as he waits for his next call.

I'm still moving. "Stop it," I whisper, covering the mouthpiece with my hand. He's still looking up at the ceiling, still faux-tapping his imaginary pen, and going to lengths to avoid my glare.

I'm inched back again. "Stop it," I say a little louder, and the man on the phone asks me if everything is okay. Duncan's now acting out a drum solo and bobbing his head to some imagined tune. I kick at his feet but he pushes me back again until my chair is two feet from my desk and my headset is threatening to disconnect. "Stop it," I say again through gritted teeth, but Duncan's lost in hammering out a rhythm on what looks to be a thirty-piece kit. His sneakers are now all the way under my desk, dirty red undersides taunting me like a matador's cape.

I roll my chair back to my desk, ask the man on the line to please repeat his credit card information, wad up a piece of paper and launch it, with all my strength, into Duncan's face. But somehow, I'm wide. I miss Duncan and the paper wad sails over his head and straight at Skip standing nearby, observing my meltdown. He catches it before it hits his face and gives me a pitying look.

"Oh shit," I say, too loud, and again have to assure the man on the phone that everything on my end is fine. I cover my face with my hand, stare down at my desk, and don't move until I'm clocked out for lunch.

* * *

The next day I'm in the break room finishing a coffee and trying to pick my fingernails inconspicuously when Duncan sits in the chair next to me. He's wearing a bowling shirt, for Christ's sake.

"Hey," he says, "does this smell rotten to you?"

He waves a ham sandwich near my face and I recoil.

"I'm not smelling your sandwich," I say, horrified.

"I can't tell if it's off," he says. "Please?"

"No," I say. "Go away." He's worse than my brother.

"Alright," he says, "but if I get food poisoning, I'm gonna barf in your trash can."

Is this harassment? I call harassment.

"So, tell me something about yourself," he says.

"That's a vague question," I say. "I wear a size seven shoe. Good enough?"

"What was your major?" he asks. "I assume you went to U of A, otherwise you killed the owner of that mug and carry it around as a trophy."

I give him an aggrieved look. "Finance."

"Cool. It's good to see you putting that degree to use. So, you probably love Ayn Rand, huh?"

"Never heard of her," I lie.

"I liked *The Fountainhead*. All that 'ideal man' stuff is junk, but I liked what she had to say about nonconformity. I had a show a couple of years ago about artists who stop themselves before they ever produce any work at all because they're afraid. I think self-censorship is gonna drive everyone out of the arts until all we're left with is the corporate crap they hang in hotel lobbies."

I look at Duncan, really look, and realize the new buddy system isn't some grizzly torture designed to send me screaming from the building, but an opportunity for me to better know my co-workers, people with whom I'll likely spend years. And I responded by attempting to throw a paper wad in my co-worker's face. What am I, nine? I also realize, watching Duncan squirt ketchup onto his ham sandwich, that I don't know a goddamn thing about anyone. "A show?" I ask. "You're an artist?"

"I'm a photographer," he says. "I've had a few exhibits. In fact, I've got a new one opening in a couple of weeks, if you'd like to come."

Yikes, no. I already almost screwed the boss. No need to alienate another co-worker. "Sorry, but no thanks."

"It's called 'Rule 34.' Have you heard of 'Rule 34'?"

"No."

"It's this joke on the internet that states, 'If it exists, there is porn of it.' Like Calvin and Hobbes, My Little Pony, Lego versions of Darth Vader and Harry Potter, anything. If it exists, there is porn of it. No exceptions. So, for this show I took ordinary objects and made them sexual. Toasters, lawn furniture, my sister's old Trapper Keeper—they all have a sexual identity to someone and that's what I tried to show in my photos."

"Sounds deep," I say, yawning for emphasis.

But Duncan is unruffled. "You're sarcastic," he says. "That's cool. I'm probably the first person to ever photograph a Trapper Keeper giving a blowjob."

"You just said that if it exists, there's porn of it. Then by your own rule, Trapper Keeper porn already exists."

Duncan laughs. "Well, maybe, but mine's artistic, right? This is Trapper Keeper erotica. How's that?"

"Okay," I say. "I'll consider coming to your show, but only because you said it's erotica."

* * *

I'm having the bad dream again about the texture. When it reaches my toes it's a thousand frost-hardened needles that spread like liquid up and out. I can't move because something is holding me down. I can't squirm or turn my head. I can't breathe. I can't—

My phone is ringing and I'm awake, I'm grabbing at it blind, and it's my father on the line. He's back in town, calling to say he wants to have lunch. I'm too tired to say no or stall or only say yes after telling him how selfish and cowardly I think he's been. I just say yes.

My mother's out so I don't have to lie and say I'm taking up hot yoga. And three hours later I'm sitting at a café, I've finished my cappuccino, my sandwich bread is soggy, he's thirty minutes late, and a gang of old ladies is shooting me murderous glances because the place is packed and they want my table. I take out my phone and pretend to text so I can't see their sour eyes goading me out of my chair, but as soon as I start punching keys at random, my dad slides into the chair across from me, out of breath, like he ran here.

"Hi," he says and steals a chip off my plate.

I murmur a greeting and throw my head toward the old women, making a face to say, I told you so!

"I'm sorry I'm late," he says. "I left the motel late and then there was an accident on West Ina, and…anyway. How've you been?"

I shrug and edge a dill pickle around the rim of the plate.

"How's your mom?"

"She bought a dog."

This makes him smile. "That's good. That's real good."

"Danny started a charity of undetermined purpose. He's become a real Jerry Lewis."

He nods, and when I ask him if he's going to eat, he says no, he's not hungry, and so I decide to eat my sandwich slowly so he'll have to do all the talking.

"New Zealand's really beautiful," he says. "You know they eat spaghetti on toast for breakfast?"

I say nothing and he looks down at his hands which, now that I look at them too, are far more wrinkled and age-spotted than I remember.

"I don't know how much your mother has told you about the separation."

"Some."

He chews his lip. The radio blares "Semi-Charmed Kind of Life" and I resent having to sit for this conversation in a bright room full of happy lunchers. This is a conversation for a sagging living room couch or a parked car during a rainstorm or an empty bar or nowhere at all. It's maddening—how everyone else's life keeps bouncing along the whole time you're sitting there wishing you could scream or cry or move at all. There's a big truck parked outside the window beside us and the sunlight gleaming on its chrome bumper means I can either look at my father or stare straight into the sun. I choose the sun, daring it to blind me, but have to look away after a few seconds, everything now replaced by a shifting red light.

I think my dad's been staring at me. "You asked me a while ago how I chose to work on Alzheimer's and I wasn't honest with you. I wanted to work on Parkinson's—everyone did after L-Dopa came out—but a semester into my PhD program my advisor left and all the other professors doing Parkinson's research went with him." He puts his hands up and for a second his eyes look past the restaurant ceiling, up to heaven. "So, I made lemonade. And here's the thing all these years later: It still just tastes like lemons."

He shakes his head and rolls a straw wrapper between his fingers. I'm surprised at this admission and touched he remembered our conversation. I need to say something but I have no comfort to offer, no wisdom. "You spent your whole career working on something you weren't even interested in? Aren't you resentful?"

He scrunches his mouth up and thinks a second before nodding. "But people who get into research are idealists, right? That's one thing your mother and I had in common when we first met. We genuinely believed a whole spectrum of diseases were going to be wiped out in our lifetimes. And that we'd be an instrumental part of that. And we've made gains—I don't want to diminish anything we accomplished. But I spent a lifetime expecting to finally get fulfillment at the next corner and then the next and it just…You shouldn't live like that, always holding out." He shakes his head again. "But I can't sit here and tell you not to let yourself get boxed in, either. Sometimes you put yourself in that box. Sometimes it's the right thing to do. Sometimes you don't have any other choice."

I'm watching his eyes fall on the empty cup, the soggy sandwich, anywhere but me.

"Mom told me. About why you guys got married."

His eyebrows go up a second but then his face gets solemn and he nods.

"So then what—you felt like you got rushed into marrying and now you want to get those years back?"

"It's not simple like that. I don't regret marrying your mother. Or having you kids. Not for a second. But it's also time I started living for myself. You can call that selfish. Maybe it is. But that's what I need to do right now."

Something pulls at the back of my throat. Here, at this Formica table, I need to understand what our relationship is going to be, if he's planning to move across the country or dart away to a different hemisphere anytime he feels the wall at his back.

"Are you interviewing for other jobs?" I ask. "Are you moving to Pennsylvania?"

He answers this with a hand up over his face. "Shit, Mona, I don't know. I'm worried about you, not me. Quit that telemarketing job. Start painting again. Why did you ever stop? You loved it so much."

"Oh my God, I'm not quitting my job. If Mom heard you say that she'd have a heart attack."

"Do you want money to take an art class again? I'll pay for it."

"So, you're just not going to have a job? Are you retiring? I don't understand. You can't just do nothing."

"I don't know. I might travel. I might teach a little. I'm not in a great hurry to figure it out. The one thing, though, is I'm going to take your mother out to dinner and apologize for all the hell I've put her through. And we're going to work out all the financials so she's provided for. And then she's free. She deserves someone a lot better than me, and I know once I'm out of the story she's going to find him."

Now I'm the one to avert my eyes. "I don't think that's how she sees it. She thinks you, well…" I shouldn't play her hand, say that she thinks they're going to get back together. Jesus, I shouldn't even be mediating the dissolution of my own family. Shouldn't adult children of divorce get the privilege of distance, watching the boat sink from the safety of a far shore?

"Everything's going to be fine," he says. "You just listen to what I said. Don't be living for the next thing. Either be happy with what you've got, or move on."

I think of all the times my mom has changed her hair over the last few years, her makeup, all an attempt, I'm now thinking, to make my father notice her. I think of this and his words—Or move on—seem so cold. I get up too quickly and overturn my cappuccino cup and the old women who've settled into the table next to us click disapproval.

"Hold on. I brought you this from New Zealand." My father produces a plush bird wearing a pink hoodie, the phrase, I ♥ NZ embroidered across the front. "It's a kiwi. Strange little creature. Did you know it's the only bird with nostrils? They might even be evolving to no longer use sight."

"You brought me a stuffed bird that's going blind."

"They don't need sight to survive. The extra input from their eyes is just noise."

"Well, then, I know the feeling."

* * *

My mom is at a women's leadership retreat for the weekend so the house is empty when I get back from lunch. Pepper defends the front door, nipping at my ankles and producing the most savage sounds his eight-pound body can muster. I nudge him away with my foot and he reluctantly abandons his post and takes up his favorite spot in the slant of light coming through the patio door.

I've had too much coffee today. I sit at my laptop and click through a dozen links in as many minutes, unable to focus. On the local newspaper's homepage there's an ad taking up half the screen, a gyrating bear advertising online degrees. I stare for a long time, unable to understand why a purported institution of higher learning would use such a bizarre gimmick. The bear's eyes threaten to disconnect from his head with each hip thrust and a murderous smile stretches across his face. The fifty or so degree programs advertised have been reduced to three-letter abbreviations tiled across the bear's stomach, bouncing each time he moves to a silent tune. I avoid the tile marked FIN which I can only assume denotes finance and try to guess at the others. Finally, I click his chest to see what will happen and three windows open at once. It's an online university of dubious accreditation, with a catalog offering an astounding array of majors. I keep scrolling and scrolling, there must be two hundred options, and I get very sad.

The only alcohol in the house is tequila and I tell myself it's too early for hard stuff, even by my loose standards. Out of habit I go to my desk drawer and the pencil case is in my hand before I'm aware of removing it. I lay out my materials and realize, for the first time, how similar the process is to painting. The artist chooses her brushes, mixes her paints, readies the canvas, and gets to work, her hand guided by some combination of mental calculation and divine inspiration. I pick up the razor. I'm working on delineating Mona Lisa's veil from the background—a hard line against a hazy grove of trees. But the line doesn't feel strong enough. It's the marker distinguishing subject from landscape and it has to be perfect. I push the blade a little harder into my leg and yelp: my hands are jittery from over-caffeination and the razor slips, cutting further and deeper than I had intended. To my horror, blood pools at the surface and starts to run down my leg and onto the white carpet.

My hands shaking, I unwrap packages of gauze but they're soaked through in seconds. The calm I had begun to feel while working is gone, replaced with clanging, gut-shaking, panic. There's so much blood, more blood than there should be. The cut is miles from my femoral artery, I know I'm not going to die, but I can't stop the bleeding. I can't stop it, can't stop it…Red splotches multiply on the carpet, faster than I can stem the flow. And I'm barely able to focus on the wound, envisioning the conversation I'll have with my mother when she finds the mess.

I press an old sock to the cut, elevate my leg, and take deep breaths until finally the bleeding subsides. When I can stand, I see the damage. A bloodstain the size of my foot has set in, the once-virginal plush now looking like a crime scene. I spend half an hour bent over the stain, attacking it with all the fury contained in a bottle of carpet cleaner. And one thought recurs with each forward thrust of the cleaning cloth, something I've known for a while and pushed stubbornly away like a child: I have to stop cutting. I know I have to, but where do I get the control twenty-three years too late?

When I'm done the stain is diminished but not gone. I think it could pass for wine. I'll throw some dirty laundry on top of it, pretend it's not there. I'm packing up my supplies when the phone rings, startling me so the pencil case falls to the floor and everything spills. I pick up the phone and hear wind rushing through the receiver.

"Mona," Paulette squeals, "how are you, dear?"

The cut on my thigh throbs. There are razor blades all over the floor and my wastebasket is full of blood-soaked gauze. "Never better," I say. "How are you?"

"I have good news," she says. "Job Seekers is back on! The library is going to let me use one of their conference rooms. I'm calling everyone to let them know we're meeting tomorrow."

"But I have a job. Why are you calling me?"

"Well, you're one of my success stories. I thought it would be nice if you came and spoke about your search process. I know everyone would love an update."

I took the job, kicking and screaming, because my mom knew the owner. What kind of example am I supposed to be? "I don't know. I'm not sure I'd be any help."

"Of course you will," she says, the wind picking up on her end. "We're meeting at nine tomorrow morning, main branch. And I'll bring refreshments."

I hang up, still unconvinced, and slowly put everything away, burying the bloody gauze at the bottom of the garbage can outside. I expected that a full-time job meant I would have fewer problems, maybe an answer or two to the questions always at my heels. Instead I feel more adrift now than ever, the rocks on the shore more jagged, and the ocean deeper, all-consuming, and filled with bigger, hungrier monsters.

You earned it

The library conference room is leagues nicer than the church annex and our refreshments have been upgraded as well: leftover chocolate Easter eggs in a cross-shaped candy dish. Dara's absent, and Randy, and there are new people in the group—middle-aged men and women holding their résumés like paper offerings, a familiar mix of hope and wariness on their faces. Chasen enters and is so happy to see me he demands a hug, and so I find myself enveloped in his ham-like arms, my nose filled with the piney scent of his deodorant.

Paulette opens her binder and goes through the routine, and everyone stands and tells their story. In the crowd today there's a laid-off janitor, an accountant forced out of retirement, a divorcee who needs money for school tuition.

Paulette announces me and I stand, feeling the weight of twenty sets of eyes, each person ready to receive my wisdom or at least steal buzzwords from my résumé.

"I work at a call center," I begin. "It's a pretty good job." I look to Paulette. "I don't know what I can talk about. I got the job through a family friend."

But Paulette is unfazed. "How many jobs did you apply for?"

"Five hundred seventeen."

No one says anything. Paulette lets that figure sink in.

"And how many job interviews did you have?"

"Twelve. I got close at a financial firm but it didn't pan out."

"You were tenacious," Paulette says. "You kept going, even when you had no hope."

"I guess." I look at the floor. "You don't really have a choice."

"And is working at a call center your dream job?" she asks.

"God no," I snort, then apologize when I see Paulette's disapproving look.

"And does that matter? Are you going to have this job forever?"

"No," I say. I pause and I think about my next words. "I'll work there until I can find something better."

"Thank you, Mona," Paulette says and I take my seat feeling something new, something the opposite of shame. Something, if I dare to admit it, almost like pride.

When the meeting is over Paulette asks what I think about the new digs.

"It's nice. You can't hear the toddler story time so that's an improvement."

"Are you okay?" she asks, pushing a lock of hair out of my face. "You look tired."

"I'm fine," I say, not wanting to burden her. But she gives me a long look, something concerned and expectant and altogether motherly and I decide she probably, for whatever masochistic reason, *wants* to hear what's going on. "I guess I thought, after I got a job, that I'd be happier. Like, my life would look like one of those stock photos of people in an office, where everyone's leaning in at a conference table and smiling at the guy giving a presentation, and everyone looks alive and engaged and thrilled to be in that conference room, listening to that presentation. And that's not what it's like. My deskmate is obnoxious, my boss is afraid to be in the room with me, and I spend every day counting the minutes until I can leave. Is...is that normal?"

And Paulette laughs. She laughs so long I pretend to look at my watch. She finally quiets down, wipes her eyes, and holds my shoulders. "Honey," she says, "that's every job. There's nothing wrong with you. Just count your lucky stars you don't work at a poultry plant—my father pulled gizzards out of chickens for a dollar an hour. You're going to be fine."

I must look unconvinced because she adds, "And you know what my dad did when he came home from work? After he showered and washed off as much of the chicken smell as he could? He'd go out to the shed every night and make these," and she fishes a small, wooden crucifix out of her purse. It's very light but extraordinary in its detail. The Christ figure looks regal; his eyes are closed but his jaw is square and set and solemn. His torso is draped in a garland of roses that extends across the arms and falls off the sides of the cross. Paulette's father must have used a needle to carve some of the finer details.

"It's beautiful," I say, and I mean it, handing it back.

"I have them all over the house—he must have made hundreds of them, all a little different." She looks down at the crucifix and smiles faintly before putting it back in her purse. "But the point is, your job is just what you do. It's not who you are. Do you understand?"

I nod slowly, trying to let her words sink in. "Yeah," I say. "Makes sense."

I get in the car with my new knowledge strung like beads around my neck. I realize I've missed Paulette. But I'm not sure what to do with what she said. It's just what I do; it's not who I am. So, who am I?

* * *

Taking the concept of Casual Friday too literally, Duncan shows up to work in novelty slippers shaped like beer mugs and I have to spend the entire day watching a parade of people, including Skip, come by our conjoined desk to admire them. At one point, Duncan and Nadine get so engrossed in a conversation about humorous footwear ("Bacon socks!" Duncan hoots. "How could I *not* buy them?") that I have to shush them and remind them I'm on the phone trying to raise money for cave salamanders.

At lunchtime, eager to sit in my car and soak up as much warmth as I can before returning to my frigid desk, I'm waylaid by Duncan who stretches one of his long legs out in front of me, blocking my path.

"I need food," I say. "What do you want?"

"You coming to my show tonight?" he asks.

"No," I say. Then, smirking, I add, "I have to wash my hair."

"I figured you'd back out," he says. "A finance major such as yourself couldn't possibly appreciate an homage to Diane Arbus. Art really isn't for everyone."

"I know who Diane Arbus is," I say, hand on hip. I won't stand here and have my intellect insulted by someone in beer slippers.

"Good," he says, dropping his leg and allowing me to pass. "See you at eight."

* * *

That night I'm sitting in my bedroom clicking through every link on the homepage of the *New York Times*, lining up excuses. I don't feel like driving. I'm already in my pajamas. Duncan's a buffoon. Other work people might be there. I'm a blight on society and should be locked away lest I infect others with my cynicism…the list goes on. I read one final article in the Health section about how people in their twenties have fewer friends than at any time in history, a cosmically hilarious and portentous indication I should go. What's the worst that could happen? He'd be amazing, I'd feel inadequate, and I'd come home and drink a lot of rum. Sounds like any other Friday night.

The exhibit is in an old church in a rapidly gentrifying area not far from Downtown. When I walk in, I'm stunned by how many people are there. I imagined Duncan's "show" would be ten or twelve photos hung in a wine bar in a nod to supporting local art, but this is legitimate.

It's a solo exhibit of about forty pictures, some black and white, some color. Well-dressed people are drinking and schmoozing, and a photographer is walking around harassing guests into posing with the art.

I see Duncan standing under a sign that says, "If it exists, there is porn of it." Being a head taller than everyone, he's not hard to spot. He's next to a black and white picture of two chairs engaged in what appears to be doggie-style sex. A woman holds a tape recorder up to him and he's gesturing a lot as he's speaking. What I wouldn't give to have a soapbox.

Since Duncan's busy I walk through the show and check out what kind of sick stuff has come out of his perverted brain. There are electric mixers engaged in S&M, lawn furniture in a gangbang, and an eerie, phallo-centric one of a bunch of pencils with detachable erasers. Everything's got this fuzzy, low budget, 1970s pornographic feel—if the subjects were people and not objects, the men would have thick mustaches and the women would all have feathered hair. I'm impressed. And a little grossed out. And a little turned on.

The Trapper Keeper picture is better than I'd imagined: it's a blue and green binder with dolphins silhouetted against a full moon on the cover. The Trapper is bent low over a book which is splayed open—a freshman economics textbook by Greg Mankiw—and the two are definitely engaged in a lewd act. I'm trying to see if I can read what's written on the open pages of the textbook when Duncan comes up to me smiling.

"You made it," he says. "Thanks for coming. You know, you're the only person from Sunshine who showed up. It means a lot to me."

"Yeah, no problem," I say. I'm happy for him, I guess. It's nice to be rewarded for doing something you love.

"So, what do you think?"

"They're…" I search for the right words and decide to be honest. "They're nasty. They're completely disgusting. But like, good disgusting. Interesting. I like them."

"Thanks, thanks." He seems giddy. "I started out with still-lifes. Like, telephone cords and uncooked pasta; random stuff. Anything with great shape. I spent all this time studying Edward Weston. He did these amazing photos in the thirties of peppers and radishes with sensuous lines and shadows. From the still-lifes I moved into furniture and I ended up wanting to do something on sexualizing ordinary things, turning a book or a teapot into something sexy."

"You get off on teapots?" I ask.

"I'm more of a toaster guy," he laughs and someone taps him on the shoulder. "I'm sorry," he says. "I gotta go, but please stay. Get some wine. It was good seeing you."

"Go," I say. "Enjoy your moment. You earned it."

Later at home I'm buzzing, and not from the wine. I'm worked up about something else, though it takes me a while to figure out what. I feel happy, which is strange. Happiness and Mona go together like snails and salt. I have a stirring, a friendly little undercurrent of something familiar, in my stomach. I'm staring at the wall and letting my mind drift over the evening when I figure it out, and the realization feels like cold water: I'm going to finish Mona Lisa. Tonight. Now.

I touch the tip of the blade and feel determination, a sensation so large it blocks all other inputs and becomes a mantra pulsing in my brain. I know what to do. Certainty is something I haven't felt in a long time and it is as comforting to me as the razor on my thigh.

"'Mona Lisa, Mona Lisa men have named you.'" I sing to myself as I work, the melody and my hand moving in tandem.

"'You're so like the lady with the mystic smile.'" I'm a virtuoso, a conductor in the final movement. I'm General Patton pushing North through Sicily. I'm approaching nirvana, lord of my infinite universe.

I'm so close. All that's left is her smile and it needs to be flawless. Total confidence—that's what I want. My leg hurts. I don't usually work this long. Blood is running down the sides of my thigh and collecting on an old beach towel, but I can't stop. One more cut, at the corner of her mouth...

That's it.

She's done.

I dab away the blood and look at my picture. She's beautiful. I'm stung by the irony that da Vinci and I both spent the same amount of time crafting our Mona Lisas: four years. It's a long time to meditate on one face.

I'm crying. Is it because I've finished the only piece of art I've created in as long as I can remember? Is it because now that Mona Lisa's finished, I'll have nothing to do tomorrow?

More blood is starting to collect at the surface so I open another package of gauze. It's over. She's over. The grim project is finished and I feel relief that it's done and pride over how she looks and terror because I'd always told myself that when she was finished, I would be finished, that I'd throw away the razors and that the whole experiment would one day exist only in my rear view. But what will I do if I have a bad day tomorrow, and the tomorrow after that? What if I find my hand holding the pencil case? What if I never let go?

No. Don't think about that now, I tell myself. Enjoy your moment. You earned it.

Waving and drowning

The Monday after Duncan's show I walk into work and there's a pink donut on my desk.

"Hey," says Duncan, grinning. "I got Krispy Kreme this morning. Figured you'd like one."

I thank him, trying to think of a joke I can make about Duncan's donuts, but he's already started talking about something else and I miss my opportunity.

"I had an awesome weekend," he says. "After my show on Friday my friend and I went to midnight bowling and I almost bowled a perfect game. Then my other friend had a pool party on Saturday. I ate, like, three burgers and two steaks. Man, I love meat. Then when I came home, I found a twenty-dollar bill in the parking lot at my apartment. Just sitting there like the universe was saying, 'Hey, Duncan, go buy yourself a pizza and enjoy the game on Sunday.' And then the Suns beat the Spurs in overtime! Best weekend of my life. What did you do?"

Finished something that's controlled part of me for four years. "Nothing." This guy talks a lot. We have to sign into our terminals by a certain time in the morning or else we get points off our time card.

"Nothing? From the time you left my show on Friday night to the time you sat down right now you did nothing? You existed in a vacuum removed from all time and space and hung in suspended animation for an entire weekend? I don't believe it."

"I finished something I'd been working on for a while."

"That's cryptic. What did you finish?"

"Umm." I don't know why I said that. It invited questions. I should have lied and said I went to the mall. "I was knitting a sweater."

"A sweater? In spring? In Tucson?"

"Yeah, well I'm not going to wear it now. It's for winter."

"I knit," he says. Obviously. "What's it look like?"

"It's black," I say. "With, like, sleeves."

"Does it have cables or intarsia?" he asks. "Is it shaped? Did you use straight needles or circular?"

"Yes," I say, taking a bite of my donut. "Mmhmm."

"We could knit together," he says. "I'll bring my stuff tomorrow. We can work during lunch."

"Absolutely," I say, putting on my headset so I can end the conversation. "Sure thing."

* * *

And the next day, as promised, Duncan comes into the break room at lunch swinging a tote bag full of yarn and whistling. I tell him I left my knitting supplies at home and he spends the rest of the lunch hour starting a sweater and going on about the merits of Fair Isle versus mosaic knitting, while I read a copy of *The Economist* I found in the women's restroom. I punctuate his conversation with the odd, "Mmhmm" to pretend I'm following, but really, I'm just growing anxious about the looming debt crisis in Europe. They never should have gone to the Euro.

The next day he's at it again. He's almost finished one sleeve, and now he's droning on about shaping, whatever that means. Nadine joins. She's working with some hairy yarn in neon orange, supposedly making a baby cardigan, though it looks like she's slaughtered a Muppet and is now weaving a suit from his skin. I tell Duncan I left my supplies in my foyer, and I'm *super bummed* I can't join his knitting circle. Instead I open my laptop and, tapped into Sunshine's paltry Wi-Fi, try to find an apartment I can afford out of my pitiful salary.

On Thursday it's the same thing: Duncan's needles going click, click, and his tongue going flap, flap, while Nadine wrestles with her yarn and pleads with it to stop knotting. I pity the baby receiving this gift.

But on Friday, while I'm thumbing through a gossip magazine and trying to guess which celebrity's cellulite-ridden ass is shamed on the front cover, Duncan enters the break room without his tote bag and sits beside me.

"I don't think you really knit," he says, pulling a ham sandwich from a baggie and winking at me.

"You got me," I say. "I'm more of a needlepoint gal."

"Are you obnoxious all the time? Or do you save it for work?"

"No, I actually save it for your mom."

"Have dinner with me." He's stopped smiling and is staring me down. How did we go from a *your mom* joke to this? His serious face is such a departure my gut reaction is to roll my eyes, but I don't. I have to be polite. I'm going to have to see him every day for months, if I'm unlucky, years. There's no way I'm going on a date with him. I learned my lesson. I don't need to add "Office Slut" to my résumé. But there's no reason to be mean. He's probably a good guy.

"No," I say. "I don't date co-workers. I went to your show, and that was great, but I don't want things to be weird."

"Why would things have to be weird? I'm not asking you to move in with me. It's just dinner. And I'm pretty broke, so it'll probably be Subway."

He's being so nice. Oh please, see that I'm being nice, too. This time I'm being nice. "I just can't," and as if to underscore my resolve I see Skip pass the break room.

I pack up my lunch bag and return to my desk, clocking in fifteen minutes early. When Duncan sits down, he puts on his headset and turns his chair away from me, and I spend the rest of the day talking to his back.

* * *

Chapter 6: This is where my thoughts would go.

This is where my thoughts would go if I had them right here in this blank space la la la la la but nothing is coming organized it's all a jumble of What Now and What's the Point and You Stupid Bitch and fuckfuckfuckfuckfuck...

In half an hour I've written one sentence bereft of point or punctuation and I delete that and then I delete everything else because when I look back over what I've written I feel physically ill, like I took a handful of pills and now that I realize they're in my system I'm afraid and wish I could reach down into my gut and pull them out again. I lean into the toilet, heaving and spitting, but nothing comes and I lie back on the damp bath mat and name birds in alphabetical order so that I don't do anything crazy. Albatross, blackbird, crow, dove. I get to thrush before I can sit up again.

This is when I would cut. This is when I'd have my razor and gauze and I'd have something to occupy my mind and I'd be working and moving forward and making progress and accomplishing and instead I'm spinning, drifting, treading, kicking, screaming. I know the addicts' mantra is one day at a time, or one minute at a time if it's that kind of day, but I can't spend every minute of my life when I'm not at work naming birds and fanaticizing about pieces of me to hurt. I breathe, I stretch, I jump up and down, I even shout. My mother's taken her car in for a service and I'm the only one at home except the dog who's rightfully terrified of my unpredictability and cowers under my mother's bed.

This is not sustainable. This is madness. This is torture. This is a brain and heart lacing fingers together when one ought to check and balance the other and meanwhile the fingers harden into a cage and I can see out, but little good it does because I'm here trapped, hostage, waving a white flag no one sees. Waving and drowning.

* * *

I chug a beer and watch a compilation of baby pig videos and by the time my mother is dropped off by the service shuttle I've calmed enough to be presentable. The car's going to be a while and she asks me to drive her to campus. I don't plan on staying at school but it's unseasonably comfortable outside with a fresh, strong breeze that lifts the collar of my blouse and tickles the back of my neck and causes a dry leaf to skid along the sidewalk. Besides, there are too many hours still in the day. I decide to take a walk.

It really can be a beautiful campus. We don't have buildings dating back to colonial times, or lovely banks of pines and glistening lakes. Arizona is no backdrop for quaint stories about prep school boys and their tweed-jacketed instructors. But Old Main, built during the Victorian period and still standing at the heart of campus, has a humble elegance. A dogged, perseverant charm that weathered decades out in the desert before air conditioning, before statehood, before two world wars, the invention of flight, and the breakup of the Spice Girls. Old Main is the epitome of American optimism. It takes rugged idiocy to plant a university in a place where nothing grows, there's no water for most of the year, and temperatures frequently top three digits. But somehow it worked. There are more than a million people in Tucson and, one day, when California plunges into the Pacific Ocean, we'll be the next Left Coast.

When I was a kid, sometimes my mom would bring me to campus with her and I always begged to throw pennies in the Berger fountain at the west end of Old Main. I never did it once while I was an undergrad. As I pass it now, I reach in my coin purse for a penny, but I don't have anything in there except an old Tylenol and a piece of gum. I want to do something, though, to mark the occasion of having been an adult, a college graduate, for almost a full year, even if it's mostly been a year of shit. I remember reading in a freshman orientation pamphlet about how dangling your feet in the fountain is a U of A tradition, so I perch on the edge of the water, slip off my shoes, and dip my feet.

The water's cold and I want to withdraw as soon as I'm in. But it feels important I follow through, sit with the unpleasantness, and let go. I feel foolish but there's no one else. I gradually relax, swirl my toes in the cool blue, and try to listen for birds. I take a deep breath, fill my chest with air until I can't take in any more. I let my body deflate, my shoulders slump, my spine collapse. I sit, my mind clear, listening to the hypnotic sound of the water breaking over the cement and enjoy a few heartbeats of peace.

Something stirs in a flower patch nearby and I look just as a rabbit, a cottontail, pokes its head up and sniffs the air. Then a smaller head appears, and another, and another. Babies! The bunnies are plump, bluish-grey and downy, unlike their gamey-haired mother who looks powerful and streamlined. The mother brings her front paws to the ground, stretches out her body, and then stands erect again. Her nose quivers and her ears are alert but she looks at peace. Her round eyes squint like she's smiling and I know she's enjoying the afternoon the same as me. The babies huddle as one. They blink out of unison and I wonder what they make of the strange world they've inherited. I don't breathe, not wanting them to leave. I want the moment to stretch forever, me and the rabbits, the breeze, the fountain.

The babies run to their mother and duck under her breast and, for a moment, I think I've frightened them into hiding. But I can see movement under her, tails wiggling, bodies shifting, and I realize they're nursing. My heart hurts from the cuteness and I sit awestruck at nature and love and serendipity and it's too much. I might die. If I could stay here like this, forever, I think I'd never have another problem in all my life. This is enough. Just this.

The wind picks up. The fountain hums. The babies drink.

And then as unexpectedly as they came, they scamper, acting on some unseen threat, some vibration in the ground or hostile murmur in the wind. They break out across the lawn, the mother in front and the babies close behind, disappearing behind a cluster of palms. Don't leave me, I want to shout. I watch the trees for a while, hoping they'll come out the other side or return to the fountain to sun themselves but they're gone. I have a strange, tender feeling spreading out across my chest that instead of blood, my veins are filled with warm milk and honey. Here in the fountain, in sunshine that feels, for once, nurturing not cruel, my heart feels a little warmer perhaps, or coated with bluish, downy fur.

I step out of the fountain and put on my shoes but I don't want to go home. The bookstore isn't far so I walk in that direction, not sure what I want to buy.

Being a Saturday and near the end of the year, the store is almost empty and most of the textbooks have been pulled from the shelves and sit in cardboard boxes stacked in the middle of the aisles. I remember coming here to buy art supplies when I still wore the kind of sneakers that lit up when I walked, and I go on instinct to the basement, to see if they're still there. The basement lighting is dim and I'm relieved to find I'm the only one here. As I walk through the aisles, I trace my fingers along pads of white paper, stubby tubes of oil colors, etching sets and sharpening stones, polymer clay, scraps of felt, pencils and knives and pens in every color, thickness, or purpose. I swing my arms back and forth like a child. I ignore price tags and allow each item on the shelves to speak to me with an openness to creative thought like I haven't experienced in years. A number 10 red sable brush is a woman's face as she exits an elevator, unsure which way to turn. A bottle of

Hansa yellow paint is the sun washing out the horizon early in the morning from the top of Mount Lemmon. A 12" by 16" linen canvas is an ocean, boundless, geometric form stretching infinitely. The world is blurry down here, smudgy, allowing only important lines and shapes to delineate themselves. In the low light I have to touch everything, bring it closer, slow my pace and pay attention until one crystalline thought shatters the haze and I understand: I want to paint the rabbits.

As I'm standing in front of the watercolors the painting starts to form in my head. The mother will stand straight up…no, she'll stretch out, her front paws in the foreground and her feet leading the eye back. Her head will cock toward me, her eyes squinting and her ears relaxed, as though caught unaware by the close of a camera shutter. The babies will cluster together in the left foreground beside a clump of pansies, their bodies melting and merging with the purple flowers, the watercolors making it all imprecise. I want the scene to have a tilting, precarious quality like *The Night Café in Arles* by Van Gogh, where the viewer senses the painting rushing toward her and away from her at once and her eye can't settle on anything for too long. But the picture is still vague, an old, eight-millimeter film with no sound, and I'm afraid it'll fall apart before I can fix it on paper. I grab paint and brushes and paper, pay in a rush, and almost jog back to my car.

* * *

Back in my bedroom the feeling's changed. I take the supplies out of their plastic bags and line them up on the floor. I retrieve my old easel from the garage and set it up near the window. I prepare the paints and shake out my hands, everything is ready. But staring at the empty white sheet the nausea comes back as well as a twisting in my stomach, a push and pull simul et semel like two sets of hands on either side of a door. I can't do it. I can do it. I can't.

"Just pick up the brush," I say aloud. But my hand ignores me. "Pick it up," I say again, but the conviction is gone.

I have a little bit of pot that Danny gave me, a malnourished joint left at the bottom of the purse I took to the pimps and hoes party. I light it now and sit on my bed in the hope of receiving the narcotic muse. Carpe cannabis. I try to welcome it, try to summon the openness I'd enjoyed at the bookstore. Let it come in, I tell myself. Be receptive to the experience, greet it naked and unafraid. But that's the problem with openness: Anything can come in.

The texture is back. I watch it form at the corner of my room nearest the door and bloom up and out of the carpet eating my slippers, a stack of magazines, a dirty bowl, the television remote. I want to move but I don't. I sit there and watch it consume my desk and chair, my bedside table, the wall opposite my bed where all my awards hang in neat rows like mounted heads. The closet disappears, the pile of dirty clothes, the window, the easel, and at last the edges of the bed. The texture swallows everything until I'm an island and like a little girl I draw my knees in close, close my eyes, sit perfectly still, play dead, pretend I'm not there at all.

Memory is a goddamned slippery eel. Or is it a Swiss cheese? Or is it a fog dissolving in morning sun? Or is it a garden path long overgrown and impossible to find? Or all of these? Or none? But when I try grab the eel or close the holes in the cheese or part the fog or hack beyond the vines to find the way there's nothing. Just ghosts and shadows.

I remember being eleven, and how the sun glinted on the backs of the dolphins breaching the water at Puerto Peñasco. I remember my cousins making lewd comments while Shakira strummed her guitar on the television in the living room. I remember the adults being gone, Danny perpetually in a bedroom with his Legos. Our middle cousin, Javi, pelting me with peanut shells while I tried to paint, aiming them at my hand each time my brush neared the canvas. Then hot breath, too close to my face, and my disgust at breathing in someone else's exhaled air. And the texture is on me and all around. Rough and grey it bites my knees and scratches the delicate skin on my cheeks and it's a rug, I realize with small relief—it's a rug meant to scrape sand from dusty feet. I'm on the rug and I can't get up, I can't scream. The dolphins on the canvas melt in streaks of blue and grey like colored tears. There are a lot of tears.

I feel the heat of the memory like a pan too long on the stove, but I can't see the fire. Memory is fickle, I've heard my parents say a thousand times. Even when a person is young and their memories are intact, they're always fungible, improperly recorded, easily suggested into some other narrative. If all we're given are these faulty, gullible sacks of tissue and goo with which to pilot our lives, then no wonder no one knows anything. I open my eyes and I don't try anymore. Those bones, if that's what they are, want to stay buried.

I don't remember why I was limping when I came back to Tucson. I don't remember if I brought any of my paints back with me after that trip. I don't remember if I left Mexico vowing to make a sharp turn in my life, veer out of the arts and steer blindly towards a vocation wholly antithetical to anything done for its own sake. That would be a neat story, wouldn't it? To chart the forking paths of a life, label each direction with concise narration: "This happened and then this and the reason is very easy to explain…" I could try to fill in the gaps, make justifications, lie to myself while biting into a pan de polvo that suddenly I can see my entire life with Proustian clarity. A la verga.

Fuck this texture. Fuck sitting here and not moving and not doing what I want. I pick up the paintbrush with an anger in my throat I can taste. I lay out the rough shapes of the mother and the three babies in greys and browns, just shadows waiting for light to touch them and make them real. I build up the background, layer over layer, green, yellow, white. It takes me a few tries to get the right smudge, to give it a seamless watery look as though the whole painting were floating atop a pond and one breath could dispel the image. But the years are coming back, the hours spent in this exact corner of the bedroom working and reworking to get a picture just right and the body remembers, the hand knows what to do and I can feel my chest fall and the bile edge back down my esophagus until I'm fully absorbed into the liminal space between the real world and the rendered.

In an hour I step back and look at what I've done and I'm so pleased I clap my hands and bounce a little on the balls of my feet. And I feel as I bounce what I gave up. It feels amazing.

My mother calls to say she's going to the movies with a friend and when I put the phone back onto the counter the clatter reverberates in the empty house. I hang the painting on the refrigerator and step back and put my thumbnail in my mouth, now unhappy with the curve of the smallest rabbit's ears. But I squeeze my lips and turn around and go back into my room, vowing not to let myself spoil what I could just as easily celebrate.

Back in my room I'm a struck match looking for something to light next. Television on a Saturday night is a wasteland, a graveyard of failed shows and a dumpsite for networks' toxic runoff. To keep busy, I decide to clean out my purse. I take out all the wadded-up tissues, gum wrappers, and gas receipts and throw them away. I pull all the hair out of my brush and throw that out, too. I hold the purse over the wastebasket and shake, and I spritz a bit of perfume into the lining, a little Promiscuous Pink to make everything I own smell like cotton candy.

As I'm putting things back into the bag, something catches my eye in the wastebasket. It's Duncan's phone number. He gave it to me the day of his show in case I got lost on my way to the gallery, a fair assumption given my difficulty finding Sunshine's office. Well, I don't want to throw that away. I might want to call him if I need a ride to work or if I have a question about knitting. I smile and I put it back in my purse.

I check the clock and it's still early. I could call Ashley, see if she wants to go to a movie, but she'll want to see some beastly romantic comedy and today feels so hopeful I don't want to spoil it with ninety minutes of bad writing. I open my laptop but can't find anything to read. It's a Saturday night: everyone should be out enjoying life, not sitting at their computers waiting for a plane to crash so they can read about it.

I dig Duncan's number out of my purse again and evaluate his handwriting. It's sloppy and canted, but doesn't scream serial killer. I pick up my phone but hesitate; there's no going back from this call. If this goes badly, I may have to leave my job, never show my face in the telemarketing industry again. Through my parents' connections in pharmaceuticals I may be able to find work as a human lab rat, getting injected with hair growth cream and testing untested herpes ointments. Okay, fallback plan is taking drugs for money. As long as I have a backup career. Okay, I'm making this call.

Duncan picks up after the third ring.

"So," I say, twirling my hair and trying to sound bored, "did you still want to get dinner?"

"Sure," he says. "I already ate but I'm always up for seconds."

He'll pick me up in half an hour.

When I get off the phone I'm seized with panic: I'm sober and I haven't showered. I probably can't remedy the sobriety situation— showing up for another date reeking of booze is perhaps not a good idea. I can shower quickly and shave my legs, though I won't have time to dry my hair and put on makeup. Oh God, why did I call him? Butterflies are thundering in my belly, feeling more like caged bats, but I manage to shower, shave, floss, dry my hair, apply lip gloss, and change my shoes twice by the time he's at the front door.

I predict he'll be driving a ten-year-old Honda Civic that smells of melted crayons and has an ironic hula Jesus mounted on the dash, and I'm wrong on all accounts. He picks me up in a late-model Korean car that smells like cupcakes and has a very un-ironic Strawberry Shortcake air freshener dangling from the mirror.

"Why would you *not* want your car to smell like frosting?" he asks.

He's chatty, telling me about his afternoon spent playing video games. I listen for once, holding back thoughts of whether I'm showing enough cleavage or worrying that I forgot to put on perfume. I'm trying to relax and forget I'm on a date. Duncan has a curious practice of raising his eyebrows a lot as he speaks, and each time he does it his nostrils flare and his face becomes a caricature like a stage actor exaggerating himself for the folks in the back. It's endearing, though, as if he's afraid I'll lose interest if he's not hamming it up.

He takes me to a burrito place in a strip mall. We carry our food to a small corner booth by the salsa bar amid the shrieks of children playing nearby.

Here's a problem: How am I supposed to eat a burrito in front of a date without getting red salsa caked under my nails and cilantro between my teeth? Duncan's unconcerned—he looks like a boa constrictor about to swallow a goat. He holds his burrito up and practically unhinges his jaw, fitting the whole circumference into his mouth before taking a bite. Juice streams down his chin and almost spills onto his t-shirt before he catches it with a napkin. I have a knife and fork, but I get the feeling he'd make fun of me for using them, so I lift up my own burrito and tear out a small bite.

He's finished before I've gotten a third of the way through. "I love this place," he says, and burps, though he has the forethought to hold his hand over his mouth while he does it.

"So, what did you do today?" he asks, draining his soda.

"My day was actually kind of good," I say, looking into my plate. "I was on campus over by the big fountain and I saw a bunch of baby bunnies. Then I walked over to the bookstore and, kinda on a whim, I bought some watercolors and painted them—the bunnies, I mean. I haven't painted since I was a kid, and it came out really well. I think? I guess. I'm kinda proud of myself." I pick up my burrito and take a big bite and I'm not even bothered by the cilantro I'm sure just slid between my incisors. "I think it was your show," I continue, food still in my mouth. "I think seeing your photos like, kicked off something in me that maybe wanted to get back into painting. That and the fact I have nothing else going on in my life besides work. And that's no good because I think I'm really bad at my job. Have you noticed that? Like, really bad. I don't have the personality to upsell people on their charitable contributions. Then I drive through the RV showroom every morning and get some horrible Beach Boys song stuck in my head for the next twenty-four hours. And am I crazy or is someone putting cinnamon in the break room coffee? I think I'm gonna lose it if I have to work there much longer."

Duncan slides his straw in and out of his cup and it makes a hollow, skidding sound. "Why don't you tell me how you really feel?" he says, smiling. "So, elephant in the room—"

"Yes," I look down at the crumb-strewn tabletop, "I'm 'Sad Millennial' and no, I don't want to talk about it."

"I was going to say if this goes anywhere, I think we have to tell Nadine, but sure, okay. Is that like a TV show or something?"

"It's nothing," I say, feeling a flush on my cheeks, but Duncan is unaffected. He puts down his cup and reaches across the table for my hand, and I release the straw wrapper I had been rolling between my fingers. He lines up his hand with mine, showing the size disparity between us, and laces our fingers together and squeezes.

"I'd love to see your picture," he says. "Do you want to show me?"

* * *

My mom isn't home yet so the house is dark. Pepper howls before my key's in the lock, but when I hiss at him to shut up, he trots away and I lead Duncan to my room to wait while I grab us beverages.

Duncan is the first boy ever to be in my room, Danny and my dad excepted. I mix us identical vodka cranberries in coffee mugs, and when I enter the room he's sitting on the bed. When he takes a sip, he coughs and looks wounded. "Jesus," he says, "you've got a heavy hand."

I shrug. It didn't sound like a judgement.

"You were going to show me your picture," he says, and puts the mug on the bedside table.

I hold up the painting and he takes it in. His silence is disconcerting, though I don't know what noise I'd expect him to make while looking at a painting. I take a gulp from my mug and feel my face get hot.

"I love it," he says and, for the first time tonight, he's not smiling. He's looking hard into my eyes, trying to see something I'm not sure about.

"Thank you," I say, now bashful. I look around my room, avoiding his eyes. "It's just this stupid watercolor. I mean, who paints rabbits? But I think it turned out…nice. A little better than what they hang in hotel lobbies."

"Don't say that," he says. "I think it's beautiful. What I like best is that it looks rushed, like you were trying to jot down something from a dream. The sun-dappling is impressive—you've obviously got a lot of talent. How come you didn't tell me you could paint?"

I shake my head. "I don't really do that anymore. Today was a lark or something. I used to do Model UN, too, but you don't see me walking around arguing about nuclear disarmament."

"You deflect a lot," he says. "My mom does that too when she's trying to avoid talking about her 'social drinking,'" and he uses air quotes to underscore his sarcasm. "I think you should paint. Everyday. If you bottle up something like that," and he motions to the painting, "you'll drive yourself crazy."

I give a short laugh and have another drink. "We'll see. Whatever. No biggie." Big biggie. Big, big biggie. "Um, so what's your favorite movie?"

"*Dumb and Dumber.*"

"Favorite salad dressing?"

"Ranch," he says, "but it has to be Kraft."

"What's the stupidest thing you've ever done?"

"Going to community college instead of a university."

I bite my lip and take a mental note to not disparage U of A in front of him.

"Who's the most famous person you've ever met?"

"Stan Lee," he says. "He signed a Spider-Man comic for my little cousin."

"What time do you go to bed at night?"

"It depends," he says, "on whether I've got something better to do. What's your angle?"

"I don't have an angle," I say. "I'm just trying to get to know you."

"You're getting crucial details about me from what kind of salad dressing I like?"

"Yeah, why not? I couldn't date someone who liked Thousand Island."

"Did you win all those awards?" and he gestures to my wall, my legacy in die-cast lead and enamel.

"Yeah, I did a lot of extra-curriculars. See the one with the American flag on it? I came in fourth in the national spelling bee. I got to meet the Vice-President and they let us sit in first class on the plane home. It was awesome. And that one, the plaque with the eagle? That was when my Model UN team took state." I laugh. "It's a funny story, actually—"

Duncan interrupts. "Do you miss it?"

"Model UN? Not really."

"No, winning. Do you miss winning?"

Yes! "No," I say, trying too hard to sound honest. "Sometimes. It's just that, I feel like this isn't how my life was supposed to turn out."

"This?" Duncan turns his head and motions around the room. "Living in a sweet house in the best part of town, with a full-time job, a reliable car, free air-conditioning, and a college degree? Plus, you're smart, pretty, and apparently artistically talented? This isn't how you wanted things to turn out?"

Unexpected kindness is hard to bounce back from. "But it's all relative," I argue, looking down into my drink. "This is where I started. Twenty-three years later and I'm still at my base point. If anything, it feels like I've moved backwards." I don't feel like I've drunk enough to be this honest.

He gives a short laugh. I'm worried it's condescending and I brace myself for the lecture I'm about to get for being callous and blind to other peoples' problems and how he had to put himself through community college working two jobs. My life could be exponentially worse, I know it. But I'm just being honest. I hope he doesn't think I don't have problems. My leg still hurts if I cross it wrong. Things are not all peaches. If he thinks I don't have problems he can get back in his cupcake-smelling car and piss off. But I hope he doesn't.

Then he says, "You're right. I shouldn't tell you that you don't have problems. I'm sorry." Holy. Crap. His hair falls over his forehead and makes me want to reach out and brush it away, tuck it behind his ear. "I'm not going to assume anything about you," he says. "I promise you that." Then he leans back against the headboard, takes off his sneakers and makes himself comfortable, like he's going to stay a while. "So, would you rather know *when* you're going to die or *how*?"

But I'm only half listening to his question. Oh, Christ. I think Mona's in love.

Breaking cycles

Chapter 7: Fun with fractals.

I've been to enough late-night weed sessions in dorm rooms that I've gotten into a number of drug-enhanced discussions of fractals, what they are, what they can illuminate. I've heard a lot of locuras about them, the worst of which being that they're some kind of blueprint from God, like a magical binary code imbedded in us. But if we take the magical part out and see fractals for what they are—an efficient way of continuous, self-organizing expansion—then we can appreciate the dazzling symmetry of a Romanesco broccoli, the jagged selfsame coastline of Norway, or a price fluctuation of a particular stock tracing a similar arc whether the time period is a year, a month, or an hour. Take apart a Jackson Pollock painting and there are fractals in the drips and drabs, order in the chaos, a rhythm infinitely repeating so that close up or far out, you're not sure if you're looking at paint splatters, tree branches, or clusters of neural networks.

So, fractals can prevail in finance and art and nature and geography, but what about in human relationships? Can the connection between two people fall into a pattern such that small parts mimic the whole? For instance, when my mother comes back from dinner with my father, furious and crying because he sold his E-Class and handed her a check, when all she wanted was for him to say he was coming back home. "He makes me feel like an obligation," she sobs. "Like I'm a bill he has to pay every month." And I remember his words about how putting himself in a box was the right thing to do at the time, and suddenly the whole pattern is clear: one person offers love and the other offers duty, and duty can look a lot like love but it isn't, and love can become duty when it isn't reciprocated, and both sentiments hollow a person over the years and they fill with resentment and the only thing that feeds resentment is revenge. This is what I see when she calls him three hours and three chardonnays later and tells him her whole life was a mistake, that she wishes they'd never met, that she knows he'll die alone because he's incapable of love.

And then I wonder if this fractal relationship can be inherited. Am I an independent shape or a subordinate arm of a larger pattern, doomed to reproduce infinitely the mistakes baked into my design? Do the small moments of my life foretell a larger arc? Can we ever gain enough perspective to see?

Duncan was not exaggerating when he told me his neighbors were colorful. When I pull into his apartment complex, I'm almost sideswiped by a fourteen-year-old pushing a baby stroller, smoking a cigarette, and shouting angry Slavic into a cell phone. When I slam on my brakes she spits on my car and shouts something that sounds like an ancient Balkan curse before resuming her conversation.

I was told to look for the building with the couch out front and it's hard to miss: a red velvet loveseat sits on the sidewalk, attended by a crew of five close-cropped young men in track suits. As I turn off my engine, I can hear Eastern European rap wafting out of an open door, angry words over heavy bass and a harpsichord. Before I get out of my car, I start to lock my sunglasses in the glove box. I'll be damned if any Serbian gangster's getting his hands on my Wayfarers. Damnit, Mona, be nice.

I've been invited for dinner. Duncan said he would be making spaghetti and needed someone to microwave the sauce. He answers the door in bare feet and I still have to crane my neck to greet him.

His apartment is small and poorly lit, sparse and shabby. But I like it. Like all guys his age, Duncan appears to have invested all his money in an entertainment system: wall-mounted flat screen, surround sound, three game consoles that I can see, and a mountain of DVDs and video games hiding a tangle of cords. It's not nearly as nice as Skip's house, though what it lacks in high end furnishings, it makes up for in art: dozens of photos line the walls, some framed, some tacked up with pins. Looking at them, I can watch the evolution of a boy with a camera into a man with a gift for capturing the best of people, of things, distilling his subjects into their essence until they are platonic forms like love, virtue, and knowledge. I stop at one, an older woman with a face half submerged in shadow, wearing purple eyeliner and looking brightly out at the camera, and something about her face reminds me of Duncan, an inner joy and comfort in her own skin. I wish I had the same look.

"Is that your mom?"

"Yeah," he says, looking down at the bottle of wine I'd brought for us to share. "That was right after her first trip to rehab. I wanted to have a picture to remind her what she looks like when she's sober." He looks at the bottle a second longer before untwisting the cap. He pours a taste for himself and a little more for me. "I guess, here's to breaking cycles."

We toast and I head to the kitchen to assist. I'm making the sauce, which consists of opening a can of mushrooms into a plastic bowl, covering them with a jar of Ragu, and microwaving for a minute thirty. We dine on paper plates as Beck plays in the background and the apartment occasionally shudders from what I'm informed is his upstairs neighbors trying out wrestling moves in their dining room.

After dinner we retire to the couch and flip channels, laughing at the earnestness of the announcers as they promise better network coverage, more miles per gallon, lower cholesterol, fewer calories, whiter teeth. We settle on a rerun of *The Sopranos*: it's the episode where Paulie and Christopher get lost in the woods and almost freeze to death. By the time they're fighting over who eats the last Tic Tac, Duncan and I are making out.

Kissing Duncan is strange at first. Our tongues are fighting for supremacy, each of us confident in our make-out style and unwilling to compromise technique. He favors a probing, thrusting motion where I prefer a lapping, swirling combo. We settle for alternating—lap, thrust, swirl, probe—and eventually fall into a rhythm until I'm no longer paying attention to method or movement and I'm just enjoying being in his arms, smelling the laundry detergent in his t-shirt, and riding the giddy high of maybe having a new boyfriend. A boyfriend! I think I have a boyfriend! I can call him up on a Wednesday and ask him out for sushi and it's not weird. I can buy him a pair of Valentine boxers with cupids on them and that's alright. At Christmas we can take obnoxious pictures of ourselves in festive hats and make greeting cards out of them that we'll send to our mutual friends, other couples, because we'll be a couple.

I'm getting ahead of myself. After an hour on the couch Duncan wants to take the party back to his room and my joy deflates. I follow him to the bed, telling myself that I can say no. Say I'm on my period. Say I want to wait a while. Say I want to leave my jeans on. Say I'm not ready to do…that. But it's a lie. I am ready, and I tell myself I can find a way around Mona Lisa, distract his eyes and his hands tonight and every night until after we're married and it's too late for him to turn back.

He pulls me toward the bed but I draw back. He tries again and I resist, my brain churning with excuses, anything to keep our momentum while concealing my secret.

"Before we go any further," I begin, clearing my throat, "I want you to know something."

He's sitting on the bed about to take off his shirt. What does he think I'm going to say? Herpes? Foot fetish? Third nipple? A third nipple would be heaven right now.

"I have some…scars on my leg." I motion quickly and rush to finish before I can say something stupid. "They're no big deal. But you might feel them and I don't want you to freak out." I look at the floor, ready to turn around and leave. I'm not answering any questions. Too much already. And he's not going to see them. Ever. I'll walk around in basketball shorts for the rest of my life if I have to.

"Oh, thank God," he says, exhaling. "I thought you were going to say you have herpes."

"Oh yeah," I say. "Well, that too. It's only contagious when I have open sores…" He kisses me mid-joke and brings me onto the bed. I maneuver under the covers and stay there and his hands never wander down to my thighs, respectful even during sex. In bed the awkwardness of our first kiss is gone. Any stubbornness I had melts, egos are bare, and we rise and fall to the rhythm of our racing heartbeats, quiet exhalations, and the metallic creaking of the mattress springs. When it's over I retrieve the wine from the living room, swigging from the bottle in Duncan's arms while we listen to his upstairs neighbors screaming at their television.

* * *

Having a boyfriend is as wonderful as I'd imagined. I feel like I'm watching my life go through one of those eighties' movie montages where the happy couple tries on wacky hats, catches a fly ball at a baseball game, and zips around a track in go-karts while some ghastly John Mellencamp song plays over the action. My younger, meaner self would have scoffed at so much Hollywood drivel, but the last few weeks with Duncan have been blissful, romantic, and rage-free, a state of being that feels perpetually effervescent, floating up and doing cartwheels in the air like

Charlie in the Wonka factory. We even went to one of Nadine's coven meetings at the pagan bookstore and I barely rolled my eyes when they debated the spell casting abilities of beeswax versus soy candles.

I haven't watched the news in weeks. Who cares if the Euro goes belly up and celebrities are dying in swarms? I'm in love and I want to focus on nothing else.

I painted a portrait of Duncan. His brown eyes are stairs ascending deep into his brain and his face is a clock, the mechanisms open and churning, moving his lips and flaring his nostrils as he smiles and welcomes you close. He called it Dali-esque and hung it in his living room, and I have this silly fantasy of us becoming one of those famous art couples like Frida and Diego or Georgia O'Keeffe and Alfred Stieglitz.

I can feel things changing, like finally putting on glasses and seeing the world clearly. I wake up and I want to get out of bed, want to use my new eyes and walk the red dirt with new feet. I want to paint, I want to draw, I want to kiss Duncan until my lips go numb and then crawl into his arms and fall asleep listening to the steady drum of his heart. I want to smile; I want to sashay. I find myself blushing alone in my room remembering a word or a glance or a line of freckles drawn down his back. I think I might scream if I get any happier. All this bliss seems unnatural or unhealthy and yet I'd gladly overdose on it, feel it expand my pupils and constrict my veins and flood my brain with dopamine until all I see are a thousand diamond sparkles.

One night I go over to Duncan's apartment and, after kissing me hello, he steps back like he's appraising my face. I'm about to ask him what he's doing when he reaches down to the coffee table and picks up a camera and points it right at me.

I had dreaded this day. I don't like getting my picture taken. I'm always pulling some face, some mangled expression of disgust, surprise, and psychotic laughter, like something from a nineteenth-century medical study of lunacy and the grotesque. And here I am dating a photographer.

I bat away the lens but he brings it up again and, out of a spirit of cooperation inspired by puppy love, I smile, staring down the barrel and fearing what he sees on the other side.

"Don't smile," he says. "This isn't your eighth-grade school portrait. Look sultry."

I laugh, spitting a little as I try to compose myself and channel my inner Marilyn.

"That's good," he says. "Now look serious. Academic. You're Madeleine Albright addressing the UN and things look bad for Kosovo."

I bring my fist up under my chin in mock seriousness. Click.

"Okay," he says, "now you're an ER nurse and you've just worked a double shift and your bus is late and you've got to walk seventeen blocks home."

I let my mouth droop, my cheeks fall, and I drop my head to the side, telegraphing weariness from every cell.

"Good," he says. "Now you're Mona, but you're eighteen and you just found out you didn't get into Harvard."

My face twitches. It's involuntary, only lasts a second. I make an exaggerated frowny face to play along but in the back of my brain I know that twitch was a physical response to an imagined slap.

I say I don't want to play anymore and we sit on the couch with macaroni and cheese and watch two hours of sitcoms. When an infomercial for acne cream begins, Duncan turns off the TV and wants to go back to his room.

I follow him but I'm still smarting from the Harvard comment and his obliviousness to the steely exterior I erected for the last two hours to punish him. I want him to apologize without me having to make it into a *thing*, but he's going to force me to spell out his mistake. It's beyond obnoxious.

"What's wrong?" he asks.

"Nothing."

"Are you angry because I took your photo? You're beautiful. I want to take a million photos of you."

"No," I say, "I don't care if you want to take my picture. I mean, I do care. I'd rather you didn't. But I don't like you making fun of me while you're doing it. It feels…predatory."

"Predatory? Jesus, is that what you think? I'm sorry. I didn't mean to make fun of you. But don't say I'm a predator. That's not cool." He pauses and I think he's finished speaking but after a moment he continues. "I've gotta say something." Uh-oh. "You're very closed off. Not just tonight, but always. Maybe I said that to try to get to you a little bit because it feels like there's this wall around you. I want to see all sides of you, but you don't give me any access. We've been going out for a while and I feel like I barely know you. It's like trying to hug someone who won't uncross their arms. I know superficial things—you like bagels, you hate basketball—but I don't know anything about *you*. What differentiates *you* from the millions of other girls who eat bread and hate sports? Our first date you told me about painting and how much you dislike working at Sunshine and all this stuff, but since then I feel like I can't get a complete answer out of you. You just give me sarcasm or vague half-answers and it's making me crazy. I've asked you to tell me about your parents. Not what they do—I know how they make money—but who are they? Do you get along with them? Were they good parents? How does it make you feel that they're splitting up? You won't tell me anything." I'm already crying when he says, "I can't keep seeing you if you're going to be like this. I need more. I'm sorry if you can't do it, and I'm not going to force you, but this is the way I have to have it. I can't be with you if you won't let me get to know you."

I want to leave. Get off the bed, storm out, erase his number from my phone, quit my job, move away and pretend this relationship never happened. But something's holding me here. A fragment of me, the tiniest shard of my psyche that's responsible for rational thoughts, apologies, regrets, grown-up plans, kind words, and doing what's right is pinning me here, forcing me to deal with this. Now. Not never, not tomorrow, not later tonight when I've had a chance to drink a pint of rum and fire out a series of angry, incoherent texts, but now. You're an adult, the tiny voice demands. Answer him.

I'm wearing jeans and a t-shirt so taking off my clothes, kneeling on his bed, is awkward. I pull my shirt up over my head and unhook my bra, laying it beside me. I sniff loudly, girding myself for what will come next, and I unbutton my jeans, pull down the zipper, slide them off, and let them drop to the floor. I can't hear them hit the carpet and I can't hear the upstairs neighbors bouncing a tennis ball against their floor. I can only hear my own kettledrum heartbeat. My vision blurs and tears spill down my chin and onto my breasts. I unfold my legs from underneath me and lie, stretched across Duncan's bed, Mona Lisa in full view, darkened every few seconds by the shadow of an oscillating fan.

Duncan's quiet. My eyes are squeezed shut so I won't have to see his face, repulsed, mortified, eager to get me out of his room and out of his life. I lie there so long I get drowsy. My mind wanders out into tangents and mini-dreams about floating away in a hot air balloon and getting lost in a Moroccan souk. I jerk awake because something's tickling me. Something's touching my thigh. I look down and Duncan is kissing me, kissing Mona Lisa, tracing my scars with the tips of his fingers and lowering his head again to brush his lips across her face. He sees me watching him and he brings his face to mine and we kiss, and in that instant my mind is blank, my heart has stopped, I lie very still, and I'm conscious only of Duncan's hands as they comb through my hair and run down my body. For the first time in my life, I am beautiful.

Cultural anthropology

A couple weeks later Duncan is trying to convince me to let him photograph my scars.

"If I had done that," he says, "I'd wear short shorts every day. You know people pay thousands for body art like that."

I'm looking at a bleach stain on his living room floor. If I keep my eyes down, I think, I won't have to answer.

"I mean," he begins, looking embarrassed, "I know you weren't doing it because you were in a good place." He stares at the bleach stain too and continues from there. "But I think you did something incredible. Maybe it doesn't seem like that to you, now, but she's beautiful. If you let me take your picture, I think it could," he pauses, searching, "unburden you."

He's still not sure how to address my situation. Is it a creative outlet or the physical manifestation of years of unchecked mental illness? Now that she's healed and the swelling has disappeared and the scars have turned more or less uniformly white, she looks a little more human, a little less like Frankenstein's monster. After a lot of pacing around my room and convincing myself I'm probably no longer in the running for Secretary-General of the UN, I finally agree to let him photograph her. If only for posterity. One day I may get her lasered off; when I'm old maybe I'll want to remember what she once was.

Duncan sets me up on his bed. He's draped a white sheet across his duvet and hung another on the wall to give the pictures a solid, clean background. I feel like I'm about to do something sordid so I drink some wine. He keeps telling me to unclench. First, I'm clenching my fist, then my teeth, then my fist again. Duncan threatens to make me smoke a cigarette if I can't relax and sit still, so I focus on naming world capitals in alphabetical order and I ignore the clicking of the camera and the lens getting closer and closer to my leg.

Abu Dhabi, Bogotá, Canberra, Djibouti. His camera is almost on top of me now. My skin warms under the heat from the tungsten lights. Duncan's upper lip is sweating and I fully understand the phrase, 'feeling like a piece of meat.'

Freetown, Gibraltar, Helsinki, Islamabad. He moves my arms up then down, drapes one across my stomach, and with each click of the shutter he demands another adjustment: too much arm, not enough ankle, tilt your head, close your mouth, look up here, now over there, point that foot, crook your elbow. I'm exhausted. He keeps turning the lens, looking through the finder, frowning, and then pressing buttons and starting the process again. After an hour I'm bored and my arm is falling asleep.

"Are we almost done?"

He takes his time, but finally smiles and puts down his camera.

"That was great," he says, and pours two glasses of cheap champagne. We toast our first joint artistic venture and, after a quickie on the couch, he drops me off at my house. I go to sleep that night debating whether I'll keep my name when we get married or hyphenate. The alliterative, Mona Mireles-Moore, is delicious on my tongue.

* * *

At work the next day I check my e-mail before lunch and there's one from my mother reminding me about Danny's graduation this weekend. My father is planning to attend, one last family hurrah before we splinter into our separate orbits. Spending a morning with my parents sounds odious but I suppose I'm duty bound.

"Do you want to meet my parents?" I ask Duncan when he finishes a call.

"Both your parents?"

"It's going to be weird," I say, "but it'll suck less if you're with me."

He nods his head and puts a thumb up, making the back of my neck tingle. I stretch my hands up in the air and sigh. I have a plus one!

I'm about to go to the break room when Duncan rolls his chair next to mine and opens a laptop. Before I can say, "No, not now, let's do this tonight," I'm looking at a picture of Mona Lisa in full, gory color. Every skin cell on display in high definition, every cut reproduced livid and pure on the screen. It's like watching a time lapse of the last four years of my life, and all the happy things are edited out. I can follow her lines and remember everything. Her right index finger—that was the time Ashley slept with the cute guy from Derivatives who told me I looked like Maggie Gyllenhaal. And the draping above her left shoulder—that was when I recommended the Finance Club buy a bunch of New Zealand dollars just before they lost half their value. My every failure and misery looking at me through a screen. I look at my boyfriend. He couldn't be happier.

"Amazing, right?" Duncan asks. "Here, look at this one." He pulls up another photo, this time it's my whole body. My face is close to the camera and my body stretches back so you can't make out much below my knees and I appear partially melted. I have a scared, searching look on my face, like a patient with some rare combination of symptoms who just wants to be told they have a disease, any disease, if only to put a name to their torment. I try to put on the same look now, hoping Duncan will allow me to escape to the break room, but he's looking at the Mona on the screen, the Mona he bottled up and can take out and look at whenever he wants.

He's saying something and scrolling through the images, there must be hundreds, and I'm watching my face flicker across the screen. It's me and Mona Lisa, then me, then her, until I'm not sure who's on whose leg and who made who and both of us are getting nauseous.

"I've already spoken to someone at the Goodman Gallery and they were super interested," Duncan says. "This could be big." Now Duncan's looking at me. He wants me to say yes, go ahead, use me to get famous, recognized, accepted. And I do want those things, for him and me. I want to scream his praises from the top of Mount Lemmon, bang the drum for him until he's bigger than Richard Avedon, bigger than Ansel Adams, but if I have to look at another picture of myself, I will scratch my eyes out. These were for later, for healing or distance or closure or something I'd hoped I'd feel when I saw them. Not for an audience with Duncan's name neatly printed on a brass plaque beneath them.

"I'm freezing," I mumble. "I'm gonna go sit in my car."

"Okay," and he closes the laptop quickly. Finally, I think, worried. "Do you want company?"

"No," I say, forcing a smile I hope looks genuine. "No, you stay."

* * *

I'm quiet that night. We're sharing a frozen pizza on his couch and Duncan's watching basketball. The Suns are in the playoffs and he's paying so little attention to his food he keeps missing his mouth.

"So, I wanted to talk about the photos," I say after enduring sports for twenty minutes. "I don't want them in a gallery. It's too much. You wouldn't hang a bunch of suicide notes up and call them art, or install videos of people's most embarrassing moments. I just…I can't do it. I hope you understand."

He's got to promise me he won't show them to anyone. One day when I'm old and I've had kids and a career and my youthful indiscretions are four decades behind me, maybe then I can look at the photos without suffocating. But not now.

"Fuck!" he screams and I realize I've been upstaged by Steve Nash getting a personal foul. For a moment I wish I had a demure, bookish boyfriend who wouldn't know the free throw line if he tripped over it. "Sorry," he says, muting the television and facing me as soon as the commercials come on, "I couldn't hear you. What did you say?"

"I said I don't want you to show those photos to anyone. They're embarrassing. Just promise me."

"Embarrassing? They're amazing. They're cultural anthropology. You shouldn't be ashamed of what you did. I'm not." Weird how sometimes coercion sounds like empowerment.

"You're not the one being asked to air their most intimate secrets in public. I don't want to be seen. And I don't need a bunch of mouth breathers looking at my leg and judging me."

"Mouth breathers." He nods his head. "If it makes you feel better, we could administer IQ tests to anyone trying to get into the show."

"I'm serious." Heat rushes to my cheeks and up my ears. I see Duncan glance at the muted game and I wish I had a rock to throw at his precious Suns, but I plow forward anyway. "You're asking too much. I let you see it, I let you take pictures, but that's where it stops. That's where I need it to stop."

Duncan sighs and looks up at the ceiling and I want to shake him. I feel tired of him trying to make me into a better person.

"You're right," he speaks to the ceiling, "that I'm asking too much. And I apologize. But I still think you should do it."

I fling my hands down on the couch and make a guttural sound. He's not listening to me.

"Hold on," he says, and now I roll my eyes up at the ceiling, refusing to look at him as he speaks. "You've got to separate Mona Lisa from her origin. You went through a lot. I'm not belittling it, please believe that. But what came out of it is incredible. I spent hours looking through photos online—there is *nothing* out there like this. And showing a picture of what you did isn't the same as showing a picture of what you went through to create it. That's still yours. That's private. And you can choose to reveal that or not. That's where your power is. That's always yours."

I don't respond.

"And moreover," he continues, "I don't think you're going to move past this without reckoning with it. In AA they talk about how you're powerless over your disease, how you need to surrender yourself to a higher power, or whatever you want to call it. I think you're still being controlled by your cutting and I think the way to get out from under it is to stop giving it this power over your life. Yes, it's terrifying. Yes, people will judge you. But ultimately, you're confronting the monster and pulling off its mask."

What if what's under the mask is uglier?

"This isn't 'Sad Millennial' all over again. This would be on your terms. But art has to be witnessed to be finished," he concludes. "That's when you know it means something."

I'm done with this discussion. I keep my arms folded and my eyes averted until he looks away and picks up the remote. "If you're not going to speak, I'm putting the game back on."

I get up and get a beer from the fridge and I feel a side-eyed look from him as I untwist the cap and throw it skittering onto the coffee table. We watch the rest of the game in silence, punctuated by an occasional "Fuck!" or "Yes, yes, yes!" from Duncan. In ninety minutes, the Suns lose and Duncan sulks, so I say goodnight and go home, neither of us feeling like keeping company anymore.

It's after ten o'clock and there are lights on when I come in. My mother is at the kitchen table surrounded by plastic file boxes and all I can see is the top of her head bent low over papers. I ask her what she's doing and she jolts awake. When she raises her head, a paper is stuck to her cheek. She pulls it off, yawns without covering her mouth, throws her head back, and groans. I see a box of cookies on the table and, from this angle, it looks empty.

She puts her head back on the table and I get a good look at her, wondering when her roots turned grey, when did her hands begin to wither? I look around the house and everything is strange. There are dirty pans on the stove and a small avalanche of unopened mail spills over the counter. There's a stack of clean towels on the couch, a pair of socks on the floor by the patio door, and I can hear the toilet running in the bathroom. Small things, housekeeping errata most mothers would overlook, but distress signals from my mom. Have I been with Duncan that much? Does she need me here more? How didn't I notice before? Shouldn't she have said something? Asked for help? For me? Should I have known?

She sits up again. "What time is it?" She yawns before I answer and moves on, "How was your day?"

"Fine," I say, bringing her a glass of water. "I watched a basketball game at Duncan's."

"And when do I get to meet the young man?"

"Well, it looks like he's coming to Danny's graduation, so I hope things aren't weird."

My mom sighs. "Me too."

"We actually got in an argument tonight," I say. "He, uh, took my picture and wants to show it to a gallery. But I don't want people looking at my picture so I told him not to do it. I don't know what he's going to do."

"Well, he's got to respect your wishes. If he cares about you, he's not going to do anything you don't want. But," she takes a proffered napkin and wipes cookie crumbs off her face, "it's a great honor to be the subject of a work of art. I assume these are tasteful photos." I roll my eyes so she continues. "You know your father and I named you after Mona Lisa."

"I thought you named me after Grandma Lisa."

"That was a happy coincidence, but no. And we didn't name you after the painting, either, but the woman. She's captivated people for five hundred years. I think, in a silly way when we were young and newly pregnant, we hoped you'd do the same. You meant so much to us," and I can see her eyelids quiver, "I think we thought that one little girl could bring meaning to the rest of the world, too."

"Yes," I answer, "that was very silly."

She nods. "We'll see."

Chapter 8: A before B.

Paul Gauguin was a successful stockbroker. He only decided to pursue painting full-time when the Paris Bourse crashed in 1882. Jeff Koons was a commodities broker for much of the 1980s. They're certainly more exception than rule but they are also precedent. Maybe there isn't one path to be followed and there aren't necessarily sunk costs being honored. Instead I could choose to see the last year as a necessary first step, A before B, to gain the insight and wisdom to have anything interesting to say in the first place. I don't know about bringing meaning to the world for Christ's sake but I can put one foot in front of the other. I can start there.

Being pushed

The morning of Danny's graduation I wake up to a text message from Duncan:

"Still want me to come today?"

We haven't spoken since the Suns game.
Still angry, I respond,

"It's your life."

Then I spend fifteen minutes debating how to write him back and remind him to wear a tie.

I lie in bed as long as I can, prolonging the start of what will be a long and draining day. Danny's graduation ceremony is this morning, followed by the charity check presentation at his frat house where Duncan will meet my parents. Then I have a few hours to go home and pack before driving to Scottsdale for Ashley's sister's engagement party. I can imagine, under different circumstances, being excited by the promise of drinking champagne twice in one day, but spending the morning pretending my parents aren't engaged in bitter separation, and introducing them to my boyfriend, with whom I'm also not on the best terms, has put a pall over the festivities. Then to repeat the whole performance again in the evening, serving as a buffer between Ashley and her family, has me wondering if I could pretend to have strep and call the whole day off.

No dice. My phone buzzes again and it's my brother reminding me we're supposed to "be cool" to one another. A minute later my mother knocks on the door to make sure I'm awake.

"I'm going!" I shout. "Keep your damn pants on!"

An hour later we're sitting through a ceremony, and to kill time during the protracted speeches, I obsess over what Danny's going to do with the money. Now that I'm a tangential part of the non-profit world, I consider myself an expert in charitable giving, and I'm a little hurt Danny hasn't told me what he's got planned. I'm so worried he's going to give it to some nefarious cause like buying silicone butt implants for underprivileged models in Brazil it's all I can do to keep from jumping out of my seat, running across campus, and storming the frat house demanding answers.

I'd also like to escape the singular hell of sitting between my parents as they battle each other with coughs, eye rolls, and prolonged looks at their respective phones. I think you've achieved full maturity when you can identify and condemn your parents' childishness. I'm going to see Duncan in an hour and I'm trying to remain positive, imagining a morning where my parents are well behaved, Duncan and I make up, and everyone enjoys a mimosa in the sunshine. Then my father blows his nose into a handkerchief and my mother mutters, "Good grief," and I spend the rest of the ceremony counting backwards from ten thousand.

After every student in the College of Social and Behavioral Sciences has had their opportunity to walk the stage and shake hands with Dean Alvarez, we leave. The sound of students and their families taking photos and shouting congratulations across the lawn is heaven after a solid hour of the marching band droning a tepid *Pomp and Circumstance.*

When we get to the Chi house it's hung in red and blue, crepe paper and balloons strung from every rafter. Inside there are a lot of people in suits, people like my mom, and she glad hands them all as soon as we're through the door. Trapped in this temple to Bacchanalian excess and playful chauvinism my father looks uncomfortable around so much unbridled testosterone, and he folds himself against the wood-paneled walls and waits to be escorted to his seat.

I spy Duncan in the back, charmingly out of place in rumpled khakis and skater shoes, like an overgrown high schooler waiting for his homecoming date. I want to leap into his arms, forget our fight, and prove I can make a relationship work where my parents failed. We don't have to mimic a bad pattern. We can be happy, I know it.

He smiles shyly when he sees me and I feel myself smile back.

"I've never been inside a frat house." He points behind a nearby couch where a sagging blow-up doll lies face up, her eyes heavenward and mouth agape in permanent bewilderment. "It's exactly like the brochures."

"Well, you came," I say. "I guess you're not mad?"

"I was never mad," he counters. "You didn't do anything to make me mad. I'm frustrated, perplexed, maybe pleading, but I'm not mad."

This quarrel is diffusing faster than I could have hoped. All he has to do is accept culpability and we can skip on to the next chapter. "So, you admit you were wrong."

His forehead wrinkles. "I was wrong to ask you to do something that I think will help you?"

"Yes."

He pauses a moment and then bends down and says, in a whisper I've never heard from him, "Sometimes love means being pushed."

I shake my head, as though the motion will knock into place the words I've heard, *love* and *pushed* fighting for primacy in my mind, but instead they spin, reckless, out between Duncan and me, and I can't catch them and soon they're gone. Despite the cold thrust of an air conditioning vent angled above my head, my armpits are damp inside my dress. Someone drops a champagne flute and I'm shuffled aside as a circle opens up around the debris. I look at Duncan—we're separated now by broken glass and a small pool of pink rosé—and I imagine how much he might want to leave. This was a terrible idea.

My brother finds us at this moment. He strides up, mortarboard playfully askew, and punches me on the arm.

"Where's your dude?" Danny asks and I point to Duncan, the champagne cleaned, now able to cross the living room.

"He's tall," Danny says, ever the keen observer.

Duncan comes over and introduces himself and he and Danny spend a moment chatting about the Suns. I'm searching the crowd for my mother. I'd not only like to get these family introductions over quickly, but I'm also confident Duncan and I won't continue our conversation while my family is around, maybe shunting the awkwardness until tomorrow or next week or never.

I see my father sitting on a folding chair speaking to a young woman with red hair. I wave but he doesn't see. They're deep in conversation. I figure her for a secretary or some administrator's daughter—she can't be more than a few years older than me. I'm about to call out to him when he sneezes and bends down to blow his nose, and as he does, the young woman pats his back. It's not a tap or a stroke, but a wide circular motion that she repeats for several revolutions, and as I watch those unlined hands work across my father's back I hear myself say, "Oh," and I cover my mouth.

I look back at Danny. Did he see? No, Danny and Duncan are forecasting the Suns' chances at a playoff victory. My brother uses the word, discipline, several times.

I look back to where my father was sitting, but now he's gone. I'm on my tiptoes, peering over and through the crowd, when I hear my mother behind me.

"What a pleasure to meet you," she says to Duncan and I'm dizzy, the people and the sounds all foreign and unreal, actors in a movie I want to turn off. I grab a glass of passing champagne and gulp it, the two tablespoons of alcohol doing little to rescue me.

My mother leans close and whispers, "He seems very nice. He's tall, huh?"

I don't say anything. Does she know? Does she know *who*? It's unlikely there are things happening on campus outside my mother's awareness, and yet I feel I must be protective, shield her from any public revelation that will bruise her heart and career.

I've turned to look for my father over my shoulder so many times I get dizzy. Duncan asks what's wrong but I brush him aside, too distracted and upset to talk. It feels like the ground shakes, like something's about to erupt.

One of the brothers approaches to escort us to our seats and Danny excuses himself. Duncan, my mother, and I are seated in front of the grand fireplace which boasted, until a few hours ago, a garland made of panties. Someone steps on my toe and I look up to see my father trying to move past me into the next seat. He leans across me to shake Duncan's hand asking, "Are you the boyfriend?" Duncan answers in the affirmative and my father whispers to me, "Kinda tall, isn't he?"

I hear someone hiss my name and turn to wave at Ashley, lovely in pink bouclé, sitting in the back of the room with Samberg's parents. I wish Samberg could go to Scottsdale tonight and serve as Ashley's human shield, but he's got family in from overseas and was forbidden from missing any graduation festivities.

Someone taps a microphone and I turn back around. My brother appears up front with Dean Alvarez, a representative from the national Chi fraternity board, a good-looking man wearing a flag pin who I assume is a politician, and a smattering of other grey-haired men in suits. The Vivaldi playing in the background is silenced, Danny removes his graduation cap and clears his throat, and the room settles.

"Ladies and gentlemen, Dean Alvarez, Dr. Lessig, Senator Fraily, Mom and Dad: I'd like to thank you all for coming," he begins. I wince—he and the senator have the same hair.

"As you know, due to some unfortunate outliers in the Greek community, the university requested that fraternities and sororities complete a community service project this year. Now, there were those who felt this requirement was unfair, given that it punished many for the actions of a few…" I look at Dean Alvarez; his face is turning red. "But," Danny continues, "my brothers and I saw this as an opportunity to make our mark on the university. To change the world. To use our network of brothers, friends, alums, and supporters to raise money for a worthwhile cause. And we did it. As of this morning the Daniel Mireles Fund has raised almost a hundred thousand dollars. Give yourselves a round of applause, folks. That's amazing." Danny grins and the audience roars. The brothers cheer and whistle and one starts a short-lived round of, "USA! USA!"

"Now, I know what you're all wondering," he says, and I grip my seat, prepared to hear the most wasteful, self-aggrandizing project ever conceived for a hundred grand. He named a classroom after himself. No, he named a chaired professorship after himself. Oh God, what if he named a chaired professorship after one of his heroes? The Ronald Reagan Endowed Chair in Race and Poverty Studies would just about be the worst thing he could say right now.

"Ms. Smithers? Can you come up here, please?" I turn around and freeze. Paulette is stepping through the crowd, her orange hair contrasted against a dowdy blue pantsuit. She gives me a wave as she walks past and smooths down the creases in her pants when she joins my brother up front.

"For those of you who don't know, my sister, Mona, has had a little trouble landing a job after graduation. But Paulette Smithers has been there all along helping her with networking and building up her confidence and teaching her not to give up."

I slump lower in my seat, feeling like one of those pitiable two-legged dogs they sometimes feature on the evening news, scooting along best they can on skateboards.

"I was inspired by Paulette's mission of helping put Arizonans back to work one at a time. How many people have you helped place into jobs?"

"Oh, I don't know," Paulette says, bumping the microphone with her mouth as she leans in to speak. "A couple hundred or so."

More applause. "Did you hear that?" Danny asks. "Paulette is a true hero, and someone who represents the character and values we uphold here at Chi Chi Theta: integrity, citizenship, honor, and pride."

I let out an audible groan, a little one, but loud enough that Duncan pokes me gently in the ribs.

"You recently lost your meeting space, is that correct?"

Paulette nods.

"And your work in Job Seekers is mostly voluntary, right? You don't get paid by any of the people you're helping?"

"Oh no, I do it because I love it. Losing your job is one of the most stressful things a person can go through. It's good for people to know they're not alone."

"Well, we want you to know you're not alone either." He signals to two brothers standing nearby and they pull a giant novelty check out from behind a chair. "I, Daniel Mireles, chairman and trustee of the Daniel Mireles Fund, am honored to present to you, Paulette Smithers, this check for the all new Job Seekers Community Resource Center. From the brothers of Chi House and the Grand Chapter of Chi Chi Theta, please accept this donation and get the people of Arizona back to work!"

People are on their feet cheering. My mother is crying. Paulette's face has gone translucent like skim milk and one of the brothers has a hand on her back because she looks like she's going to fall over.

I'm not sure how to feel as I make my way to the front of the room. I'm so happy for Paulette I'm sure I'm almost as pale as she is. I wasn't exactly ready to find out my brother is a goddamned super hero. My dad grabs Danny and me and holds us close in an uncomfortable, needy hug, my brother and I smooshed so close together I have to turn my head so our lips won't touch. Finally, we're released and my parents continue their effusions.

"The most beautiful thing anyone's ever done," says my dad.

"How did we get so lucky?" my mom asks.

"Is that cake?" Duncan escapes to a buffet and I turn after him, mentally pleading for him to return with more champagne.

Paulette's face has regained its color and then some: she's now red and wet from tears and she hooks her arms around Danny and clings like she'll drown if she lets go.

"—an angel. An angel from heaven," she's saying when I tap her on the shoulder.

"You had no idea?" I ask. "What did Danny tell you?"

"He just said his fraternity was giving me a service award. I thought it was a little strange but he was adamant I come so I said, Sure. Why not?"

"Well, what are you going to do?"

"My head's spinning. I can get a workspace, computers, some staff to do workshops and training. But this is going to make such a difference. *Such* a difference, I can't even begin to thank him. And you." She holds my shoulders and I can feel my body warm under the sunlight of her smile. "God put our paths to cross for a reason," she says. "And I'm so thankful He did." I wouldn't have said it in so many words but I agree. I am so thankful, too.

When I turn back to my family, my brother is shaking hands with the senator and my mother looks star struck.

"Mona," she says, "I want you to meet State Senator Fraily. Senator, this is my daughter, Mona. Senator Fraily," and my mom's tone indicates I should stop slouching and looking wistfully at a passing tray of cake, "has just offered your brother a staff position in his upcoming campaign for Congress. Isn't that wonderful?"

Seriously?

"Seriously?" I ask, though I manage to evoke surprise rather than disdain. "Congratulations, Danny. That's awesome." What's a word that means happy, jealous, floored, and proud all at once?

Duncan returns and I have to repeat the story for him, my voice snagging on the word 'Congress.' "Danny's getting his dream job," I say, and Duncan puts his arm around me.

"Thanks," Danny says, grinning and running his hand through his thick, Republican hair. And I see him, I really see him, from before, when we were kids in the backseat of the Acura, fighting over the last Goldfish at the bottom of the bag our mom tossed back to keep us quiet; and a year ago, sharing weed in his bedroom on the third floor of the frat house, bouncing a tennis ball on the wall until one of the brothers stormed in and threatened to burn us both alive; today, a day he'll probably remember as one of the best of his life. And now the future, striding marble halls and regaling the Georgetown elites with stories of boyhood indiscretions off in the desert. I see all this and I realize with the impact of a meteor: *He's* the golden child. Maybe always was. Not me. I may have gotten the brains, but he got the real genetic bounty. For the first time in my life I have the feeling the most successful Mireles kid may not be me, and it doesn't feel bad. It doesn't feel bad.

He and my parents pose for a photo with the senator and their faces betray nothing, just another happy family. People start to drift out. Ashley squeezes my arm before she leaves and I promise to see her this evening. The senator has moved on to other potential donors and I'm starting to think I've made it through the worst part of the day, that my family isn't barreling towards some hideous confrontation, and that I can escape the charade in one piece.

I'm about to say my goodbyes when Danny starts speaking to our parents again. "So, we're all here together. Pretty nice, right?"

My mom and dad make eye contact for the first time all morning, their eyes holding the same mix of embarrassment and remorse. I catch

Danny's eye and shake my head slightly, just enough to warn him he's about to be crushed.

"What I'm trying to say is, nothing has to change," Danny says. "You don't have to move out," he says to our father, "and you can bring Dad back to the lab," he says to our mother. "That was a bump in the road. Everything can go back the way it was. Things don't have to change."

"Danny," my dad says softly, and he looks like the words are causing him physical pain, "your mother and I are not going to work things out. I'm sorry. We'll always be a family for you and your sister but we can't be married anymore. I'm so sorry."

"I don't understand why you can't, at least, *try*."

My mother is chewing on her bottom lip and turning pink and she grabs Danny by the shoulder and leans into his face, and he looks sick, like he's guessed what she's going to say. "He cheated. End of story."

"I said it was a mistake, for Christ's sake," my father whispers. "And I didn't know she was going to be here." He looks at my mother. "I swear it."

Then, as if on cue, the usurper approaches, somehow sensing that the moment couldn't get any more unbearable and wishing to ferry us all into the tenth level of hell. My father shakes his head as she approaches but she either doesn't see or doesn't care. He introduces her to Danny, Duncan, and me as his acquaintance, Charlotte. I look at my mother and realize what a superb actress she is—her chin remains high and her expression is impassive, haughty almost, some deep reservoir of self-preservation holding her features firm against what must be oceans of despair and rage.

Charlotte works for Dean Alvarez and was asked at the last minute to accompany him. She looks calm, chewing gum with her arms crossed like she was waiting in line at the airport, though I suppose I can't expect her to get on her knees and grovel before us.

"Charlotte, it's so lovely to see you again," my mother says, ice in her voice. "And don't worry about the plumbing bill." She leans to

Danny, Duncan, and me to catch us up. "After the donor appreciation dinner I had to pay someone to fish her cell phone out of our guest bathroom toilet. Six glasses of Pinot don't agree with most people." She turns back to Charlotte, no longer chewing her gum and looking ill. "You were very entertaining, though. Your impression of Dean Alvarez's limp was something no one is going to forget. Ever. Too bad he missed it."

Charlotte drops her eyes and steps away without a word, and my father goes after her probably to apologize.

"Wait," I say, "she was at that dinner party you threw a few months ago?"

My mother nods.

"Dad knew her already?"

She nods again.

"And he let her come anyway?"

"Your father was so nervous he ladled gravy all over Dean Alvarez, so he left. Then that girl got drunk and threw up in our guest bathroom. Everyone else left, and when your father was putting her in a taxi she…" my mother pauses and clears her throat, "she made their relationship known. Between that and sneaking off to secret job interviews I just exploded."

I hear her words but none of this makes sense. My father's unhappy, but sleeping with another woman? It's so out of character. It's so—I close my eyes and try to remember that night and when I picture my father his eyes are small and slightly yellowed and full of hurt. And all at once the pieces come together and I see it: the times I've caught him staring out the window at nothing and how he startled when I touched his shoulder, unaware I was even in the room; the forgotten meetings, the late appearances, the drastic upheavals in his personal and professional life; how he seemed for the last year to be floating higher and further, until he was almost invisible, no more than a pinprick in the vast, blue sky.

My mother pulls in a big breath. "Obviously, he didn't want you kids to know about that young woman. I still don't understand it. You know, I play the night back in my head and at times I swear it seemed like he didn't even know her."

And then if he knew something was wrong, if he knew he only had a few more good years…

My father comes back and before anyone else can say anything he puts his hand up and speaks and his voice is almost frantic. "I'm leaving," he says. "I'm going to travel—Vietnam first, Cambodia. I have enough saved that I can live for a couple of years, at least. After that, if I'm still around, who knows?"

"You're leaving?" Danny asks.

"What do you mean, 'If you're still around'?" My mother's features are drawn and her eyes search his face.

"Nothing. I didn't even want to tell you I was going. I'm sorry. I'm so, so sorry for this whole…mess. But I need to go. It's something I've thought about for a long time and, as hard as it's going to be, I'm telling you that I need this. I have to go."

"What does that mean," Danny asks, "that you *have* to go?"

"You still haven't answered me," my mother demands. "What the hell do you mean, 'If you're still around'?"

Of course he can read the signs far better than me. Spending his life researching and recording exactly what happens when the adult brain slides down from decay into total revolt, allows the paths to overgrow, the fog to descend—my father better than anyone knows what might happen next, how the clock may hold but few lucid hours. And instead of submitting, he's running.

I cover my face with my hand, massage a pain above my right eye. I don't know what to do. Should I say something? Leave? Duncan is using his height to his advantage—his hands are on my shoulders but he's looking over everyone's heads and through a window, leaving us to our private turmoil below. I look up at my father again and he's exactly the same, nothing changed, still the same absent-minded professor, and so I doubt myself, tell myself I don't know anything. Except I do. And I know he wouldn't want me to say anything.

"Have your fun then," my mother concludes. "The rest of us are going to stay here in the real world." How could she not see as well? Or maybe she's too close.

For the longest minute of my life my parents, my brother, and I stand in the frat house, in a room full of happy graduates and their families toasting with beer and champagne, two dozen young men ready to set sail for bright horizons, and the thing uniting my family is our collective desire to not cry in public.

My father says he's going to go, that he doesn't want to spoil any more of Danny's big day. He shakes Duncan's hand, hugs Danny, and when he hugs me, he whispers, "I'm sorry," barely above a breath, into my ear. I hold him hard for a second and then let him go and as I watch his back disappear into the crowd I believe, in that second, that somehow it's all over, that I will never see him again.

"Shit," my mother says when he's gone, and runs both fingertips under her eyes. "I need to go. I'm speaking at the medical school in half an hour."

She leaves and Danny and I look at each other and then down at the floor. And finally, Danny claps his hands together and says, "Hey, he's gotta do him, right?" And I can see he's already rearranging the elements of the story, telling himself that my father isn't a sad and frightened man trying to recover a lost life, but a swashbuckler setting his course for the Far East, seeking individual fulfillment like a Mexican Übermensch. I open and close my mouth once, twice. Now that my father's gone, I don't know what I saw. I don't know anything. I just know I want to cut.

Danny hugs me goodbye and leaves to adjudicate a flip-cup related dispute. This leaves Duncan and me alone in the living room to process the seismic movements of the last few minutes. He puts his arms around me and it feels good, it really does, but the need to cut, once embedded, will not be ignored. I pull away. There's a half bottle of champagne on a table nearby and I pour a healthy amount into a Solo cup and start drinking, each gulp helping a little to beat back the thunder in my chest, stomach, and brain.

"What's going on?" Duncan asks. I only shake my head and take another drink. "Come on," Duncan pushes, "you can talk to me. You don't have to hold everything inside."

"Everything's fine," I hear myself say, even as my inner monologue shrieks like a feral crone, Liar! Liar! "Like Danny said, he's gotta do him, right?"

The look of concern on Duncan's face, instead of melting my defenses, makes me feel like a taunted bull. And the irony doesn't escape me that my father and I are apparently genetically predisposed to be unable to ask for help.

I can see Duncan's getting frustrated, which, in its own perverse way, feels like a victory. "It's barely noon," he says, indicating the cup. "Are you going to be alright to drive?"

"Excuse me?"

"I don't want to have an argument right now. I'm just saying take it easy. I know what I'm talking about."

"Are you seriously saying I have a drinking problem? *That's* what you think I should hear right now? Are you fucking stupid, or just cruel?"

"Don't do this."

"Too late. You wanted a fight? Now you've got a fight. You're an asshole."

He covers his face with his hands and pulls them down slowly. "Forget I said anything," he says. "Anyway, you're not really yelling at me right now. You're yelling at your dad."

"Oh, gee, thank you, Dr. Freud," I mock. "What would I ever do without your stunning insights?"

I drop the undrunk champagne on the table and run out the door and down the steps. The sun is everywhere in the cloudless sky. The heat wraps around me, sneaks in between my toes, burns the tops of my ears. I can hear Duncan coming after me but I don't turn around until we're on the street. "This isn't working," I say. "I thought that meeting my parents would be a bad idea and it was. I'm sorry for taking up your time."

"That's it?" Duncan asks, his voice finally betraying anger or hurt or both. "You're done? Fine." He crosses a grassy median to his car and turns around. "You're a coward!" he shouts and then gets in his car and slams the door with a crash that sends three turkey vultures high into the blue sky.

The right choice

Back at my house I'm livid, neither the champagne nor the drive home doing anything to calm me. The dog growls when I come through the door and I shout at it so that its tail tucks under its body and it retreats to lie in front of the refrigerator and attend its wounded feelings. I go in my room and hurl things indiscriminately, shoes, papers, graphing calculator, and the throws are accompanied by grunts like a tennis player launching a serve.

After I've exhausted my throwing arm I collapse on the bed, overcome with sudden itchiness. My scalp itches, then my neck, and from there the itch travels down my belly to the sides of my thighs and the backs of my calves. I scratch like I have mange, disgusted by the amount of dead skin cells I'm dusting over the duvet, but unable to stop. The itch doesn't come from anywhere specific but leapfrogs over parts of my body, touching down long enough to set my skin afire and then landing somewhere else so that I writhe like I have demons. I break the skin but the blood on my forearms and down my shins does nothing to stop the itch. I scratch and scratch and scratch until I'm out of breath. Then, as quickly as it came on, the itching subsides, and I know.

I take the razor and gauze and isopropyl alcohol out of my desk drawer. I clean the blade and lean over my leg and it's automatic, a ballerina getting into first position. My breathing slows with anticipation. In a few seconds I'll be calm, in control, I'll be myself again.

But I wait.

I can't cut Mona Lisa. She's done. I've got to think of something else.

I could do a pendant, a companion piece to La Gioconda on my opposite thigh. A portrait of Leonardo himself, creator and creation preserved together in a macabre tribute to the High Renaissance? I could do another Mona Lisa, this time casting myself as the subject, though that feels unforgivably narcissistic.

I sit with the knife hovering above my skin, my virgin thigh calling out to be punctured, penetrated, brought to life with the tip of my sharp knife and the artistry contained in my hands, but I'm blocked. I have no muse, no lightning strike, no image so compelling I must carve it out before it eats me alive.

I feel sick, actually. I don't like looking at the two legs together, one scarred, one pure. I feel shame, intense, backbreaking shame. Not the shame of cutting. All cutters know that feeling—the invisible hand tugging at your clothes to make sure they cover you, or the third eye that scans the room, watching for someone who knows, someone who suspects, someone whose eyes linger a little too long down there. I've been wasted. Mona Lisa isn't something to celebrate. She isn't an achievement. She's a ragged and ghoulish reminder that I'm deeply, fundamentally, and now, for the world to see, scarred. All those plaques and medals on my wall are bullshit. Accolades, lines on a résumé and cheap pieces of plastic. But Mona Lisa is real. She's the only trophy I get to keep, the one triumph I've got to carry through the rest of my life. And after I die, the morticians embalming my body will remove my clothes and see her, still smiling, still cryptic, and they'll know my awful secret. The one thing I've done, the one thing I've seen through from start to finish, my one accomplishment in my adult life, is looking me right in the eyes, mocking me, and I'll never be able to look away.

I want all these feelings to go. I want to have never carved myself. I want to be a different person with a different past and a different future, somehow wriggle out of my old skin like a snake to reveal a fresher, unsullied exterior. I want so many impossibilities that conquering cutting seems like another pointless wish, and yet my hand holds steady above my thigh. And I remember something: I haven't cut since I painted the rabbits.

Slowly, unfamiliarly, I pull back my hand and put the razor in the case, pack up the gauze, the alcohol, zip it up, and shove it into the oblivion of my desk drawer. I've lived on the other side—happiness, purpose, pride in myself—and for the first time I have too much trust in tomorrow to throw it away on a bad afternoon.

I pull the dog away from the refrigerator and hold him on my lap and stroke his head and apologize for shouting. After a bit of trembling and a few attempts at escape, he finally sniffs my hand and licks my palm and then rests his head on my knee and falls asleep with his tongue halfway out his mouth. We sit like that for a long time, Pepper and me, listening to the gentle hum of the dishwasher, and I think how beautiful must a dog's soul be, that they can so readily and sincerely forgive.

* * *

The drive to Scottsdale is two hours barreling through a parched landscape of saguaros and rocks broken only by the occasional rest stop. In downtown Scottsdale I'm waylaid by a traffic circle enclosing a fountain set with charging horses. Luxury SUVs zoom past me and I miss my exit once, twice, three times before I get an opening. Then I have to cross a river twice before I find my bearings and get on the right road.

There's something vulgar about the green, sloping hills of the golf course against the craggy, bone-dry foothills. It reminds me of a deer head I once saw in an antique shop where the antlers had been painted bright pink and the whole head dusted in glitter. I leave my car at the valet stand and walk through the grand colonnade to the lobby, where I'm informed by a pert young woman in a sun visor that the party is in the Maricopa Room. I go back outside, walk past three fountains, hang a left, and find the party by following a trail of yellow rose petals scattered on the travertine.

I'm early—two violinists are tuning their instruments when I enter and the repeated, dissonant notes climbing ever slightly higher are a good soundtrack for round two of a stressful day. I don't see Ashley so I go to the bar, an imposing wood and copper affair presided over by a ten-foot-high fresco of a galloping steed. The bartender fixes me a vodka tonic and finishes it by throwing two lime wedges in the air and landing them simultaneously in the glass. Something about him reminds me of Duncan and my face falls, remembering that Duncan and I had planned a special dinner out for our two-month anniversary.

"Mona!" Ashley squeals and I turn around, my eyes widening as I take in her outfit. The eighties must be back. Her sequined dress is shaped like a giant blazer, shoulder pads and all, the bottom hem hanging about a centimeter below her backside.

"Wow," I say. "You know you can't bend over in that, right?"

"Oh my God," she gushes, "my sister spilled red wine on her dress and it was like the fucking apocalypse. She literally cried for thirty minutes. My mom had to go to Nieman Marcus and they had the same dress but it was a size too small, so she's in the bathroom right now putting on two girdles and taping down her boobs. If she has a cherry tomato, I think she'll pop the seams." Ashley and I snicker until we see Crystal emerge from the bathroom with ruffled hair and a look on her face like she just witnessed a limb amputation. She looks left and right and then puts her head in the bathroom to call forth her other daughter. Ashley's sister appears, red in the face and stuffed, sausage-like, into a white ruffled and sequined dress that makes her look like a cockatoo moonlighting as a stripper.

I go through the requisite pleasantries with Ashley's mother and sister—you look beautiful, stunning location, no, it's not *too* hot— and afterwards find myself marooned conveniently near a mountain of shrimp while Ashley greets other guests.

I'm working on my fourth serving of brie en croute when I hear a man say my name. I turn around and see eyes the color of shadows, a short, salt and pepper beard, and fine lines about a kind face. He smiles. I know him from somewhere but his name is escaping me.

"Raymond," he says, holding out his hand. I shake but must look confused. "Ashley's father," he adds and I apologize for not recognizing him. While he and Crystal may be intertwined like a caduceus, he's always maintained distance from his daughters, dropping checks and gold jewelry like leaflets from a plane and retreating again to his office. Ashley once told me when she was a child, she thought Wavecrest and Hawthorne Ridge were children he had somewhere in another part of town, and it wasn't until she was older that she realized they were housing tracts he was building.

"Are you having fun?" he asks.

"Yeah." I clutch my drink to my chest and twist the straw between my fingers. "This country club is nice," and I try to flatten my voice, inflect as though I've seen dozens of private clubs and this one only ranks somewhere in the middle.

"My wife and daughters enjoy this…pageantry," he says, breaking his gaze on me to look out on the crowd. "I've never had the nose for it." Pageantry does seem the right word. I'm the only female, other than the catering staff, not in sequins. Most of the women look like they need a decent meal, and there's a palpable distrust fogging up the room. I can see it in the forced smiles, the canned laughter, the way everyone acts as though they're on camera all the time. I'm suddenly shocked that when Ashley made her escape, she didn't run further.

"It's not so bad," I try to mediate. "There's an open bar." Then, realizing the foolishness of my comment, I look down into my glass and wish I could hide in between the ice cubes.

"You're in finance, aren't you?" he asks, putting an olive in his mouth and letting the pit fall into a napkin.

"Not right at the moment. I'm working at a call center, but I don't like it."

"No," he agrees, "I'd imagine not."

"I started painting again, actually," I say, testing how it feels to tell someone. "Like Ashley. I stopped for a long time but picked it back up." I think of the painting I made of Duncan's face and wonder if he's already taken it off his living room wall. "I don't expect anything to come of it—monetarily—but it's nice to have something to think about, something a little more meaningful than this," and before I can stop myself, I hold out my hand to the room, denigrating the party before the host. My face reddens. "I'm sorry," I say.

Mercifully, he laughs. "Don't be sorry. That's the only honest thing anyone's said to me in weeks."

"I don't know why I just told you all that. I don't even think Ashley knows I paint."

"Painting," he says, "is like arranging the past and the present and the future into something you can see all at once. That's an important skill—you shouldn't be ashamed."

I'm blushing, deeply. Crystal taps a fork against her wine glass and the room quiets for a speech from Ashley's sister. I expect Raymond to excuse himself and join his family but instead he leans in closer to me.

"Ashley told me you were looking for a job in finance. Do you know anything about hedge funds?" he whispers while his eldest daughter rhapsodizes about her marriage proposal in Cancún.

"Lots," I whisper back. "I ran the investment portfolio for the finance club at U of A. We averaged twenty percent annually for the two years I was in charge."

"Not bad." He raises an eyebrow. "How would you like a job?"

I'm breathless. I can't hear the speeches, can't hear the scrape of forks against fine china. I only hear my heart and I feel, somewhere in my ribs, the sensation of a knot untying. "A job?" I whisper. "Doing what?"

"I'm starting a hedge fund. The Recession hit us hard but I think we've seen the bottom and I want to spread my risk for next time. I need an analyst," he muses, stroking his beard. "I'd start you small, see what you can do. But if you can bring in numbers like you had in school, you'd shoot right up."

He sees my frozen expression and adds, holding up his hands, "There's no pressure. But Ashley gave me your résumé recently and said you were the hardest worker she knows. I only take the best. And the job is yours if you want it."

"I'd have to move," I say, more to myself than him. "The hours would be long. The pay is…"

"Ample," he finishes for me. "For those who've earned it."

Ample. The word swells like a round red apple and is just as sweet. Ashley never said anything, maybe not wanting to get my hopes up. I want to hug her, shower her with thanks. After a year of kicking, the door is finally open wide. Why am I hesitant now to walk through? "I don't know what to say. Thank you. I'll need to think about it."

"You're clever," he leans away, breaking the privacy of the moment. "I know you'll make the right choice."

The speeches have ended. Ashley teeters over to us and Raymond hugs her and tells her how much he enjoyed her tribute to her sister. The lie comes so easily it takes me a moment to register it as a falsehood. Then I find myself telling her the same lie and adding that I adore her dress. Raymond excuses himself and, without him standing beside me, our conversation feels like a dream.

The appetizers have been replaced with main courses. A suffocating scent of rosemary wafts from a tray of chicken breasts and people now surround me, jostling me left and right to reach the food. My palms are sweaty and running them down the lace front of my dress does nothing to dry them. I tell Ashley I'm going to the bathroom but instead I escape to the courtyard, blinking up at the stars on a moonless night.

What the hell just happened? I pace in circles, my heels making a light, percussive sound against the tiled patio. I've been offered my dream job. Why do I want to run away?

Of course, I have to take the job. I'd be an idiot not to. I'd get to leave Tucson. I'd have my own apartment. And money. I'd have money! And prestige. I'd be able to brag about my job to strangers I met at parties: "Oh, you're a software engineer? That's cute. I work at a *hedge fund*." I'd be able to cast off my minimum wage shackles raising pennies for second-rate charities and devote a hundred hours a week to a cause, if not worthier, at least more profitable: lining my bosses' pockets with filthy, filthy lucre and waiting for bonus checks to rain down like confetti until one day I'd be the boss and could dispatch my minions to scour the earth for an ever lower beta coefficient.

And the spreadsheets. I'd make so many spreadsheets. My brain would perform data regressions in my sleep, sleep which would occur on a cot in my office because I wouldn't really have time to go home and make it back for the opening bell. And painting would have to be put on hold. I have a sentimental moment imagining packing up my paints and easel again, piling them back into the cobwebbed corner of the garage to be found again only in the event of my mother's death. Spreadsheets could be like painting. What did Raymond say? A picture that captures the past, the present, and the future in one glance? Spreadsheets could do that. Painting was only ever a hobby anyway, a silly diversion from my boring, low-paying job. Other than painting and sleep and free time and social activities, what would I be giving up? Duncan? He's gone anyway, probably having already replaced me with a large pizza and a DVD of the Suns' greatest playoff highlights. I have nothing to lose, everything to gain. Si nil habes, nil amittere potes.

And yet something holds me to the patio, preventing me from running inside, shaking Raymond's hand with all the vigor of a drowning woman clutching a life preserver, and grabbing the gold-plated keys to my new life. It's the memory of the second time I cut myself. The first time was so spontaneous as to be almost accidental, a hole kicked in the drywall in a moment of blind rage. But the second time I cut it was planned, premeditated, and performed with the intention of creating something. I wanted, with that second cut, to make a living embodiment of my anger that would exorcise me of all my hurt and leave me, to the world at least, normal. These best laid schemes were nothing more than that, but I feel I've turned a page, battled that monster and can limp away victorious. And it's this thought that holds me there, worrying that if I take the job, by my silver anniversary I'll have to wear a tent to the office to hide all the scars.

On the patio, I can still see my father's eyes from this morning, someone so desperate to escape he'll run stumbling to the other side of the earth just to eke out a little happiness before it's all over. I see my mother who believes so fully in the fictions of her life that she can no longer see what's right in front of her. I see Duck Ford and his belief that the world is good when everyone acts in their own self-interest, and it seems to me that greed proliferates in a world where people live without friction, whether they're careless or carefree. I never believed anyone would truly want to live their life over again because it all seemed so meaningless, that most of a life is the boredom between disasters. But it feels now like I'm being given the opportunity to live my life over again, and I choose yes. Enthusiastically: yes.

The enormity of my task pushes down on me until it's hard to walk. I sniffle, taking tentative steps back to the party. The skin on my thigh prickles underneath my dress, a tactile reminder of the life I don't want. I splash cold water on my face in the bathroom. In the mirror I'm resolute—I just hope I can keep the same composure when I close this door.

Raymond is leaning against the bar. Behind him, the bartender attempts to roll a bottle of rum behind his head and misses the catch, shattering glass amid the gasps and squeals of his female audience. Raymond smiles when he sees me, the light of an overhead chandelier warming his expression in a way that makes me think I can't tell him no. I let my hand drop to my thigh and, through the thin fabric, I can feel the outline of Mona Lisa's face, her mouth always smiling up at me.

"I think the bartender might have overestimated his showmanship," he chuckles.

"I can't do it." I force the words out before they retreat and bury themselves where I can't find them. "I appreciate the offer so much—I can't tell you what it means that you want to give me this opportunity—but I just can't. I'm so sorry."

His face goes solemn and he nods. There is sadness, actual sadness, in his eyes at this news and I bite the inside of my cheek to keep from retracting everything I just said. "You should take some more time. Think harder about what you're doing," he offers. "You should never close the door on an opportunity."

Oh god, don't make this harder. "I can't do it."

He shakes his head and, seeing Crystal on the other side of the room arguing with a caterer and gesticulating with an empty martini glass, wishes me a good night.

I take a seat at the bar and put my head down, the copper rail cool against my forehead. The words 'You're an idiot' form a wall of sound that blocks out all inputs so that I don't hear Ashley saying my name until likely the fourth or fifth repetition.

"Where have you been?" she asks. "My mom is wasted. She's throwing a fit because she thinks the caterers brought the wrong cake."

I look over. Raymond's pulled Crystal behind a plant and she looks so wounded and righteous, it's hard not to feel sorry for her.

"And the worst thing is," Ashley says, "no one other than my dad is even embarrassed. Everyone here is as drunk as she is." She leans against the bar with her head in her hands. "I hate Scottsdale."

Raymond and Crystal approach the bar. Crystal is swaying slightly with her eyes half closed, and an unmitigated sneer pulling up one corner of her painted mouth. Raymond looks tired, sighing before he speaks, presumably to show how exasperating his family is. "I'm getting the car," he says to Ashley. "Watch your mother." And he stalks away, a gust of wind outside the door stirring yellow rose petals under his feet.

Crystal's somehow found another drink. It's pink and fizzy and the carbonation leaves a slight sheen on her upper lip. "That color," she points an unsteady finger at Ashley, sizing up her dress, "is doing you no favors."

Ashley throws her eyes up to the wood beam ceiling. "You said so, Mom. Thank you for the constructive criticism." The last words come clenched together and I realize that Ashley should probably be studied in a lab so scientists can uncover how a person can turn out so relatively normal despite being raised by an asshole. I also decide that, since Ashley won't tell her mother where to stick her nasty comments, I will.

"Shut up, Crystal."

She regards me boozily, her acid tongue at last slowed by liquor.

"Ashley's an amazing person—a way better person than you could ever be—so shut your ugly mouth." Ashley's hands are covering her face so I can't gauge whether she's amused or mortified, and I keep going. "And you know what's sad? I think you know how awesome she is and that's why you pick on her. Because you're jealous. Because you know she's happy and you're not. And do you know why I feel sorry for you?" I catch Ashley's sister out of the corner of my eye, squealing as she and several friends start throwing cake at each other as the caterers look wearily at the mess. "You backed the wrong horse."

Now Crystal points her finger at me, fighting to find the words to skewer me and send me back to Tucson smarting and shamed, but all that comes out is, "I'll call the cops."

Before she can hit me with more zingers, the bartender appears, taking Crystal by the arm and leading her out to Raymond waiting in the car.

With her mother retired Ashley bows, flashing the entire bar staff in the process, and then wraps me in a long embrace. She finally lets go and says, "You know she won't remember anything you said tomorrow, right?"

"Thank you," I say, keeping a hand on her arm. "For giving your dad my résumé. I think it's not going to work out this time, but thank you. That could have changed my whole life." Ashley squeezes my arm back, and I know she thinks I made the right decision, too.

The cake fight is getting rowdier. Chunks of fondant are landing dangerously close. "You wanna blow this popsicle stand?" I ask.

Ashley grimaces. "Go back to my parents' house? Not really."

"Then let's go back to Tucson. Screw it. Samberg can bring you back to get your car."

Ashley blinks. "Can we do that? Just go back tonight?"

"Why not?" I don't mention that I'm afraid if I see Raymond again, I may prostrate myself begging back the job.

"Okay," Ashley says, dodging a lump of white frosting that lands unnoticed on the bartender's rear end. "Let's go."

The drive back is jubilant. We're AWOL and unbound. I drop Ashley off at Samberg's and she kisses my cheek before exiting the car in bare feet. "Thank you!" she screams as I drive away.

After leaving Samberg's place I'm on Campbell Avenue and I find that my blinker is on at a stoplight. I turn left, going far down Prince back towards the highway. I pass a cemetery, a mobile home park, a used car lot, several small homes behind chain link fences, and park in front of the building with the red, velvet couch out front. I climb the stairs two at a time but at the front door I hesitate. It's the middle of the night and I don't know what to say.

> "Hey, I want to apologize. I was wrong today. I'm wrong a lot of the time. Sorry about that."

Through the door I can hear Duncan's phone ping with each message. It sounds like a quacking duck and I try to not let the noise diminish the seriousness of what I'm saying.

> "You're the best person I know. And you make me want to be a better person. You make me so happy even though I may not show it. And I know you want the best for me. I know I've been wretched but I want the chance to do better. I've never asked anyone for help before but here I am. Please. I love you. I LOVE YOU!!!! By the way I'm outside."

I wait for a response. Nothing. Three minutes, four, five. We broke up this afternoon—he couldn't possibly have a girl in there. I don't want to harass him, beyond the barrage of text messages I've just sent, at least. I'll count to sixty and if he hasn't opened the door or texted back I'll leave.

I'm on fifty-five when the front door opens and Duncan holds out his arms. Folded into him, breathing his warm scents of laundry detergent and deodorant, I know I made the right choice in Scottsdale. Over Duncan's arm I can see my painting still on the wall, my past, present, and future coalescing into one, and I hug him tighter.

Epilogue or,
A reason to keep showing up

The grocery store is packed. I should have known not to go to Safeway on Super Bowl Sunday. Looking at other people's carts, you would have thought doomsday was coming and the only way to survive was to binge on Cheetos and Coors Light.

Were the lights always this bright? "Walking on Sunshine" blares overhead and I try to block my ears while simultaneously rolling my cart forward. I pleaded with Duncan to go to the store instead, spare me the torture, but he's grilling meat and doesn't trust me with his precious steaks, caution that's probably well-founded.

I only need a few things but everyone's in my goddamn way and they're remodeling the store so everything's where it shouldn't be. I'm stalking up and down the aisles searching for peanut butter when I hear whispering behind me, two girls:

"You ask her."

"No, you."

A tap on my shoulder. "Excuse me." I turn around and it's two teenagers. The one who speaks is still in braces. "Um, like, are you 'Sad Millennial'?"

A way out. I could say no. I could ignore her and flounce away. I could take my stand here in this grocery store and demand to know why she found the worst day of my life so entertaining. My chest is tight and I can taste the bile coming up the back of my throat like green hate.

I let out a breath. "Yeah," I say, trying to relax my face, "that's me."

The girls exchange a giddy look. "Oh my God," squeals the one with braces. "Can we take a picture with you? You're like, our hero at school. The government teacher even showed your video in class as an example of like, opportunity inequality or something."

My smile in the selfie looks genuine, untainted by bitterness or regret.

In my car, I head north towards my parents' house, but after going half a block I remember I don't live there anymore and have to turn around and go south. ~~I'm unemployed,~~ ~~I've never had a boyfriend,~~ I live with my ~~parents~~ boyfriend in a perfectly adequate ~~the most boring~~ town ~~on the planet~~ for the time being ~~and I hate myself~~.

Duncan and I are living in a duplex near the university. In the winter, when the leaves are gone, I can see my freshman dorm from our front porch. It's a nice little place—hardwood floors, barbecue pit in the backyard—and we have a guest bedroom that we converted into a studio, half for Duncan's photos, half for my painting. I wouldn't say we always work in perfect harmony—I had to put a line of tape on the floor to remind him to keep his crap out of my way—but ninety-nine percent of the time it's great.

We had to get a functional studio going because, after Duncan showed the photos of me at the Goodman Gallery show, we had people calling us for weeks, wanting more, wanting anything we could get out the door. Duncan was invited to participate in an exhibit highlighting young artists in Tucson. Naturally he wanted to show the photos of my scars, and I agreed, after much hand-wringing, and pacing, and one unspeakably uncomfortable conversation with my mother. She cried, she asked if it was her fault, and when she calmed down, she said she was impressed I'd been able to achieve linear perspective on my own skin. I called my father in Phnom Penh. He left a few days after Danny's graduation, before anyone could stop him or suggest he see a doctor, and he's been slowly touring Asia ever since. He said if I'd done it, I must have had my reasons, and then told me that in New Zealand, ancient Maoris marked lineage and achievements on their skin with tattoos formed by making deep cuts and mixing their blood with pigment.

"Being able to withstand pain was a point of pride," he said. "Maybe after that, they could cope with anything."

Duncan had the idea that I should do a painting to go along with the pictures, and I ended up painting a self-portrait, probably my best work yet. It's a weird one. It's me as Saint Bartholomew, the disciple of Jesus who brought Christianity to Armenia and was then skinned alive, a gruesome scene of high drama rendered in many classic paintings. In mine, I'm lying naked on a table surrounded by people pulling at my skin, ripping it from the muscle. Blood everywhere. But if you look closely at the people pulling, they're all me. They're dressed as men and women, and each have different clothes and body types, but the face is the same throughout. Trippy, huh?

We displayed them together and everyone went mental. This Arizona arts magazine asked if they could use my painting for the cover of their next issue, and an art dealer from Phoenix said he had several clients lined up to buy Duncan's photos.

Don't get too excited; we still work at Sunshine. But having a painting to come home to after work is so magical, so life affirming, I wish I could apologize to myself for robbing me of the opportunity. If my car's leaking brake fluid, or Duncan and I can't afford to do anything at night but sit on the couch and play gin rummy, or my dad forgets to call for weeks at a time and I don't know if he's dead or alive or just hitchhiking through South Korea, if everything in my life is going wrong and I want to scream at the unfairness of it all, I always have my half of a studio, my paint, my mind, my work. And I may not always be productive, I may go to bed feeling like the day was a waste, but I have a reason to keep showing up.

But it's more than that. When a wound opens up the instinct is to close it, sew it tight, make it look good as new. But sometimes the fissure reveals a deeper wound, something undiscovered that craves daylight. When the skin is ready it doesn't have to grow back in its old shape. It can develop new contours, it can bend or discolor or warp, but it's just as strong if not stronger. Scars are proof that you have healed. The person under the new skin finds others like them, the walking wounded. They go forward, shoulder to shoulder, stuttering, staggering, but together.

When Duncan helped me pack my things for the move, he found my cutting supplies in my desk drawer and asked if they were coming with us to the new apartment. I took them, ran my thumb lightly over the razor's tip, inhaled the clean, clinical odor of the rubbing alcohol and gauze pads, while the memory of cold, mercury pain filled me.

"Of course not," I said, and dropped them in the trash on top of my ribbons and plaques, my Model UN awards and science fair certificates. It was that easy, shedding a skin that no longer fit.

I turn into our driveway and I can see through the living room window, Duncan's got the game on. It's been raining and the wildflowers are in full flush, and when I step out of the car the air is fresh and full of rain scent and the sun coming through the pregnant clouds is gold. Through the window I can see them all: Paulette, Chasen, Randy, Nadine, Danny, Ashley, and Samberg, smiling and chatting. And I'm happy. Content. Blessed by abundance I might not deserve yet. I hope it never ends.

Acknowledgments

It is a long and, at times, agonizing process to turn a book from a fevered idea into something printed, bound, and beautiful. *Mona at Sea* took ten years to write and publish, beginning one morning in 2011 when I hurriedly typed up the first words after they came to me in the shower. But long as the process was, it was made far less agonizing and far more fulfilling thanks to the love and support I enjoyed along the way.

I want to thank Andrew Gifford, founder and director of the Santa Fe Writers Project. When I'd nearly given up hope Mona would ever see publication, Andrew sent me an email that changed my life. He is a tireless champion of writers and small presses, and his belief in me and my work lit a light inside me for which I will be forever grateful.

Thank you now and forever to Nicole Catherine Schmidt, who took my manuscript to new heights with her masterful edits. I could not have asked for a better editor and I am so grateful we were together on this journey. Thank you to Monica, Wendy, and everyone else at SFWP for all your work getting Mona (and me) ready for the big time. And a huge thank you to Carmen Maria Machado for shortlisting my novel for the SFWP Literary Awards.

I also want to give sincere thanks to Lena Yarbrough for her energy, edits, and enthusiasm. Special thanks too, to Ursula DeYoung of *Embark* for including an early chapter of *Mona at Sea* in her magazine. In no particular order I also want to thank the following friends and readers for their support, either artistic or moral (and I apologize if I'm leaving anyone out but I can't remember who I talked to last week, much less ten years ago): Neil Abrams, Galadrielle Allman, Karragh Arndt, Sarah Bardeen, Elizabeth Bernstein, DB Finnegan, Judith Flores, Jim Gavin, Jacqueline Hampton, Barbara Hawkins, Kurt Wallace Martin, John Putnam, Laura Schulkind, Deborah Shaw, Anita Sinclair, and Eric Wallace.

Special thanks too to Cynthia Warren for her incredible cover and for bringing Mona to full-color life.

Thank you, Fiona and Teddy, for being wonderful and filling my life with so much joy always. And of course, of course, of course, I couldn't have written this book without Larry. Thank you for supporting me in all the ways one person can support another, and for believing in me all the times I didn't want to go on. The greatest thing in my life was meeting you.

About the author

Laurence James

Before becoming a writer, Elizabeth was a waitress, a pollster, an Avon lady, an opera singer, and a telephone fundraiser. Her essays and short stories have appeared in *The Idaho Review*, *Ploughshares Blog*, *The Rumpus*, and elsewhere, and have received multiple Pushcart Prize and Best of the Net nominations. Originally from South Texas, she currently lives with her family in Oakland, California. This is her first novel.

Find out more at elizabethgonzalezjames.com.

Also from Santa Fe Writers Project

If the Ice Had Held *by Wendy J. Fox*

Melanie Henderson's life is a lie. The scandal of her birth and the identity of her true parents is kept from her family's small, conservative Colorado town. Not even she knows the truth: that her birth mother was just 14 and unmarried to her father, a local boy who drowned when he tried to take a shortcut across an icy river.

"Razor-sharp... written with incredible grace and assurance."
— *Benjamin Percy, author of* The Dark Net

eightball *by Elizabeth Geoghegan*

Fueled by an abiding sense of loss, the eight stories in this collection take you on a journey across the exploded fault lines of intimacy, unfolding across cities and continents.

"The quiet power of Geoghegan's voice reaches both heart and bone."
—*Francesca Marciano, author,* The Other Language

Magic For Unlucky Girls *by A.A. Balaskovits*

The fourteen fantastical stories in *Magic For Unlucky Girls* take the familiar tropes of fairy tales and twist them into new and surprising shapes. These unlucky girls, struggling against a society that all too often oppresses them, are forced to navigate strange worlds as they try to survive.

"A wonderful, truly original work."
—*Emily St. John Mandel, author of* Station Eleven

About Santa Fe Writers Project

SFWP is an independent press founded in 1998 that embraces a mission of artistic preservation, recognizing exciting new authors, and bringing out of print work back to the shelves.

Find us at www.sfwp.com